Hold On TO ME

LUCIA FRANCO

For Mattingly Churakos
You helped make a dream a reality. This novel wouldn't have been possible without you. Thank you for seeing the light when I couldn't.

MORE NOVELS BY LUCIA FRANCO

ONE

ALYSSA

A blast of heat billows against my cheeks when I step outside the new rental house. My hair instantly frizzes. The bottoms of my bare feet burn against the pebbly, red dirt road as I make my way to the mailbox at the end of the street. I draw in a lungful of air, my lips parting from the high humidity. I feel like I'm breathing in hot air. I'm not used to this weather and quickly discover I don't like it. Back home in California, all the roads I'd lived on were paved, and the temperature was always a cool seventy-five degrees.

"Son of a bitch," I mutter when a tiny, sharp rock digs into the ball of my foot. Balancing on one leg, dirt wedged between my toes, I swipe away the embedded stone and continue walking.

South Fork is the smallest town I've lived in. It has a population of only a few thousand people. I'd been forced to leave the beautiful Pacific Coast because my mother had found love and then lost it for what felt like the hundredth time. I didn't have to really leave California, but my mom is my only family. The thought of staying behind hadn't been a factor for me. Not to mention, I can't exactly support myself yet, what with being a student. I wish I could say college has been some of the best years of my life, but I can't. I'm tired of moving. I crave stability. I want friends to talk to and hang out with. It shouldn't be so difficult to obtain, but it is when you've been raised by a parent who chases love.

I was shuffled around as a kid. In the last three years, I've lived in eleven houses with two different "father figure" men in my life my mom had insisted I needed. I attended three high schools in two counties. I'm about to begin my second semester at a new community college.

Flipping down the mail door, I grab the stack of envelopes lying inside. As I sort through the credit card bills my mother will probably never pay, the roaring sound of engines catches my attention. I glance over my shoulder and look past the heat mirage glistening in the middle of the road. Two guys on four-wheelers are headed my way. A large cloud of dust follows behind them until they stop right in front of me.

I stand still, quietly assessing them. Typical looking country boys—barefoot, no shirts, and wearing raggedy shorts. They're built a bit huskier and not too lean, something I appreciate. Everyone is on a low-carb diet in California. Both guys look similar, except one has toffee-colored eyes, and the other has the deepest green eyes I've ever seen. His hat is on backward, allowing the sun to pick up on the specks of yellow in his eyes. They're energetic, and I stare at them longer than I should.

"Hey there, sugar," green eyes says. A crooked grin

tugs at his mouth, and his lazy southern drawl moves something deep inside me. "Are you new to the area?"

I nod. "I just moved in about two weeks ago."

"Where did you move from?"

"California."

"What brought you down here?"

I turn to look at the other guy, who asked the question. "My mom wanted a change of pace. She told me to close my eyes and point to a place on the map. So that's what I did."

It's my go-to lie, and the most believable.

"It's just you and her?" he asks, and I confirm. "I'm Jace, and this guy"—he hitches a thumb toward his friend with the green eyes—"is John."

John throws a leg over his seat and stands. He reaches out an open palm, and all sensible thoughts leave my brain when I slide my hand along his calloused skin. He is undoubtedly attractive in a rough around the edges kind of way. His scuffed-up shorts sit low on his waist, exposing his toned stomach and the muscular indents around his hips.

"If you need anything, let us know. We'll ride on over."

My brows angle in confusion. "You'll ride over on those things"—I point to the four-wheelers—"and do what exactly?"

"Those things," Jace says, his tone teasing. "Have you ever ridden on one of these things, princess?"

"My name is Alyssa."

"Sugar plum?"

"Alyssa."

"Pretty girl?"

"Wow, I'm in the presence of a comedian. No, I have not ridden one of those things."

Chuckling, John steps in. "Well, this is called a four-wheeler, not a thing, but I'm assuming you already knew that. Wanna take a quick ride with me, and I'll show you how it's done?"

I want to. It honestly looks like fun.

"Maybe another time. You're filthy and covered in mud. Not really my thing. No offense or anything."

John clutches his chest. "Oh, I think she just insulted me." He jokes, eyeing Jace. "You have a lot to learn. You live in the South now. We get dirty here, and so will you."

"Doubtful, considering I wasn't raised to play in the mud. Pigs play in the mud, and I'm not an animal."

The two friends look at each other and then burst into laughter. "We weren't raised to play in the mud, sugar plum. It just sort of happens."

I shift my feet. "How does it just happen?"

"When we go muddin' or party down by the river. Mud just happens. You'll see," Jace says.

"Mud just happens," I repeat each word slowly, completely dumbfounded. Now I've heard it all.

"Mud happens," John repeats with a wink.

"That doesn't make any sense," I say with my nose in the air. "Mud won't happen to me."

"Mark my words," Jace says, "it's inevitable."

"Is that how you guys down here talk? Mud happens? You sound silly."

Jace gives me a challenging, playful stare as he says, "Say it with me. Mud happens."

"I'll pass."

They both shoot me a grin that causes my stomach to tighten. They're trouble.

"We need to get going. We're late to meet a friend. But I guess we'll see ya around. Welcome to South Fork," John says.

"See you around," I say.

Cranking the gas, their engines roar back to life. John clutches the gear and glances over his shoulder at me. "Later, sugar."

"Bye, princess," Jace says.

The urge to flip them both off is strong, but I don't. I watch John and Jace take off, a puff of dirt flying up behind them. When they're halfway down the street, I turn around and walk back to the house.

It looks like I just got some of that southern charm I've heard of, and I'm eager for more of it, especially coming from John.

TWO

ALYSSA

I enter the lecture hall, and the door closes behind me with a loud thud.

Heads turn in my direction. I hate being late.

"Can I help you?" the professor down in the front asks.

I pull my schedule free from my folder and walk toward the middle-aged woman. She glances down at the paper when I hand it to her.

"Welcome, Alyssa Winters," she says with a genuine smile and hands the schedule back to me. "There are some open seats in the back. Come see me at the end of class, and I'll get you a syllabus."

"Thank you."

I walk back up the aisle and pass seven rows of desks before I find an empty seat. They're spaced out so I can comfortably walk between them. I pull out a pencil and my notebook once I'm seated. I tune into the lecture, trying to catch as many words as possible and jot them down. After a page or so of notes, my skin prickles with awareness. It's the kind that feels like I'm being watched. It's not like I know anyone here, yet the sensation is getting stronger. I scan the room and do a double take.

Two rows over, I spot John leaning back in his chair with a pencil dangling between his lips. His appearance catches me by surprise. I almost didn't recognize him with his hair brushed. Yesterday it was wild and disheveled, and he was a dirty mess. Today he's cleaned up and looking suave.

My eyes fall to his mouth. His tongue flicks the tip of the eraser and the pencil bobs. One corner of his mouth tugs up into a grin. My stomach tightens at the sight. A flush of heat crawls up my chest. I bet he's a huge flirt and loves being one. My gaze meets his, and I still. My cheeks burn. John is already looking at me. He pulls the pencil from his mouth and starts bouncing it between his fingers, the eraser tapping lightly on the desk. I blink rapidly and face forward, refocusing my attention on the professor. A few moments later, John scoots into the empty chair next to me. I pay no attention to him and jot down another line of notes despite his best effort to get me to notice him. From the corner of my eye, I can see a full-blown grin on his face. I try not to return the smile, but I ultimately cave. I turn to look at him, and our eyes meet again. He waves inconspicuously, and my stomach drops.

"Hi," he whispers.

Then I notice it. A dimple. John has one dimple right above his jawline when he smiles. Dimples are my weakness. They fall somewhere between being a good ol' boy and a rebel. He has a flirtatious dimple and hazel green eyes. Plus, he has a southern drawl. I'm in trouble. Big trouble.

"Young man," the professor says, grabbing John's

attention. "Stop flirting, and focus on the reason why you're here. Eyes up front."

"Yes, ma'am."

John winks at me and then does as the professor asks. He spends the next two hours sneaking glances my way.

Class ends, and I quickly gather up my books. John waits for me while I get a copy of the syllabus. As we exit the room together, he hooks an arm around my neck and rests it on my shoulders. He tugs me closer to his side. We walk together down the hall as if we've been friends for years, not having just met only recently. I look up at a grinning John.

"Figured since you're new here, I could walk you to your next class. Where are you headed?" His voice is right near my ear.

I look at my schedule. "Physics."

"Ouch. Not my kind of class, but I can lead the way."

I hold my books tighter to my chest. "Thanks, Johnny."

He gives me a little tug, and I catch a hint of something that causes my stomach to flip-flop. Unlike the expensive fragrances guys wear back in California, John smells earthy and rich, like freshly cut grass on a sunny day. I wasn't expecting John to wear cologne, or own any, but he is. It's subtle, but enough to cause me to lean in and get a better smell of it.

"Huh."

"What is it?"

"No one's ever called me Johnny before."

"Really?" I feel stupid for calling him that now. "That's your name, right?"

"I would've corrected anyone who said that, but I like it

on your lips." He pauses. "Know what else I'd like on your lips, sugar?"

John's brows waggle and his eyes gleam with wickedness. I playfully elbow him in his ribs. That stupid dimple is all I can focus on.

"If you call me those stupid nicknames, then I get to call you Johnny."

"Fair enough."

"Are you going to be late for walking me to class?"

He shakes his head. "No. I have a break for the next two hours."

"What do you do in between classes?" I ask.

John drops his arm from around my shoulders and holds the door open for me as we step inside another building.

"Depends. Schoolwork. Sometimes I hang with my friends. Wherever the day takes us. Where's your schedule?"

I hand it to him.

He scans it. "These are the hours you're with me, Alyssa. We have two classes together."

"Lucky me," I say sarcastically. "I'm surprised you even remembered my name."

"I didn't. It's at the top of your schedule."

I glance at him from the side of my eye.

"What? I'm being honest." Laughing, he returns my schedule and asks, "What are you doing after class?"

"Not talking to a guy who can't remember my name, that's for sure."

"Ouch. You wound me." He jokes. "Hang out with me. Let me make it up to you by showing you around town."

"No."

"Why not?"

"Because I don't know you."

"But that's how you'll get to know me, by hanging out with me," he states obviously.

A low chuckle rolls off my lips.

When we reach the classroom, we turn to face each other. John is charming, and it makes me feel shy.

"Thanks for walking me to class. At least I won't be late for this one."

He winks. "See you around, sugar."

The first half of the day passes quickly. I find myself standing in the dining hall by noon. I quickly grab a bottle of water and a bag of chips then leave to find my new lunch spot. Outside, groups of students are scattered about, sitting under the overhang. I take a seat on the thigh-high wall of red bricks. Bringing my legs up, I uncap my water and take a sip, then I pull out a map along with my schedule. I got lost on my way to another class earlier and walked in late. I want to avoid that if I can, so I begin studying the map.

JOHN

LAST SEMESTER I WOULD LEAVE BETWEEN CLASSES TO grab lunch with Jace and Ford. We'd pick up food and bring it back to the dining hall, hanging out there until our next class began, or catch up on work in the library. This semester is shaping up to be no different, except I polished off my sandwich before returning to school. After parking my truck, we walk to the courtyard as Ford tells me and Jace about a senior prank his little brother wants help with.

"Just hear me out before you say no. We round up a bunch of cows, like ten of them, and sneak them into the school. Gather as many frogs as we can and dump them in there. Some stray cats and dogs too. Stick dead fish in the air vents. Then we wait and watch from a distance the next morning."

"Where the hell are we going to get ten cows from? And no offense, but I don't want to get a disease trying to catch some stray animals for your brother," Jace says.

Ford ignores him and continues, "We could use Super Glue on all the locks except for one door so no one can get in that day."

"You've given this some serious thought, haven't you?" Jace asks Ford, and he nods.

"You guys are crazy. There's no way this could work. Not to mention, your brother could get expelled. You guys are on your own with this one," Jace says.

"My parents have so many cows that they would never notice ten missing," Ford says.

I sip my Coke and give some thought to Ford's wild idea. I don't have anything better to do. It could work, but before I can think further, I spot a pretty blonde sitting by herself. I begin walking toward her.

I don't know what got into me, but the instant I saw Alyssa yesterday, I had to meet her. I'm drawn to her for reasons I wish I could explain. She gives me a weird, fluttering feeling in my chest. She's beautiful. Alyssa is gorgeous from head to toe. She doesn't seem to be interested in getting to know me, or my town, so of course I'm going to make it so she has no choice in the matter. I want to know everything I can about Alyssa Winters and why she's so standoffish about making friends.

Jace's hand flies back and smacks me in the stomach, pulling me out of my thoughts. Frowning, I look at him. "What the hell?"

"I asked you a question," Jace says.

"Obviously didn't hear you. What'd you ask me?"

"Want to go muddin' this weekend? We haven't been in a while."

"Yeah, sure." I'm still focused on Alyssa as I respond. "Have you met the new girl yet, Ford? She lives near us."

"I call dibs!" Ford exclaims.

I turn my head, puzzled. "You call dibs? What are you? Fucking ten? First of all, no one says dibs anymore, dipshit. And second, you haven't even seen her yet. For all you know, she could be wearing braces, is pimply-faced with some raggedy-looking hair, and is all skin and bones. And we all know how you like 'em thick and younger than you. You still gonna call dibs then?"

Jace laughs at Ford's expression, and I find myself laughing too.

"I can't help it if I like a little meat on my girls' bones. More cushion for the pushin'."

I shake my head and guide my friends to where Alyssa is sitting. "There she is," I say with a nod of my chin.

"I think I see hearts in John's eyes." Jace jokes.

I give him the middle finger.

"Well, hey there, sugar," I say, stopping before Alyssa.

Alyssa's head snaps up to see the three of us standing in front of her. The blinding sun shines in her eyes. She tries to block it with her hand as she looks at each of us, and then settles her gaze on me.

"Johnny. Still can't remember my name, I see."

Another weird sensation rolls through me, one I've never felt before. I like the sound of "Johnny" on her lips.

"Johnny?" Jace quirks.

"Alyssa," I draw out her name, ignoring Jace. "This is Ford. You met Jace already the other day."

"Yup, she ain't my type. Pretty, though," Ford says, bobbing on his toes.

Alyssa's brows pinch together. "I'm glad because you are not my type either," she says slowly with a tone of derision.

"Are you finding your way around campus?" I ask.

She nods at me and then looks at Ford. "Is your name really Ford, or is that some sort of nickname?"

Ford lowers his eyes. Barely moving his mouth, he responds, "Yes. My name really is Ford."

"He hates when people ask him that," I say.

A smile forms on Alyssa's sweet face. Her heavy black lashes make her blue eyes brighter in the sunlight.

"We just decided to go muddin' this weekend. Since I know you have no friends yet, and I can bet you have no plans, what do you say? Wanna take a ride with us?"

Alyssa's mouth drops open. "I told you, but I'll tell you again since you seem to have a listening problem. I don't play in the mud. And aren't you a little old to be going mudding? Isn't that for kids?"

I stare into her eyes, unblinking. I love a girl with spunk, one who isn't afraid to hand it to me. Her sass is a turn-on. Typically girls beg for my attention, considering who my famous brother is, but Alyssa doesn't. She does the complete opposite, and it's a nice change of pace for once.

"There isn't much else to do around here." Jace jumps in.

"Unfortunately for you, I need to get a job. So that's what I'll be doing this weekend."

"You're going to be looking all weekend?" I question her, and she nods quickly. "Alright, you get a pass. This time. But I'll get you on the back of my four-wheeler and some mud on you soon."

Alyssa snaps her mouth shut, her lips forming a thin line.

I walk away before she can respond. Ford and Jace follow. Before I turn the corner to walk inside the building, I glance over my shoulder.

Alyssa flips me off.

I grin inwardly. She was watching me.

I have a feeling about Alyssa, and I'm going to run with it.

THREE
ALYSSA

Sharing a car with my mom means some days I have to drive her to work before school, which is usually before the sun rises, and then pick her up at the end of her shift when it's pitch-black outside.

I had my own car back in California, but we needed money when we moved here. My mom insisted I sell mine since it didn't have a lease on it, whereas hers did. I was a little aggravated I had to give up another piece of myself because of her failed relationship. However, I try to see things on the bright side. The money helped with moving expenses, and whatever was left went toward paying for college textbooks. Living in some rural town with nothing to do but watch the grass grow, one car is perfect for us.

Unfortunately, her car won't start this afternoon. I have class in an hour. School is my only hope in this world if I want to make anything of myself. I try never to miss it. Luckily the community college is on the edge of our new town. The walk won't be too bad. I'm hoping I see Johnny when class is over so I can ask him for a ride home.

I pop my earphones in and begin making the trek. I glance up at the darkening sky every few minutes, watching the clouds move. Thunder booms in the distance, the rumbling growing closer each time. I smell rain in the air and hope it holds off until I'm at school. Lightning strikes and causes me to jump. An instant later, the sky opens and rain pours down on me. I quickly shove my phone and earbuds into my purse and zip it up. Water splashes on my toes, and I look down at the small, muddy red puddles forming on the ground. Grimacing, I unbuckle my sandals and place them under my arm and continue walking. I don't want to ruin them.

I hear the roar of an engine behind me. On instinct, I look over my shoulder and spot a navy-blue truck with dark-tinted windows coming my way. Water flares up and spatters the car's underside and onto the grass. I pray that whoever it is slows down as they pass by. Otherwise, I will be sprayed too.

"I'll be goddamned," I say to myself when I see who it is.

John idles up next to me. He rolls down the window and leans on the console.

"Jump in. I'll give you a ride."

I eye the navy-blue monstrosity idling on the side of the road as I contemplate his offer. Another bolt of lightning strikes, and I jump in.

"Thank you," I say. "I'm sorry about your seat getting wet."

John brushes it off. "It's no big deal. Where're you headed?"

"I was going to school, but can you take me home,

please? I can't show up soaking wet like this. I wasn't expecting it to rain."

As much as I want to attend class, I can't show up like this. I'll have to email my professors and ask for the assignments for the day.

John turns on the radio. I feel terrible about getting his truck all dirty, even though he says it doesn't bother him. Mom would have yelled at me for this. When we turn onto my street, I glance at John and notice the small smile on his face. I wonder what he's thinking about.

"Why are you smiling?"

"That's my brother," he says.

I look ahead to the street. "Where?" I don't see anyone out.

John cranks up the stereo and points to the dashboard. "He's on the radio."

My brows bunch together. "Your brother is a singer?"

"Yeah. A country singer."

"I should have known. Country music is the only thing that plays on the radio down here, isn't it? How do you listen to that stuff?"

Creases form between his brows. "What do you mean?"

"For starters, they all have that twang and sound the same to me. They sing about their dogs riding shotgun as they prepare to play in the mud," I say, emphasizing the last word. "The girls walk around in ugly ass cowboy boots, and everyone loves fishing. I can just picture a piece of straw hanging between their lips."

John chuckles. "You forgot beer drinking."

"That goes without saying."

"Have you ever been fishing?"

"It's not really my thing."

"How do you know it's not your thing if you haven't tried it?"

"I don't, but sitting still and waiting around for a fish to bite would make my patience run thin."

John laughs. "What is your thing?"

I shrug. "Not getting dirty. Anything but country. I love the city."

He's quiet for a minute, and it causes me to look at him.

"What is it?" I ask.

"I like your straightforwardness. You're not like other girls around here. Sometimes I feel like they say what they think I want to hear. You don't seem to care either way."

Bluntness and honesty go hand in hand in California. It's all I know.

"Thanks," I say quietly.

John shifts in his seat. "What kind of music do you want me to put on? I have to be honest. I don't really care to hear about hoes getting fucked and bitches getting slapped. Not a huge fan of boy bands either," he says.

I bark out a laugh that causes a smile to spread across his handsome face. His eyes light up at my laughter.

"This is fine. It's your car."

Leaning back, I listen to the song on the radio, mainly because it's John's brother. The lyrics are full of sappy love, sadness, and a yearning to be close to someone. The emotion in his voice tugs at my heart, and I find myself turning up the radio. I bob my head. Definitely not what I was expecting, but I like it. As the song ends, I sit quietly, thinking about the lyrics.

"Your brother's song wasn't anything I expected," I say.

"What do you mean?"

"For one, it's full of heartache. Like he's singing about missing someone."

John nods. "He wrote that song many years ago after he broke up with his girlfriend."

"Aw. How sweet is that? Do they still talk?"

He grins. "I'm not sure what's going on with them. They were separated for a long ass time. Something like ten years. They're back together now."

"It sounds like he never stopped loving her."

"You could say that. They were childhood friends, then they turned into high school sweethearts."

"That's the sweetest thing ever," I say, gushing.

He shoots me a quick glance before his eyes are back on the road. "If I write you a love song, would you warm up to me a little bit?"

"Slow your roll, country boy."

We pull into my driveway. John eyes my mom's car. "What's wrong with it?"

I shrug. "Beats me. I don't know a thing about cars. It's actually my mom's car. We share it."

"Once it stops raining, I'll come back and give it a jump to see if that helps."

I look at John. "You don't mind?"

"Not at all."

I give him an appreciative smile. "Thanks."

"Wait." He stops me with his hand on my arm before I leave. "Do you use your mom's car for school every day?"

"Only until I can get a job and save money to buy a car. But I haven't had any luck finding work yet."

"How about I pick you up and we can ride together?"

"It's not out of your way? I don't want to inconvenience you."

John shakes his head. "I live three streets over."

I hesitate before agreeing. Accepting a ride from John means I have to make friends. I don't like to do that when I know I'll just have to leave again. I'm tired of goodbyes.

"It's only been a few weeks of school, and I'm already getting rides from guys I hardly know. That doesn't look good," I say. He gives me a flirtatious smile that makes my stomach flutter. "Thanks again, Johnny."

"Anytime."

I climb out of John's truck and sprint to the front door. Dropping my sandals on the porch, I stomp my feet to rid the excessive dirt caked on my skin.

I tiptoe inside the house, trying to leave as little trail as possible, as I make my way to the bathroom to remove my clothes. While John has been blatantly flirting with me since we met, I think it's adorable and sweet. He's easygoing, smooth, and full of Southern charm. I don't want to get ahead of myself, but I can see him being a friend, which scares me. Friends aren't hard to come by for me, but I choose to keep them at a distance since I move frequently. I keep things casual and emotionless and don't get attached. It's better that way.

SLAMMING MY TEXTBOOK SHUT, I LOOK UP AT THE SOUND of my door opening. Mom walks into my bedroom wearing blue scrubs. The bags under her eyes have gotten more prominent, and her dirty-blond hair is thrown up in a messy bun. She's been picking up as many shifts as possible at the local hospital to get ahead. We left California with the clothes on our backs and little cash in the bank.

"Hey, Mom. What are you doing home?"

I've been raised single-handedly by my mom, Lauren, for as long as I can remember. My dad is just another random man in my life. I consider him to be an acquaintance more than anything, like my mom's boyfriends usually are. I don't care much for the guy since he can't be bothered with his daughter, but Mom still has a soft spot for him. Deep down, I don't think she ever truly moved on from him. First loves and all that.

"I got the night off early. I feel like I hardly get to see you anymore," she says apologetically. She folds up a knee and sits on my bed. "How's school going? Make any new friends yet?"

I pucker my lips. Why make friends when we're going to leave again?

"Sort of. There were a couple of guys I met when we first moved here. I have a few classes with one of them. They're friendly and nice, the total opposite of home. For some reason, the car wouldn't start today. I started to walk to school, but I got caught in the rain. One of the guys gave me a ride home."

"That explains why I found this on the windshield."

She hands me a piece of paper.

I came by with Ford to look at your mom's car. I knocked to let you know we were here, but you didn't answer. Checked the battery. Pretty sure you just need a new one. We jumped your car and it started.

-J

I smile, my stomach fluttering again. That was incredibly sweet and thoughtful of John. I'll have to thank him when I see him next.

"Sounds like my friend thinks it's the battery. Maybe I left a light on or the door cracked a little." I trail off, wondering what could have killed it. I hope that's all it is.

"So, does this friend have a name?" she asks.

"His name is Johnny. John. His name is John."

Mom nods. "Give John my thanks, will you?"

"Yes, of course. Speaking of rides, how did you get home?" I ask with a tilt of my head.

"One of my coworkers dropped me off on her way home," Mom says. "Are you hungry? I'm starving."

"I can cook some pasta if you want," I offer.

"How about we go out for dinner instead? I'm too tired to cook, and I don't want you to cook either."

"Mom, this town is super small. I saw two fast food places and a gas station. Where are we going to go?"

She chuckles. "It is small, isn't it? Probably the smallest we've been in yet." The sadness in Mom's eyes when she looks away causes an ache in my heart. I don't want her to feel bad about our situation. "How about we ride to the next town over and grab something?"

"Sounds good to me."

SITTING IN THE BOOTH SIPPING HER COKE, MOM SEEMS awfully quiet and deep in thought. I can feel the words on the tip of her tongue.

"I know you want to say something. Go ahead."

She looks down at the table as she speaks. "Sweetie, I know South Fork is a far cry from what we're used to, but I think I'm done shuffling you around. It isn't fair of me to do that. I want to make a home here in South Fork."

I giggle. "Of all places, Mom? Seriously?"

"Yeah, why not? Who knows, you may grow to really like it here. The people seem nice, and I can't believe I'm about to say this, but I like that it's off the beaten path."

"But how do I know you won't get the itch to move again?"

She lifts her head and looks me straight in the eyes. "I promise." She pauses. "I promise I'm done. You know I don't regret having you so young, but life hasn't been easy. I've tried to find a man worthy of being your father, but that's only backfired. I don't want you to make the same mistakes I've made. I want better for you. You can't do that when I'm constantly moving you around."

My shoulders sag. I've heard this speech a hundred times in the past couple of years. She always starts with, "You know I don't regret," but it feels like she does regret getting pregnant at sixteen. Why even say that at all?

I try to make light of the subject and say, "Note to self: Don't follow Mom's footsteps. Got it."

"I'm serious, Alyssa. Refrain from falling for the charm and sweet-talking the way I did. I was young and naïve. I didn't know any better. Just because you're over eighteen now doesn't mean anything. If you screw around, there will be consequences to pay, just like there were for me. I barely make it to support both of us. Get your degree and get a good-paying job."

As if having a baby is what I want to do right now.

"Mom, I'm well aware of that."

She looks at her glass, moving the ice with her straw. "I wish I would've planned better and saved money. Now we're starting over, and it's all my fault."

I can feel the pain in my mother's voice, the guilt laced in her tone. I don't want her to feel bad. "It's okay, Mom. You've given me everything I've wanted."

My mom isn't the best role model, but she does her best. I don't fault her for my life. Could it be better? Sure. But it could also be worse. My mom is always looking for love. I have no doubt she's already scouting the hospital for the next love of her life. She's been through more boyfriends than fingers she has to count on. When she discovered that her recent boyfriend of nearly two years was married with children, it did a number on her. She thought he was the one. Two weeks later, we were gone.

"Except stability. I've moved you around too much. I was selfish."

"Eh. Who cares? It's been fun. I can call myself a world traveler." I laugh, hoping to show Mom that I'm happy.

Regret plagues her mouth, though. Thin lines curve around the corners.

Here we are in small-town USA, eating pizza while my mom preaches about stability and preventing babies. The two things she could never master.

FOUR

JOHN

I knew it. I knew Alyssa would be walking alone.

I left my house early because I felt Alyssa had no ride to school. I forgot to get her cell phone number yesterday, so I had no way of contacting her.

Idling slowly up next to her, I roll down the window. "Jump in."

Alyssa doesn't hesitate. She flings the door open and jumps inside, mumbling her thanks.

It's on the tip of my tongue to make a sarcastic comment about the door nearly flying off from how hard to threw it open, but I let it go. Something is going on with her. She's stewing. I notice her reflection in the passenger mirror as she stares out the window. Her lips are puckered together, and her arms are crossed firmly against her chest.

"Want to talk about it?" I ask.

"Not really. I got into an argument with my mom. It was dumb, and now I'm in a bad mood because of it. She had to cover a shift for someone and took the car. I think she forgot I had school because she stormed out and didn't even check if I needed a ride."

I don't let her see my grin and turn up the music. She's such a girl. Says she doesn't want to talk about it, but then lets it all out. I'm tempted to ask what the argument was about but I decide not to push my luck.

Ten minutes later we're pulling into the campus parking lot. I park and say, "Give me your phone."

"What? Why?"

"Don't ask me questions. Just hand it over."

She hands it to me, and I add my number to her contacts. "There you go. Anytime you need a ride, I'm your guy."

"Thank you," she says quietly and slips her phone into her bag.

Together we silently walk through the maze of cars in the parking lot. The discontent written on her face gives me the urge to wrap my arm around her shoulders and bring her in close. I want to erase the look. For some odd reason, it bothers me.

We're passing rows of cars and trucks when Alyssa notices Chad leaning against his vehicle. I scowl at the sight of him. He's dressed all in black and smoking a cigarette. Their eyes connect for a second too long, and I don't like it. The intensity of his gaze makes me feel like he's undressing her. He takes a puff of his cigarette and blows it out, a diminutive smirk forming on his lips.

"That's Chad," I say, breaking their stare.

"Who?"

"The guy you're staring at," I say, glaring at Chad with disgust. I can't help it. He knows how I feel about him. I really don't like the guy. "I wouldn't suggest making friends with him."

"We have a class together."

"He's bad news. I've heard some stories about how he likes to get rough—and not with guys, if you follow my drift. Rumors were circulating a couple of years back that he forced himself on a girl. Not sure if they were true because there were no charges pressed. I'm surprised he's even enrolled in college to be honest. Guess he got his GED after dropping out of high school."

"You know him?" she asks.

"Yeah, he actually lives near us."

She purses her lips. Alyssa glances one last time at Chad, her eyes narrowing. He dips his head slightly, acknowledging her, then looks away.

When we reach the courtyard, Ford and Jace are already there. Jace spots both of us and nods, his eyes landing on Alyssa.

"You two rode together?"

"I was already driving and happened to see her walking, so I made her get in. She can be a little hardheaded at times," I say, nudging her.

"I don't know what he's talking about," she says innocently.

A laugh rolls off my tongue. Looking at my friends, I say, "So, we on for this weekend?" We planned on going muddin' again.

"Yup. For sure," Jace and Ford both state in unison. "I'm always ready to get my truck dirty and drink a few beers."

"Jace, your truck is always dirty—inside and out."

Ford laughs. "When has it ever been clean? I don't even remember its color since it's covered in shit all the time."

Alyssa's face scrunches up. "Isn't that going to ruin the paint and interior?"

Jace shrugs indifferently. "I'm a dirty boy. It doesn't bother me a bit."

"Do you have a girlfriend? Doesn't she care when she rides inside your truck?"

"I have a few girls. They've never complained before, but then again, we usually hang out in the back of my truck." Jace winks playfully.

Shaking her head, Alyssa says, "I have to get going. See you guys around."

"Here, let me walk you to class," I offer.

She shakes her head adamantly. "It's okay. I can find my way. See you later."

Alyssa glances over her shoulder as she walks away and locks eyes with me. I let her go without a fight. If she needs me, she knows where to find me. Something is bothering her. I don't want to get on her bad side just yet.

A L Y S S A

I NEED TO TREAD CAREFULLY WITH JOHN. HE'S BEEN ON my mind. Since leaving him in the courtyard this morning, I've been looking forward to the next time I see him. He brings a sense of comfort to me. I'm doing my best not to make friends so quickly, but he's easy to like.

"Why do you sit out here? It's so damn hot." Someone stands over me, breaking me out of my thoughts.

I glance up and find dark brown eyes piercing right through me. The first time I saw Chad, we passed each other in the hall. Our eyes met, and I felt a tug in my stomach. Like I do now. He pulls his lip ring into his mouth, and I watch him use his tongue to play with it. I've never had a friend or boyfriend who had piercings before. It makes me wonder if Chad has any tattoos. They seem to go hand in hand.

"I'm plotting to take out my archenemies from afar."

"Funny girl," he says, and leans against the wall and crosses his legs. "What's your name?"

"Alyssa."

"I'm Chad."

"I know." His eyes darken, and I say, "John told me your name." He bobs his head then scans the courtyard. "So what do you do for fun around here?" I ask, making small talk. I hope he doesn't say four-wheeling.

Chad blows out a loud breath and raises his brows. "Not much. It's boring as fuck around here. You either work on the weekend at your family's farm, or you get a job outside of town. You can go hunting. Swim down by the river. There isn't really much to do in South Fork."

Great. I went from swimming in the most sought-after beaches to swimming in a river.

"Sounds desirable," I say, my voice dripping with sarcasm.

Chad chuckles as he looks down at me. "It didn't hurt," he says.

"What didn't?" I look into his eyes, confused.

"My lip ring you can't stop staring at. It didn't hurt in case you wanted to know."

Heat rises to my cheeks. I fight the urge not to squirm under his stare. There's an air of danger that surrounds him. It's thrilling. I've had a few casual boyfriends, but Chad reminds me of the kind of boy you don't bring home, the one a father would warn you to stay away from.

But I didn't have a father to watch out for me.

"What did your parents say about your lip ring?"

Chad huffs, and his jagged smile causes my stomach to tighten. "Mom took off when I was a kid, so it's just been me and my dad. Let's just say he wasn't too fond of it at first and tried to rip it out a few times."

My eyes widen.

"Don't worry. He didn't get very far since he was drunk and shit."

"What does he say now since you still have it?"

Chad shakes his head. "Nothing. When he tries to put his hands on me, I put mine on his right back. My dad raised me with an iron fist and a splash of vodka. After a while, you learn how to handle that." Chad shrugs it off. "Have any plans this weekend?"

"Yeah, she does. With me."

I still. That southern voice commands attention. I don't have to turn around to know it's John.

"I should have known," Chad sneers.

"Why don't you take a hike?" John suggests.

"I actually don't have any plans except looking for a job." I interrupt, trying to cut the tension.

Chad looks at me. "I'll see you around, Alyssa. Maybe I can help with your job search this weekend." He winks and then leaves.

John watches Chad walk away. His jaw is clenched. His body is radiating heat hotter than the Georgia sun. There's bad blood between them.

"You need to stay away from him. He's bad news."

The last thing I want is to be told what to do. I hate when someone tries to dictate my life. My mom does enough of that.

"So you've said. Why don't you let me be the one to decide that," I say.

"I'm serious, Alyssa. I've heard things."

"He didn't seem so bad to me."

"That's because you don't know any better yet."

I ignore his comment. "What are you doing here anyway?" I ask incredulously.

"What do you mean?"

"I figured you would be with your friends."

"You are my friend," he states plainly. "Why aren't you trying to make friends?"

"I just tried to make a new friend, but you told me to stay away from him." I shrug. "Besides, what's the point? Every time I make friends and get comfortable, I end up having to move."

"Why do you guys move around so much anyway?"

"My mom is a serial dater. All her relationships seem to end on a bad note, and she feels the need to move when that happens."

John laughs and sits down next to me. "What relationships end on a good note?"

"Well, some people have amicable splits, but that's not the point. The point is she moves after each breakup. It's ridiculous. Who does that? She swears this is it, that we're not moving this time."

We share a bag of chips for a few moments. I'm thankful John doesn't pry.

"How do you like the campus so far? It's small compared to other community colleges, but that's what I like about it."

I shrug. "It's alright, I guess. It gives me some sort of consistency, so I'm happy about that." I face him. "What's your major?"

John offers me some of his French fries. I take a few. "I'm undecided. I've been thinking about dropping out and enlisting in the Marines. My dad served. I just took the ASVAB test, and I'm waiting to hear back. My mom is sick, though; so I'd like to stay close to home, just in case. But if I join the Marines, I wouldn't be home much, would I?"

My brows pinch together. "Your mom is sick?"

John grows quiet and looks above my head, unable to meet my gaze. "She has multiple sclerosis."

FIVE

ALYSSA

My heart softens.

I don't know anyone with that disease, but what I do know about it is that it can be debilitating. I'm surprised by the conversation I'm having with John. It's unlike me to delve deep into someone's personal life, especially someone I've recently met. I'm scared of getting attached.

"Do you know what you want to do if you enlist?" I ask.

"My family was in aviation, so I was thinking of going down that path if I can, but it depends on my scores and where I place."

Tilting my head to the side, I take in John as he watches people walk through the courtyard. He has olive skin, a narrow nose, and a square jawline. His gaze scatters across the open space. He has incredible eyes that light up in the sunlight. And that stupid dimple near his soft lips really gets to me. I wish he wasn't attractive. It would make being friends with him easier.

A smile slowly slides across his mouth, and I realize I've been caught.

"Oh damn," I say, heat rushing to my cheeks. "How embarrassing."

"It's all good. I stare at you too, only I don't get caught." His gaze drifts to my lips.

"Hey," I say, breaking his stare. He looks into my eyes. "You have another dimple by your eye. I didn't notice that before."

"That's because you're too busy staring at my mouth, probably wondering if I'm a good kisser."

My mouth falls open, and I smile. "I was not!"

"Yeah, right. If you're lucky, I'll let you find out."

"Oh, you are so full of yourself, country boy. And who said I wanted to find out anyway?"

"You didn't have to, your eyes—"

"John!" A female voice carries in the air, cutting him off.

We both turn toward the source.

"Hey, Sarah," John says.

Sarah ogles John as she saunters over to him, her hips swaying as if she is on a catwalk. I can't help but notice her pouty red lips and the mountain of cleavage John seems to focus on.

"Have you met Alyssa?"

Sarah looks right through me. "Hi."

"Hey," I respond before she focuses her attention back on John.

"I've been trying to find you. Are you heading home soon? I usually ride with Chelsea, but she wants to stay in the library and study, and I have to work today. Anyway, can you give me a lift home?"

My brows pinch together. Did Sarah even take a breath?

"Yeah, that's cool. Are you ready now?"

Sarah bats her eyelashes at John, making me want to roll my eyes. She nods.

John looks at me and says, "I'll be back when your class is over to get you."

"It's okay. I can call my mom." The last thing I want to do is inconvenience him.

"I'll be back to get you. Later, sugar," he states, leaving me gawking.

The way he says "sugar" causes Sarah to actually look at me this time.

I ignore her.

A FEW MINUTES BEFORE CLASS LETS OUT, MY PHONE vibrates in my back pocket. I pull it out and spot two text messages—one from my mother apologizing for not waking sooner to drive me to school and the other from Yours Truly.

Yours Truly?

Then it dawns on me.

John.

Yours Truly: Meet me in the courtyard.

I walk to the front of the school and around the maze of people conversing with one another. A small smile tugs at the corners of my mouth when I see the tall dirty-blond. My stomach flutters with the knowledge that he came back for me. He's reliable when most people in my world aren't. I give him a good-natured shove when I reach him, and he stumbles.

"Yours Truly?" I say, holding up my phone.

John spins around, a huge grin plastered on his face as he pins me with his incandescent eyes.

"I knew you'd like it. I have you as Babe in mine."

"In your dreams, country boy. I'm changing it."

John snatches the phone from my hand. He's laughing and holding it high out of my reach. My body presses into his as I try to wrestle the phone from him.

"John, you better stop! Give me back my phone!"

"Only if you leave it."

"No way!"

"Then you can't have it back."

I cock my hip to the side and hold out my hand. "Stop acting like a ten-year-old and give me my phone."

"Only if you promise not to change it."

His eyes flirt with mine. He makes it hard to say no. I grit my teeth behind my smile.

"Maybe."

"That's not enough for me."

"Ugh. Fine. I'll leave it."

John plops it in my hand. "Ready to ride?" he asks, and I nod. Turning to Ford and Jace, John says, "I'll hit y'all up later," and waves goodbye.

John pulls me into his side as we begin walking to his truck. He gives a light squeeze to my shoulder, and I lean into him. He opens the passenger door and waits for me to climb in. Our movements feel natural, like he's been giving me rides for years. We don't exchange words on the drive home, but none are needed. It's not awkward or uncomfortable. Just easy, like a Sunday morning. After a few songs play on the radio, we pull into my driveway.

Turning to John, I say, "Thanks again for the lift."

"Anytime."

Smiling, I step out of John's truck and slam the door shut.

"Wait."

I spin on my toes, ready to question him, but words fail me. John walks around the front of his truck. His eyes hold me still. As he nears, I take two steps backward. John presses me against the door with his body, and I feel every rugged ridge of him. My hands come up, and my palms flatten against his chest. John leans in and angles his head down as he rests his forearm on the hood of his truck. He hovers above my parted lips.

"What is it about you that draws me in? Is it your beauty? Your feisty attitude? Maybe it's your blue eyes." He pauses, then says, "Maybe it's the fact that you have no idea who my brother is and actually like me for me." I don't respond as he stares at my mouth. "Tell me you want to kiss me, because I sure as hell want to kiss you," he drawls, and it's sexy as hell.

"I don't think that's a good idea," I whisper.

John doesn't move. "Why's that?"

"Because nothing good can come from a kiss."

His eyes dance with trouble, and it makes my heart flutter.

"Says who? If that's the case, you aren't being kissed right. Many good things can come from a kiss," he says. His husky voice sends a shiver down my spine. John presses his hips into mine.

"While that may be true"—I fist his shirt and hold him close—"I don't know if it's a good idea."

"May I? I promise to make it worth it," he whispers.

My heart thumps against my chest. A beat passes between us, and I nod subtly.

John tilts his head as he descends. His tongue dances across the seam of my mouth, asking for more, and I grant it to him. He holds both sides of my jaw and nips at my lips, pulling and kissing but not delving in as much as I want him to. He teases me more than he takes.

He pulls back and whispers, "See you tomorrow."

John steps back. I move on shaky knees and walk toward my house, unable to form words. I've never been kissed in such a simple way that's left me with goose bumps. It was electric.

I stand still with a smile so big my cheeks hurt as I watch John drive away, a cloud of dirt flying up behind his truck. As crazy as it sounds, I want to feel his lips on me again soon.

LATER IN THE NIGHT, LONG AFTER THE SUNSET AND MY schoolwork is complete, I struggle with falling asleep. I worry about finding a job but am at ease knowing I can finally settle in one place. There's a peacefulness in the little town that puts my restlessness at bay. It's quiet. As much as I love the city, I like the countryside a little more. Something I never thought I'd admit.

Throughout my jumbled thoughts, I keep drifting back to John. I hadn't been expecting his kiss. Did I want to kiss him? Sure. I just don't know what to think of it.

My phone chimes. Picking it up, my heart flutters at the name on the display. A smile spreads across my face. I slide my finger across the screen. His ears must've been ringing.

Yours Truly: That kiss was a mistake.

Frowning, I shake my head. Why would he say that? My lips tingle just thinking about it. I knew I should have told him no earlier. I'm bothered I let it happen now. My stomach turns to stone as I stare at the text message. Before I have a chance to respond, my phone chimes again.

Yours Truly: One kiss isn't enough. I want more.

My lips part. Damn country boy.

Me: Too bad. That's all you get.

Yours Truly: We'll see about that.

I reread my reply. Even in text form, I know it's a lie. If he wants to kiss me again, I'll probably allow it.

Actually, there is no probably about it. I would without hesitation.

Yours Truly: Do you have plans this weekend?

Me: Yes, I'm looking for a job.

> Yours Truly: With Chad? You know how I feel about him. The guy discards chicks before he can take the condom off.

While I have zero plans to sleep with him, I keep that information to myself.

> Me: He's been nothing but friendly to me.

> Yours Truly: Text me after your job hunt. We could go to the movies or grab some dinner.

Is he asking me out on a date? My fingers tremble thinking of a response.

> Me: Sounds good to me.

> Yours Truly: Good luck.

I smile to myself and toss my phone on my bed.

SIX

ALYSSA

L ooking over at Chad, he reminds me of a typical bad boy girls lust after.

His black sideways hat is propped on his head. He has one arm slung over the steering wheel and a cigarette dangling from his pierced lip. From what I've learned through John, he sleeps with any girl he can get, and parties like a rock star. He isn't the committed relationship type, which means he doesn't like attachment. I like that the most, seeing as I am not one myself. He makes his own rules and lives by them.

Chad shoots me a fleeting glance before his eyes are back on the road, and I feel every inch of his heated gaze on my skin. He takes a puff of his cigarette.

"Have an idea for a job yet? What do you want to do?" he asks.

I shrug. I asked Chad after class yesterday if he would take me to apply for jobs today. I didn't care where I got one, just that I was getting paid.

"Whatever I can get, I'll take."

"The restaurant I'm working at, Roxie's, they're looking for a part-time waitress. Do you have any experience?"

"I don't, but how hard can it be?"

"I'm a busboy, so I don't have a clue. But I know they train. We can go fill out an application if you'd like."

I look at him with hopeful eyes. "Could we?"

The panty-melting grin he gives me hits low, and I feel it all around. "No problem."

Twenty minutes later, we're leaving Roxie's. I have a new job starting next week. "Thank you so much, Chad! I really needed this job."

A sly smile slides across his face. "Wanna take a little ride?"

I nod quickly, beaming. I'm so happy I got a job that I can't wipe the smile from my face.

"Sure. Where to?"

"This place down a back road I know about." He opens his arm. "Come here." I scoot over to him and curl into his side. "Damn, girl. Those legs," he says and grasps my thigh. His grip is rougher than what I'm used to, but I'd be lying if I said I didn't like it.

"So you and John?" he asks, leaving it open for me to answer.

"Are just friends."

"I bet he wouldn't like it if he knew you were hanging out with me.

I don't tell him that he wouldn't. Biting my lip, I take a chance. "Why is there tension between you two?"

Frowning, Chad looks over at me. "He didn't tell you?"

I shake my head. "I didn't ask. But I can sense it."

"He claims I stole his girlfriend back in high school." A sardonic laugh escapes his lips. Chad takes one last drag and flicks his cigarette out of the window. "She was willing and able. I didn't have to do anything but wave two fingers at her and she came running. He never got over it."

I groan inwardly. That's not what I want to hear. It's sneaky, and breaks bro code. I want to ask more questions, but at the same time, I don't want to probe. And considering it's history, I don't want to restart any problems either.

As Chad turns off to the right and drives through a wooded trail, he says, "How's about I grab a few beers and we hang down by Whiskey River?"

I smile cheekily at Chad and say, "Let's do it."

THE SUN HAS SET BY THE TIME CHAD DROPS ME OFF. WITH my mother still at work and all my schoolwork caught up, I plop on the couch and flip on the television. Bright headlights shine through the windows and bounce around the living room. I stand up and look out the window. A smile slides across my face. John's truck turns off, and he steps out. I sprint to the front door and throw it open, excited to see him.

"What the hell, Alyssa? Where've you been?"

The delight I felt at the sight of him is instantly wiped from my face. Where have I been? He says it as if I've done something wrong.

"Why did you ignore me? I've been trying to call you," he says.

I'm still tipsy from drinking with Chad, but I manage to march to John with my chin up. Call it liquid courage. He may tower over me, but he doesn't get to demand anything from me.

"First of all, you have no say in what I do. I can hang out with whomever I want, when I want."

John waves his hand, arrogance written all over the motion. "When it comes to Chad, I do. The guy is a snake. He's trash. He's only showing interest in you because I am. Did he try to fuck you yet? Because he will."

My eyes lower and I ignore his last comment. "Second, you're not my boyfriend, so I don't have to answer to you. And anyway, my phone was on silent. I didn't see that you called. Chad was helping me look for a job." John leans down and inhales near my face. I rear back. "What the hell are you doing?"

His brows bunch tightly together. "Are you drunk?" John asks, his voice laced with accusation.

"What business is it of yours?"

His eyes narrow and then widen. "You're drunk. He took you job searching while drunk? That's real smooth." He shakes his head in disgust. "Trust me when I say he's no good for you."

"How many times are you going to tell me that?"

"Until you get it through your thick head."

I cross my arms in front of my chest. "But you're good for me, right?"

John brushes a hand down his troubled face. "That's not what I'm saying. He's bad news, has an abusive drunk of a father, and is always in trouble with the law. I don't like that you were out drinking with that trash."

"I had fun with him. Nothing happened. And anyway, Chad got me a job."

John takes a step forward. "I don't want you hanging out with him."

"You can't tell me what to do," I spit back.

He takes another step and has me boxed in against his truck. Just like the time when he kissed me.

"Think about what you're doing."

"What's there to think about?" I shrug. "We were just having a little fun after he helped me out. I didn't drink before applying for a job, only after."

"Alyssa." He breathes on my neck. That's when it hits me.

"Are you jealous?" I ask. He doesn't answer, but his silence says it all. "You are, aren't you?"

"Yeah, I am," he shockingly admits.

My stomach tightens. A part of me likes that John's jealous.

"Did you kiss him?" he asks. "Did he touch you?"

I shake my head. "No. Nothing happened."

"Good."

Even in the darkness, John's eyes stand out. They pour into mine, touching me intimately and warming my body as they travel down to my parted lips. He steps closer and is a mere inch from my mouth. He puts one hand on my hip and squeezes.

John gives me a lopsided grin as he leans in for a kiss, but I swoop out of the way. His chuckle sends a shiver through me.

JOHN

ALYSSA IS GETTING UNDER MY SKIN.

She chuckles as she moves away. She's purposely playing with me. Taking a deep breath, my head hangs as I stare at the ground. I want Alyssa. I want her more and more each minute we spend together. But then I hear she's with Chad, and the need is ten times stronger. He can't have her.

I despise that she was with him. He always goes after what's mine.

"Girl," I say, my voice low. "You better run."

"What's that, country boy?" She's flirting with me. I can hear the smile on her face even though I can't see her. "I didn't quite hear you."

I raise my head and drop my arms. "I said, you better run. When I catch you, you're mine." She giggles in response, and I love the sound of it. "I'm going to count to three." I take a step back. "And you better be gone." I pause. "One."

"Johnny…"

"Two." I take another step closer, and I hear her feet pound into the ground.

"Three." I chase her around to the back of the truck. We're going in circles and laughing at the same time.

"John!" She pants. "I don't want to play your stupid game."

I stop running and duck so she can't see me. I get low and look under my truck for her feet to see where she is.

"Johnny?" Her whisper carries through the night air. She stands on her tiptoes looking for me. "Where are you?"

Quietly, I circle the truck again then take a few giant

steps. I say nothing, just creep as quietly as possible to where she is.

"Where are you?" she asks again.

"Right here," I say in her ear.

Her shriek echoes through the air, and she jumps. Turning around, she slaps my chest, and I pull her into me.

"You jerk! You scared me!"

I laugh loudly and then wrap my arm around her back. "I told you I would get my hands on you. I wasn't kidding." I push her up against the truck. Her body is pressed to mine. She's breathing heavily. "Do you know what I want right now? To kiss you again. I haven't been able to stop thinking about it. I was serious when I said one kiss wasn't enough. You're mine, Alyssa."

Then I smash my mouth to hers. I can't take it any longer. I need to feel her lips on mine.

Alyssa kisses me back. Her tongue strokes along the roof of my mouth so seductively slow it causes blood to flow directly to my cock. I harden, and I know she can feel it. I delve deeper and kiss her back with the same tenacity. Alyssa rubs her sweet little body against mine. She nips at my lips. Her arms circle my neck, and she draws me in, but I break the kiss.

"Since we're on the subject. You don't have a boyfriend, and I don't want a girlfriend. How about we try out the friends-with-benefits thing?"

"That is the stupidest idea ever. Friends with benefits never work for anyone."

"Such a pessimistic outlook you have. Take a chance."

"With you?"

"Well, I'm sure as hell not talking about one of my

friends or sleazy Chad." My gaze turns hard, matching my voice.

She huffs. "What if it ruins our friendship? I like you. You're the first real friend I've had in a long time. I don't want to screw this up." When I stay silent, she says, "I don't know. I just don't know if it's a good idea."

"Why not? We're friends, and we have chemistry. There's no harm in it."

"It's just that... It's... We're friends, and I don't want anything to ruin our friendship. The benefits would."

I turn serious. "Alyssa, has our friendship been strained or awkward since we last kissed?"

She glances to the side, musing over my question. "Well, no."

"Then there's your answer. Nothing is going to happen to us."

"That was just a kiss, though. What you're asking for is way more."

"We'll start off slow. I want you, and I'm pretty sure you want me."

She gives me a lopsided smile.

"You don't have to tell me I'm right. I already know I am."

I want to see how far we would take it. Would she push me away? Or would she pull me closer?

"I guess we can try it out," she says, and exhales a long breath.

A triumphant smile spreads across my face. I close the distance between us with my mouth once more. Alyssa lets out a little moan and grips the back of my shirt. She holds me closer, just like I hoped she would. Before it goes any further, like fucking her against the side of my truck, I break away with a gasp. I step back, and she reaches for me. I grin knowingly at her.

"I just sealed our deal with a kiss," I say, and Alyssa puckers her lips together. "See you later, sugar."

She huffs. "That southern drawl of yours is trouble, you know."

"I know. Girls love it. Sometimes I even lay it on thick."

Her eyes lower in a challenge.

"You want to play like that? The boys around here seem to like blondes, short shorts, and tanned legs, which I have plenty of." She gives me a cheeky grin.

Alyssa sashays away, adding extra sway to her hips, knowing I'm watching. She doesn't get very far. Not even a second later, my arm wraps around her stomach, and I pull her against my chest. The feel of her against me sends a flood of sensations through my body. I like the feel of her more than I should.

"Alyssa." I breathe against her hair. "Don't play with me like that." I nip her ear. "I've wanted you since the moment I saw you, and watching you walk away like that, teasing me, makes me want you even more. So much more that I would fuck you right now if I could."

My hand slides down the front of her shorts. I cup her pussy, fingers fanning and skirting across her creamy thigh. She squeezes her legs together and arches her hips back, her ass pressing into my cock. I groan in the back of my throat from wanting her. "You have no idea how bad I've been dying to get inside you."

I begin rubbing her pussy. "Johnny… You can't." She rotates her hips on my hand, wanting more.

"Do you really want me to stop?"

She shakes her head. "No," is a whisper on her lips. "But what if someone sees us?"

"No one will," I say in her ear.

It's nearly pitch-black outside. Houses aren't close to each other here. The only light is the one on her front porch. Alyssa gyrates on my hand.

"I have one rule that you have to agree to," I say, then slide my hand inside her shorts and cup her pussy. She moans, and I love the sound of it. I can feel the wet spot on her panties and rub her where it is. "You're not allowed to hook up with Chad."

"Okay. I agree," she says quickly.

I circle her clit and listen to her panting. I can tell she's close, but the painful ache in my dick forces me to step back. If I don't, I'll pull her into my truck and fuck her senseless. I want her totally sober when we have sex.

"What... What the hell are you doing?"

She wobbles on her knees.

"Showing you how good our chemistry is." I pop a kiss on her cheek and then turn to walk away. "See you later." I jump in my truck and drive off, leaving a breathless Alyssa behind.

SEVEN

ALYSSA

I've planned my schedule so that I have my mom's car most nights I work at Roxie's.

It's been a week since I started working. Juggling work and school took some practice, but I've managed it. Chad was friendly and offered to drive me to my shift if something happens. That's a plus. I didn't tell John, though.

It's early Saturday morning, and I have the day off while Mom works. I throw another piece of white cheddar popcorn into my mouth while I sit on the couch. I've already eaten half the bag for breakfast. Putting it to the side, I brush off my shirt, grab my water bottle, and take a sip. As I cap it shut, a knock sounds at the door. I look down at what I'm wearing—a white camisole and plaid pajama pants. I haven't yet brushed my hair, so I can only imagine what I look like. I stand up, and another couple of knocks sound before I can reach the door.

"Good mornin' to you," John says, smiling. His eyes eat me up. "Is this what you're wearing?"

I'm confused. "Wearing for what?"

"To go muddin'," he says like he's stating the obvious.

A loud huff breaks from my lips. My hand slides from the door to the handle. "You're kidding me, right? I told you, I don't play in the mud."

"Do you have other plans? I was looking forward to hanging out with you. Tell me you don't have other plans."

A slow smile spreads across my mouth. John is persistent, and I like the way it feels. I open the door wider to welcome him in.

"No, I don't have any," I say.

"Good. Now go get changed. I'll wait here."

"Johnny, " I draw out his name. "Playing in mud doesn't really appeal to me."

"Alyssa, go," he demands, softness covering the edge of his voice. "Let me give you a taste of the South and how we country boys get down. It'll be fun, trust me. You might even like it."

We have a mini staring contest before I cave.

"Ugh, fine. I'll be right back."

"Wear some old clothes. They're going to get ruined."

John says for me to wear old clothes, but the truth is, I don't have any. Nothing I have is considered old, ripped, or worth getting mud on.

Yanking the dark cherry dresser drawer open, I rifle through my clothes. An array of colorful tops swirl around each other as I search for something old. My drawer is turning into a mess. I find a tank top and a pair of shorts. Slipping them on, I look in the mirror and take in my appearance. I look like a porcelain doll with my high cheekbones, almond-shaped eyes, and hair pulled tight. I grab a pair of crystal-encrusted flip-flops and slip those on too.

John eyes me as I leave my bedroom. A smirk spills across his face before he laughs.

"What's so funny?"

"You gotta change your shoes."

"What's wrong with my shoes?"

"Either put on old, ratty ones, or just go barefoot. Otherwise, you're going to have mud between those pretty little stones, and I have a feeling that's not what you want to happen."

Barefoot? Is he insane? That's gross. John starts laughing again.

"I don't see what's so funny. You know what? I'm not going."

"You should see the look on your face right now. Priceless." John's long legs eat up the space between us. He grabs me by the elbow and pulls me close. He looks into my eyes and says, "I'm just playing with you. Come on, let's go. If you want to wear those shoes, fine by me, but don't say I didn't warn you."

I don't respond. I can't. The heat coming off John's body puts me under a spell. I'm too busy getting lost in his green eyes to open my mouth and speak. I like the way he looks at me. As if I'm all that matters. If it isn't his sweet southern drawl, or his gaze that penetrates me on another level, it's the strength of his hands holding me. John is strong and radiates a protectiveness that I'm drawn to. We're all alone. I have the house to myself until tonight.

"Johnny," rolls off my lips.

His thumb traces my jaw. "Yeah?"

"What are you doing?"

John shrugs. "Staring at you."

"Why?"

"Because you're beautiful. And because I want to kiss you."

A blush fills my cheeks. "Oh."

A playful grin forms on his lips. "Oh?" he repeats.

John leans down, and the scruff from his unshaven jaw rubs along my skin as he dusts kisses up my neck. He moves over my mouth, and my lips part for his tongue to slip in. His caress is gentle yet demanding. He kisses me like there's a need to consume me, and I let him. I balance on my tiptoes and kiss him with a passion and intensity that shocks me. I want John. The touch of his hands on my body overwhelms my logic, and I melt into him. Leaning into him, I thread my fingers through his hair and lap at his mouth. As my hips press into his, he growls, and holy hell, does it make me wet. The sound is one of the hottest things I've ever heard. I'm on fire. Desire engulfs me in a haze of lust. I want him badly. His hands skate down my sides, his fingers leaving trails of heat as he cups my rear and lifts both my legs to hook around his waist. I squeeze him with my thighs, moaning as I kiss him harder, bruising my lips from the force of our mouths. Blinding pleasure runs down my spine. I ache for more. His nimble fingers dance down my thigh to the seam of my shorts, curving around my ass and gripping me hard. I moan loudly into his mouth. I can't help it. His touch is electric.

"I want you." He pants.

I squeeze my eyes tight. "What have you done to me?"

"Same thing you did to me."

"Which is?"

"We kissed. That's all it took."

"Are you calling me easy?" I say it jokingly, but he seems to take offense to it.

"Don't put words in my mouth, Alyssa. I didn't say that. All we did was kiss, and look where it took us. We're out of breath, ready to rip each other's clothes off. This feeling you give me has never happened before. Don't try to deny the chemistry between us. It's been there all along. Tell me it hasn't."

He holds the back of my nape and kisses me again, thrusting his tongue into my mouth to prove his point that a kiss was all it took.

"Tell me," John demands.

I fist his shirt in my hands. He's right. I do want him. And I want him right now.

"I want you," I say, my voice breathless. He grins, and that damn dimple makes an appearance. "I need you right now," I say.

"Where's your room?"

JOHN

I THROW THE DOOR OPEN AND SLAM IT SHUT WITH MY foot. I take three long strides to her bed and kneel on her mattress to set her down. She's wild and aggressive, trying to pull off my shirt then fumbles with my belt. I grasp the seam of her shirt and pull it over her head and toss it to the floor. My shorts slide down my legs. My erection juts out, and her eyes focus on it. Alyssa reaches for me, but I push her shoulder, and she flops back on the bed. Her perky breasts bounce, and her nipples harden. My mouth is already watering to taste them. I don't bother undoing her shorts. I grab the waistband and yank them off in one swift motion along with her panties and drop them to the floor, where they join the rest of our clothes.

"Give me your mouth," I demand.

I love kissing her.

I don't waste any time. I lie on top of her and thrust my hips against hers, making her feel my cock and how hard I am. Her pussy is warm. I slide my erection along her slit, feeling her wetness. Alyssa tightens her legs around my back and locks her ankles. She rubs her pussy on my cock, gyrating on me. Fuck. I can't wait to be inside of her.

"I need to feel you," she says, her voice breathless. "I need you inside of me."

It's as if she can read my mind. Leaning down, I pull one of her nipples into my mouth. I flick the nub with my tongue and she purrs. Her back bows, her head rolling against the bed. I reach between us with two fingers and stroke her clit. She's soaking wet and wild with desire.

"Do you have a condom?" I ask.

Alyssa shakes her head. "No, do you?"

"Yeah, hang on."

I quickly grab the condom from my shorts pocket. I rip the foil open with my teeth and then roll it down my cock. I glance at Alyssa and notice she's watching my every move. Her teeth press into her bottom lip in anticipation. Palming her pussy, I use her wetness to coat the condom, then kneel between her legs. She spreads her thighs wider to make room for me. Using the tip of my cock, I rub her clit in circles, and her hips start to move. I tease her before

I move lower and nudge her opening. I push in just the tip and stop to suck in a breath.

"Stop playing around. I want you inside of me already."

Taking Alyssa's mouth in a surrendering kiss, I surge inside of her all the way to the base of my cock. She fits me like a glove. Alyssa cries out, and her breasts push into my chest. I don't spare her a second to breathe. She feels so fucking good that I almost can't control myself. I need to get deeper. I need to push harder. I want to feel all of her.

"How's that for playing around?" I say.

I thrust into her again and again and again. Sex has never been like this. Alyssa whimpers for more, and I give it to her. I'm untamed, but so is she.

Alyssa rolls me onto my back. I look up at her in surprise and she grins. With her hands flat on my chest, she begins to ride me. Her blond hair falls over her shoulders and covers her breasts. I move the strands away so I can see her breasts bounce. She slowly moves up and down my shaft, taking every inch. The change of pace makes it hard for both of us to hold on. The only sound in the room is of us panting and our bodies moving.

"Oh fuck," I groan.

I slide my fingers under her clit and stroke her from side to side. She gasps, her mouth falling open. Her arms give, and she almost falls on me.

"You like that, don't you?"

"Yes," she whispers.

"Then get back up and ride me like you were so I can keep doing it." She does as I say, and I feel her pussy clench around my cock. "Just like that, baby." Alyssa begins to ride me harder.

"I'm close."

Her head lolls back and her breasts bounce as she fucks me. She doesn't hold back, and it makes me so hard for her. My hand picks up speed, and I work her faster.

"Fuck," she moans. "Johnny."

I don't stop as I feel my own release climbing.

"I'm almost there," I say, thrusting hard into her.

"Don't stop," she begs. "Please don't stop. Just like that."

"Not a chance."

"Right there. Oh my God. Oh my… Yes…"

A curse comes out in a guttural moan as Alyssa's pussy tightens around my cock. She rides us into a blissful wave of ecstasy. I don't stop rubbing, and she doesn't stop riding. Her hips slowly undulate against mine as her pussy contracts from the orgasm. A shiver falls down my spine, and I come undone just as she does. We pant, we moan, and screw the living daylights out of each other.

Alyssa falls forward onto my chest. She's breathing heavily. A dampness coats our skin. I wrap my arms around her back and hold her.

"That was amazing," she says breathlessly.

"That was pretty incredible."

And holy hell, it was.

I cup her cheek and bring her mouth to mine. I gently kiss her swollen lips. After a minute or so, I say, "Come on, pretty girl. We gotta get going."

Alyssa's raspy giggle makes me feel good. She turns onto her back, and I pull out of her. She extends her arms above her head, looking comfortable and sedated, and sighs.

"I'm going to skip your mudding session and take a nap. I'm kind of tired now." A small smile forms on her face. I can tell she's lying.

"Don't try me. Let's go. Get up. I'm taking you for a ride."

"But you just did." She laughs, her eyes twinkling with naughtiness.

I turn onto my side and kiss all around her face and neck. "I'm pretty sure you rode me."

She chuckles playfully, her blue eyes gleaming. "Fair enough."

Kissing her forehead, I say, "Leave the shoes at home. Trust me."

EIGHT

ALYSSA

I must be out of my mind.

I'm going mudding.

Maybe all my common sense was thrown out the window earlier when John and I tumbled between the sheets, because there is no other way I would ever agree to something like this.

I take one more look in the mirror then step out of the bathroom to find John sitting on my couch, scrolling on his phone.

"I can't believe I've agreed to this."

John's head snaps in my direction. He rakes a stare down my body and grins. "You'll have fun, trust me."

We walk out of the house, and I lock the door behind me. I take a few steps when I see his four-wheeler sitting in my driveway and not his truck. It catches me off guard. He reaches for my cell phone and keys and places them in the duffle bag that's bungeed to the back. Throwing a leg over his seat, John stands on the foot bars as he cranks on his ATV. He revs the gas and motions for me to get on. I place my hand in his outstretched one, carefully put one foot behind his, and throw my other leg over the seat.

John sits down and the machine bounces. "You might want to hold on."

I grab his hips.

Looking over his shoulder, he says, "You might want to hold on tight, Alyssa. It's okay. You can touch me. Don't be afraid." He teases.

I scoot forward and wrap my arms around his stomach and squeeze him as hard as I can. He chuckles.

"Let's ride."

John peels out of my driveway. My legs are pressed to the sides of his thick thighs, and my cheek rests on his back. We weave through the woods then travel down some back roads. The Georgia sun is hot today, and it's beating on my face. I feel free as we ride without a care.

"How fast does this thing go?" I yell.

He grins at my question, and it makes my heart drop. "Hang on, and I'll show you." John's foot clutches into third gear, and he flicks his wrist back on the accelerator. The ATV vibrates under us as we pick up the pace. My breasts are smashed against his back, arms tight around his stomach, and I smile as the wind slaps me in the face.

"That's all you got?" I taunt.

John presses the accelerator, and we fly down the dirt road. My giggles float through the air. John laughs too. I squeal when we hit a pothole and mud flies onto our legs. I lift off the seat, bounce back down, and bury my face in his back. John turns in a circle and goes back to the same spot.

"Hang on!" he yells.

Quickly shifting into gears, John races toward the

pothole once more. "Oh my God, oh my God," I chant in his ear before he hits the hole again. I tighten my arms around his waist so I don't bounce off the seat this time. Mud flies onto our legs and feet, and droplets coat my arms.

Spinning the ATV around, John stops and asks over his shoulder, "How was that?"

I meet his eyes and drop my chin on his shoulder. All I can do is give John a cheesy smile. "How was that? That was fun as hell!"

"That was only a prelude for what's to come. Just wait. It rained all week, which means lots and lots of muddy holes. Me and the guys come out here when it rains like it did."

Before I realize what he's doing, John leans over and kisses my forehead. It makes me blush.

Downshifting, he drives us into the empty muddy field. Trees are planted sporadically, potholes of various sizes are everywhere, and there's a large lake right in the center. The open land is unlike anything I've ever seen before. I find it breathtaking and peaceful. John tells me it belongs to Ford's father, who turned it into a riding spot for him and his friends years ago. There's a trail of hills, and trees to ride through. Tracks are set in the ground, circling and overlapping each other. It reminds me of a giant sandbox made of mud. This place is a country boy's dream.

Jace rides over with a longneck beer in one hand and parks right next to us.

"What the hell took you two so damn long? We've been waiting for an hour now."

"I had to convince this one to go." He hitches his thumb over his shoulder at me. "Once she agreed, I explained that her sparkly glitter flip-flops wouldn't work. Told her to get rid of them. That was an ordeal. Man, you know how girls are. She had to put makeup on, do her hair, paint her nails." John jokes.

I smack his side and stand. "He's such a liar." I go to step down but pause.

The red clay looks like it could swallow me whole. It reminds me of quicksand. I should have worn boots. And maybe some jeans.

As I dip my toe, I'm nudged from behind and lose my balance. Instead of stepping into the mud, I swiftly step onto Jace's ATV and into his arms.

"Looks like your girl is scared of a little mud, Johnny boy." Jace snickers. Jace slides his arm around my waist and positions me on his knee, where I go willingly.

"I'm not his girl."

John glares at me. Maybe I shouldn't have said that. I didn't mean to hurt him with my words, but I don't want him to think that just because we had sex we're an item now.

"I'm going to ride with Jace."

"Like hell you are," John says. He reaches for me, but I quickly pull away.

"Take me for a ride, Jace?" I ask sweetly.

"Well, sure, my darlin'," he says, starting his four-wheeler.

"Jace," John warns, then looks at me. "Get over here, Alyssa. You're with me."

I pause behind Jace, using him as a barrier. "Make me," I say, and then take off running.

"You better get back here," John yells from behind me.

I look over my shoulder and my eyes widen. John is

running after me. My heart thumps wildly against my ribs. He's quick. I pick my knees up and run as fast as possible. Splats of mud hit my thighs, up my back, and into my hair, but I don't care. I run zigzag and hear John curse behind me. I laugh. Just as I gain a little distance between us, Jace drives next to me on his ATV.

"Get on!" he yells over the engine and holds out his hand for me to take.

I hop on the footrests of Jace's ATV and hold on for dear life. He makes a U-turn and heads back in the direction I came from.

"Wh-What?" I stammer. "What are you doing? Go the other way," I plead. But Jace slows down. "What are you doing?" I tap his shoulder furiously. "Keep going!"

"You didn't think I'd screw over my boy like that, did you?"

"Well, no, but I didn't think you'd hand me over either," I say.

"You thought wrong, sugar plum." Looking at John, Jace says, "She's all yours."

John grabs me by the waist and holds me up. Jace hops off his ATV and reaches for a handful of mud. He attempts to make a mushy ball out of it as he walks my way.

"What are you doing?" I ask.

"I'm just going to get you used to the mud before we get going," Jace says, slapping the mud from hand to hand. I eye it wearily.

I try to slide my legs down John's waist, but he won't let go. He holds me too tight to wiggle out of his hold. My brows rise as Jace steps in front of me. Mischief paints his face, and I know I'm in for it.

"You better not do any—"

Jace pats mud on my cheeks. I gasp and clench my eyes shut. He rubs it in. He then runs both hands down my neck, over my shoulders, and down my sides while John holds me in a vice grip.

"We're just warming you up," John says and then sinks to his knees.

"What are you doing?" I ask suspiciously. "I swear to God, I will kill you if you do this!"

"I told you. We're getting you warmed up."

John presses my back into the mud and lies on top of me. Goose bumps break out down my arms at the feel of the watery gunk covering me. I yell, and John just laughs. Jace rubs some in my hair, and I decide I'm definitely going to kill them both. Especially John. I could easily torture him.

John gets up and takes my hand. We stand, and I thread my fingers through my hair, trying to get some of the mud out but get nowhere.

"Laugh it up, boys. I'll get you back for this."

Jace and John both chuckle as if they don't believe me.

Ford rides up. "Would you like a cold one before we get started?"

John nods. "You know I do."

"I guess," I say. I'm not a big drinker, but why not.

I watch as Ford reaches behind him and grabs three cold beers. He sticks each cap in his mouth and pops the tops off with his teeth. He hands one to me and then one to both John and Jace.

Mortified, I say, "I can't believe you just popped that off with your teeth."

"Better believe it, baby."

"And girls actually like that down here?" I ask, stunned.

Ford nods with a half-grin. His boy-next-door charm is strong, and his smile lights up his face.

Hours later, I'm having the time of my life. I laugh so much that my stomach aches and my cheeks burn. I have no idea what time it is, and I don't care. I'm having a blast and don't want the day to end. Dirt covers the four of us from head to toe, and my clothes are ruined. Now I know why John said to wear old clothes and leave my sandals at home.

"Do you think I could drive?" I ask, lifting my chin toward the ATV.

John nods. "Let's see what you got."

He reaches behind his head, fists his shirt at his nape, and yanks it off. He drops to the ground in a heap. I swallow thickly, liking what I see. It takes everything in me not to gawk at his toned body. John climbs on behind me and leans in close to grab the handlebars. His chest is pressed to my back as he explains the gears and pedals. The heat of his delectable body causes a flutter to hum through me. I fight the urge not to lean into him.

"Alright," he drawls, "this is the accelerator." John thumbs it to show me. "Here are the brakes," he says as he squeezes the bars. "And if you look down, this is the clutch. Now place your hands here and your feet on top of mine." John scoots closer, and my heart speeds up. His arms box me in and his thighs hug me from behind. The hardness pressing into my lower back does not go unnoticed. John's hands rest on mine. He flicks on the ignition and cranks the gas with my hands under his.

Gently, he eases into first gear and presses on the accelerator.

"Listen to the engine closely. You can hear when it's ready to shift into second gear. It kind of just reaches its max, and you'll know."

I listen, but I wonder if I'm hearing right. "Right there?"

John nods. "Yup. Now, you'll flick the clutch with your foot and gently apply the accelerator."

I do as he says, petrified I will screw up somehow and stall.

"You're doing great. Now just ride slow so you get used to it."

John removes his hands from mine. He slides them up my outer thighs and places them on my hips with a light squeeze.

I curve around holes and pass hills so I can get used to the feel of the horsepower under us.

"You can go through a hole if you want," John says.

I nod. I turn the steering wheel around and pass Jace, who has a grin on his face, and aim for a large pothole. Adrenaline fills me as I take a deep breath and ride straight for the puddle. The opening is much deeper than I thought, and the ATV bounces hard. Thick mud flies into the air and splatters us. I bounce off the seat, and John wraps an arm around my waist to hold me steady.

I turn around halfway and smile brightly over my shoulder. "That was so much fun! Can I do it again? Can I go faster?"

"Yeah, but only if you don't let go afterward. Luckily I was on here with you, or else you would've sputtered and stalled."

My smile vanishes, and my shoulders drop. "Oh…"

"It's all good. That's why I'm behind you." John squeezes my hip lightly, reassuring me that everything is okay.

"Well, well, well," Jace says as he pulls up next to us.

"What?" I ask.

Jace shakes his head, and Ford pulls up. "I haven't ever seen another chick drive his ATV before. This is something new, isn't it, Ford?"

"Sure is." Ford tips his beer back.

"You guys are a bunch of assholes," John says. "How would you know if any other chick drove? I don't ride with you guys all the time."

Jace grins with a twinkle in his eye. I know what he says is the truth, and something about that makes me feel good inside.

"Whatever you say. Want to take a few more spins and then head down to Whiskey River?"

"Sounds good to us. Alyssa wanted to ride a little more, then we'll go."

THREE BEERS IN, I'M HAVING THE TIME OF MY LIFE BEING barefoot and reckless. John has brought out a playful side of me I didn't know existed. I'm feeling tipsy as I balance on a huge, fat tree that fell over the river. If I'm not careful, I could fall into the water. I feel like I'm Baby in *Dirty Dancing* right now.

"Can you swim?" John hollers from land. Specks of dirt cover his face.

I spin on my toes. "Yes, why?"

"Because if you fall in, I ain't jumpin' in to save you." He jokes and takes a swig of his beer.

My arms flop to my side. "What kind of guy are you? What do you mean you're not saving me? You're supposed to save me if I'm hurt."

"I ain't the savin' kind of guy, honey."

"So if I fall in, you're just going to stand there?"

"Maybe."

His big grin contradicts his words. I wave him over.

"Come over here with me."

"Hell no."

I taunt him. "Why? You scared?"

"I ain't scared of shit."

"Then come up here with me and show me you're not scared."

His eyes scan the length of my body. "If I come over there, you have to kiss me."

I roll my eyes playfully and nod. Maybe it's the beer that makes me agree so fast, but he has some delectable lips. It's just a kiss anyway, right?

John chugs the remainder of his beer and then chucks it off to the side where it rolls on the ground. Ford catches it and puts it in the garbage. I watch as John steps onto the tree and walks toward me like he's walking on grass.

"You really thought I was scared?" He grins. "Now give me that kiss."

I stand on my tiptoes and place a light kiss on his lips.

"That's not the kind of kiss I was talking about, and you know it."

He steps away from me and does a backflip with some crazy twist off into the river.

"Are you freaking crazy!" I yell, while Ford and Jace laugh from a distance.

"Jump in with me! You won't even need a shower tonight."

My jaw drops. "Oh my God. You're serious, aren't you?"

"That's the redneck's way to take a shower," Ford yells.

"I'm not jumping into that disgusting water."

John waves his arms around the murky water and splashes me. "You just went muddin'. You have so much dirt on you that it will take more than one shower to get it all out, and you're worried about some river water?"

"It's not happening," I say firmly.

"Jump in and give me the kiss you were supposed to." He pushes.

Propping my hands on my hips, I stare at him. I can feel his enthusiasm. I'm having the most fun I've had in a long time, and John is the reason for it all. Taking a deep breath, I jump into the water and come up to see John swimming toward me. He grabs me by the waist and pulls me to his front.

"It's not so bad, is it?" he asks.

"I guess not."

John smiles at me. I wrap my legs around his waist and float with him.

"Now where's my kiss?"

"I think you got your kiss this morning, country boy."

"That wasn't part of our deal just now." John squeezes my waist, tickling me.

"John!" I giggle.

"Give it to me, and I'll stop."

"Ah, come on, Alyssa. Put him out of his misery, please, and kiss him already!" Jace yells from the land.

"Do it!" Ford shouts.

John smiles at me, his green eyes lighting up. "Yeah, just do it."

I huff dramatically. "What am I going to do with you guys?" I say, then plant a kiss right on John's mouth. I grip his face while kissing him hard.

Desire courses through my veins, and a replay of this morning flashes through my mind. His lips flirtatiously nip at my lips. Under water, he palms my butt and squeezes.

John pulls back, breaking the kiss. We pant into each other, trying to catch our breath, while Jace and Ford whistle. I want him again, just like he wants me.

Letting go of me, John dunks me under the water before swimming to the grass. He helps me out and then walks to his ATV to grab a towel from the bag strapped to the back. He hands it to me and waits until I'm finished drying off to use it.

"Y'all want to get a fire going and crack a few beers here after the sun sets?" Ford asks.

John and Jace perk up and shrug at each other then look at Ford. "We're down."

Looking at me, John asks, "What say you?"

I beam at my new group of friends. "Sounds like fun. I'm in."

NINE

ALYSSA

I take an extra-long shower, washing my hair more times than I can count, and scrub every inch of my body.

I'm sure there is still mud somewhere.

I step out, dry off, and dress. There is a chill tonight, so I pull out black leggings and an oversized sweater. I even put on a pair of sneakers instead of sandals.

The front door slams, and I pause. "Mom?"

"I'm home, honey."

"Hi!"

I flip my silky blond hair over my shoulder and blow-dry it until it's pin-straight. I apply black eyeliner on both my top and bottom lids with tiny wings to help accentuate my sapphire eyes. I finish off with a light dusting of blush and clear lip gloss. After one last check in the mirror, I head out to see Mom. John will be here to pick me up within the hour. Now that my mom is home, I want to spend time with her before leaving.

"Hey, Mom," I say, and kiss her cheek.

"Hi, honey. Where are you headed to?" she asks.

"To hang out with John and his friends. They're going to build a small fire and just hang out in the back of their trucks." I pause, my brows pinching together.

Mom gives me a quizzical look. "What did you do today?"

"I went mudding."

She barks out a laugh. "You're kidding me."

I shake my head, smiling as I think about my fantastic day. "Sure did! It was so much fun too." I drop my clutch on the counter and sit on a barstool. "At first, I was going to kill John for covering me head to toe in mud."

"Mud?" Mom makes a sour face.

"I know, I know, but then he let me drive his four-wheeler," I say excitedly. "I've never ridden one of those things, but now I wish we had one."

"It sounds like you had a blast today," she says, and I bob my head rapidly. "But now you're going out with him again?" she asks with a tilt of her head.

"Relax, Mom. He's just a friend, nothing more."

"It's not that, sweetie, but have you made any girlfriends?"

"Not really." I shrug nonchalantly. It doesn't bother me that I haven't. It's a challenge to make girlfriends. I mainly have guy friends.

"Do you need the car?" she asks.

"No, Johnny is picking me up. You'll have the chance to meet him. He's a really good guy, Mom. I think you'll like him."

She eyes me. "And he isn't your boyfriend?"

"No."

Knock, knock, knock.

I smile from ear to ear and get up. Opening the front door, the first thing I see are dimples. Be still my heart. I check him out. His distressed jeans, camel-colored boots, and white shirt tucked in the front with the rest hanging out makes him look effortlessly hot. I step to give him a hug, and his mixture of cologne and the scent of pine invades my senses.

"Hey," I say softly.

"You look beautiful." His gaze travels the length of my body and then stops on my shoes. "Wow. This is surprising."

"I'm learning," I say.

"Is that your friend?" Mom says as she comes to stand behind me. She extends her arm toward John. "I'm Lauren, Alyssa's mother. Why don't you come in for a minute?"

"Thank you, Ms. Winters. It's nice to meet you." John shuts the door, and we follow my mom into the kitchen.

"My daughter tells me you give her a ride to school. That's very generous of you. Please let me pay for your gas."

"Thank you, but that's not necessary, Ms. Winters. I'm not going out of my way to give her a lift, plus that's what friends are for," he says, looking at me. My cheeks flame under his gaze.

"Are you sure?"

"Yes, ma'am."

"It's very unexpected of you but much appreciated, especially while we share a car."

John smiles. "You're welcome."

"What are you studying in school? Same as Alyssa?"

"I'm actually undecided right now, but I've been

77

thinking about enlisting in the Marines. My father and his father served, so it's in my blood."

Mom smiles in approval. "Do you have any siblings?"

He nods. "I have an older brother—"

"He's a country rock singer on the radio," I chime in.

Mom's brows angle toward each other and she looks at John. "He is?"

"His name is Luke Jackson. He lives around here but is busy a lot and only sometimes in town. I also have twin brothers. They're younger than me."

"Wow. Your mom is a busy bee."

I groan inwardly. "Okay, Mom, are you done with the interrogation? We have somewhere to be."

Chuckling, she leans over and kisses my head. "Be safe, both of you."

"Always."

Jumping into his truck, John cranks the ignition. There aren't many streetlights at night around here, so he backs out of the driveway slowly. He turns on the radio and "Take Your Time" by Sam Hunt streams through the speakers. Yeah, I've been listening to country music, and I like it.

It's bumpy as we drive for a few minutes until we reach the large clearing in the woods. I glance around. Roughly ten trucks are lined up. Some with their lights shining on, others with the tailgates down. There are coolers on the grass next to the huge wheels. John finds an opening and parks his vehicle. We step out and make our way to the medium-sized fire pit. It's surrounded by heavy gray blocks to keep the fire from spreading. Thick orange, yellow, and blue flames crack under the starlit sky.

Without looking in my direction, John slides his hand

down the inside of my arm and laces his fingers with mine, finishing with a light squeeze.

"Johnny Boy," Jace drawls, handing us both a beer.

"Jace, you fucker. What've I told you about that?" He tips the beer back, giving Jace shit for calling him Johnny Boy.

"Hey, don't blame me. It's all your girl's fault here," Jace retorts, nodding his bottle toward me.

I take a sip of beer. "If Johnny didn't have pet names for me, I wouldn't have pet names for him. Therefore, it's his fault he's called Johnny Boy." I finish with a winning smile.

Ford snickers. "She's got a point."

"Oh, so you're taking her side?" John asks Ford.

"Nope. Just stating the facts."

"You know I'm right," I say with the bottle to my lips.

John shakes his head, trying to hide his own smile.

"Where's your truck? You brought cornhole with you, right?" Jace asks.

"Yeah, it's over there," John says and hitches his thumb behind his head.

"Sweet," Jace says. "You go drop that fancy tailgate of yours, and we'll grab the cooler and head over."

"What's a cornhole?" I ask.

"It's not a cornhole. It's cornhole, sugar." John shakes his head with a grin. "You've got a lot to learn, city girl."

John walks back to his truck. Tilting my head, I drink him in as I follow. The distressed jeans he's wearing hug his ass to perfection. It makes me want to reach out and pet him.

"This is cornhole," John says, but it doesn't register

because I'm too busy staring at his backside. "Were you just checking me out? Alyssa?"

"What? No."

A slow smile slides across his handsome face. "Liar," he states and stalks toward me. I back up blindly, rounding the truck to the driver's side and lean against it. John steps close and boxes me in. Everything about him is overpowering my commonsense.

"Johnny," I whisper. "What are you doing?"

"I can tell you're lying. Your body gives you away. Admit you were checking me out."

"I… I was not. I was looking to see what cornhole is."

His nose grazes my neck, and he leans in. My heart is racing at his closeness. "Oh, really? So the flush in your cheeks is all over a game you've never heard of? And what about your parted lips? Are those for the game too?" His tongue snakes out and slides across my neck and over my thumping pulse, making me shiver. "Either I make you nervous, or you're lying. Which is it?"

My breathing accelerates. I'm at a loss for words. John hovers in front of my mouth. I can feel his breath mix with mine. I can't move. My hands are flat against the truck. He's so close I can almost taste him. If he breathes, his lips will be on mine.

"What would you do if I kissed you right now? Would you pull away? Or would you pull me closer?"

TEN
ALYSSA

John dances dangerously close to my mouth with his own.

He presses his body firmly to mine, and I can feel every sweet inch of him. He feels so big and strong. I grip his waist and dig my fingers into him.

"You." He presses his lips to my neck. "Are." I gasp as he pushes his cock against me. "Lying," he says, then kisses my forehead and steps back.

John walks away with the most adorable smile on his face. It makes my heart skip a beat. I watch as he pulls out the cornhole boards and carries them to where Jace and Ford are. Jace eyes me and walks to where I'm standing.

"He's got it bad for you."

I give Jace a droll stare. "We're just friends."

"We don't let anyone ride our shit, unless it's in the sack," Jace says, wiggling his brows. He's so cheesy it's cute. "Then it's a free for all." Jace chugs his beer. "I've never seen anyone else ride his ATV before." He nods toward John, who is standing in front of the fire pit talking to Sarah. The smile slips from my face at the sight of her. I'm not usually a jealous girl, but it seems I am right now. "Next thing you know, he'll let you drive his fruity truck."

"It's not that big of a deal."

"If that's what you think. But what would happen if I wrapped an arm around your shoulder right now?"

My face scrunches together and I turn to look at him. "Nothing."

Jace takes a long gulp of his beer. "Wanna test it out?"

"Not particularly."

"Scared?"

I huff. "I'm not scared. Seriously, we're just friends. I don't know why you would think anything else."

"I've known John much longer than you. You may say you're just friends, but from the way he looks at you, and he's letting you drive his wheels? No, definitely not just friends."

"If you say so."

Jace steps closer. He wraps an arm around my shoulders and tugs me to him. I take another sip of my beer and eye John.

"You see that?" Jace asks, flicking his jaw toward his friend.

I feel a pang of jealousy seeing John talk to Sarah. This is precisely why I say no good thing can come from a kiss. Because a kiss leads to another kiss, and feelings are secretly woven through it all. Maybe it's the beer that's causing my emotions to bounce around and mess with my head. Jace's fingers massage my shoulder. I rest my head on his chest and close my eyes, trying to clear my unexpected feelings for John.

"You're playing with fire," Ford mumbles, walking up to grab a beer, then leaves.

I exhale a sigh just as John turns around. His eyes dance across the crowd until they land on me. His smile drops from his face, and he pierces me with a dark look. Sarah is still talking to him when he walks away mid-sentence and saunters over to where we are.

"See?" Jace whispers in my ear. "Look at him walking over here, ready to mark his claim."

I chuckle. "You're still wrong."

Jace drops his arm. "Whatever you say, sugar plum."

"Ready to play some cornhole? It can get pretty competitive," John says casually.

I sip my beer. "I am. Do you want to invite your friend to play too?"

John doesn't look over his shoulder when he answers. "Nope. Me and Alyssa on one side against you and Ford," he says to Jace.

"Fine by me, but it's really Alyssa and me on the same team since we're on opposing sides," Jace smirks.

John gives him a blank stare then picks up the little sacks in the grass and tosses them in the air. He walks to one of the boards.

"Told you he didn't care," I whisper to Jace.

"Trust me, he cares," Jace says, trying to reassure me.

Breaking away, John places the cornhole boards nine feet apart, counting by nine giant steps he takes. He distributes the sacks and then tells Ford, "You're over there with Jace."

Ford grabs another beer bottle from the cooler. He places the top in his mouth, bites down, and pops it off.

Horrified, I ask, "Aren't you afraid of losing a few teeth?" He looks at me and laughs, then walks to stand with Jace.

"Do you know how to play," John asks, turning toward me. I shake my head. "The goal is to land a sack on the board and keep it there, or make it in the hole. Don't throw too hard or too light. If you arc it high enough and lightly, it will land and slide up. You can stand behind or next to the board, but not in front. I'll go first so you can see, and then Jace will go, then you, and then Ford. Ready?"

"Yes."

John takes one last swig of his beer and balances it on the rail of his truck. He stands next to the board, swinging his arm back and forth before he lets go of the sack. It flies through the air and lands on the board, sliding up to stop before the opening. A smug smile splays across his face.

Jace is next. His sack lands on the board just shy of the hole as well.

"You're up."

I pick up the beaded sack. It feels like a mini bean bag. I was never really into sports, so this should be interesting. I begin swinging my arm back and forth then silently count to three and let go. The sack soars through the air and lands off to the side and in grass, not even close to the board. My shoulders drop. Turning around, I find John covering his mouth with his hand as he tries not to laugh.

"I'm sorry, but that was horrible," he says.

"What do you want from me? I have no aim, and I've never played a sport in my life."

"Ford," he yells over to the other side. "Throw it back and let her have another shot."

Ford throws the sack back, and John catches it. "I'll

teach you. Come stand behind the board instead of off to the side."

I stand behind the board, and John comes up close behind me. I'm hyperaware of his proximity and can feel the heat of his chest on my back. John holds my hip with his left hand. His touch burns right through me. With his other hand, he cups the back of my hand with his and begins swinging our arms together.

"Eyes on the bottom part of the board," he whispers near my ear. "Don't aim for the hole or you won't make it. Keep swinging like this. Slow and steady wins the race." My breathing grows heavier. "Just like that," he whispers, rubbing my back with his thumb. "On the count of three, let it go. One… Two… Three."

As if it's playing in slow motion, I hold my breath as I watch the sack soar. It lands on the tip of the board before falling into the grass.

"Oh man! So close!" I yell excitedly.

"That's better," John says. I high-five him, then wait for Ford to go. When it's John's turn again, he has me stand in front of him and gives me his turn. "Let's try it again," he says.

His chest is firmly pressed to my back, his stance wide as he helps me, both hands in the same spot. Heat crackles all around us. I wonder if John feels it too or if it's one-sided. He hasn't so much as mentioned what happened earlier with Jace, which makes me believe it's nothing, just like I said.

The four of us play cornhole for the next half hour, and each time John helps me. Once the game ends, I sit on John's tailgate, sipping my beer while he talks to his friends. When they're done, John jumps up and sits next to me. He hooks an arm around my waist and pulls me to his side.

"What was that stunt you pulled with Jace," he asks, staring straight ahead at the fire.

Maybe Jace was right. "What stunt?"

A dry laugh rolls off his lips. "You really want to play like that?"

"I could ask the same of you. You flirted with Sarah the first half of the night, so I hung around with Jace. What was I to do?"

"It was more like thirty minutes, and you didn't have to go and get all cozy with him."

"We were hardly cozy. More like just two friends hanging out."

"Friends don't touch like that."

I laugh. "Really? We're friends, and we touch like that."

"That's different, Alyssa. Jace is my best friend. He should know better than to put his hands on you."

I stifle a chuckle. "How's it different?"

He tightens his hold around me. I can tell I'm testing his patience. "We fucked this morning. Do you really take me for the kind of guy who goes around and fucks any girl? And just so you know, Sarah means nothing to me."

I can't stop the cringe that rolls through me. My heart drops, and I suddenly feel sick.

"No, I don't take you for that kind of guy. And for your information, that little scene you saw was Jace's idea. He played you, and I went along with it to prove him wrong."

John's brows shoot up in confusion. "What are you talking about?"

"It's nothing. I really don't want to get into it."

"I want you to tell me."

"I was proving you and I are just friends since he thinks we're more than that." John is quiet, and it makes my stomach flip. "Just because we hooked up doesn't mean we're dating," I say. "We had a little fun. That's it."

He stares at the bonfire as he talks to me. "I don't appreciate seeing you hang on Jace. You'll get a name for yourself around here. Is that what you want?"

"I think I'm ready to go home."

"Do you want him?" he questions.

"Did you want Sarah when you put your arm around her waist?"

He chuckles near my ear. "She's not you, so that's a hell no." His warm breath tingles along my skin. His lips graze my neck up to the shell of my ear. "I don't go around laying lips on anyone, or screwing them. Only to the ones I really like," John says. "I'm not a player."

I nod subtly. Deep down, that makes me feel good inside. I watch the flames in the fire pit crackle. The truth is, I do like John more than friends, and that worries me.

"Ready to get out of here?" he asks.

I nod.

After saying goodbye to his friends, we're loaded and ready to go. John pulls out of Whiskey River. I unbuckle my seat belt and scoot next to him, resting my head on his shoulder. John turns on the radio, and Kip Moore's "Dirt Road" fills the speakers. I reach over and turn it up.

"I see my girl is opening up to country music," John says.

"I have to admit that I like the stories the songs tell. I never thought I would want to listen to it, but it's growing on me." I pause. "They remind me of love stories."

John pulls into my driveway and switches off his headlights. I gather my things as John steps out of his truck. He walks around to the passenger side and opens my door. Darkness surrounds us save for the moon shining above. He takes my hand and walks me to my front door, then turns to look down at me. I swallow back the knot in my throat. Our eyes lock.

"I like you a lot, Alyssa. I'm not talking to other girls. Just thought you should know."

He leans down and presses his lips to mine, but he doesn't linger.

"I had a really good time tonight. I needed a day like today. Thank you, Johnny."

ELEVEN

JOHN

May rolls around, marking the end of another semester.

I look forward to this time of year simply for the feeling it brings. Anticipation, laughter, endless star-filled nights, and long hot days are what I look forward to. All my best memories happen in the summer.

"I heard there's a bonfire tomorrow night in that big field near the water tower to celebrate the end of the semester. You guys want to hit it up?" I ask as I climb down a tree.

"Oh yeah? Who's putting it on?" Ford perks up.

"Not sure. But who cares? It's a party," I say, reaching the ground. Looking at Alyssa, I ask, "Want to come with us?"

Alyssa shrugs. "I have to work tomorrow, but maybe after if it's not too late."

Another day is spent with my friends under the hot Georgia sun. Ford busts out his dirt bike at one point. We even manage to hook up a new river swing.

This is my life, and I love every minute of it. Summer has always been spent with my closest friends since I was a kid. I can't imagine living any other way.

I glance at Alyssa. She's wearing tiny black shorts and a black tank top. Her hair is tied into a ponytail, and just about every inch of her is covered in mud. I laugh at her repulsed expression.

"What's so funny?" she asks.

"You should see the look on your face right now."

"This mud better be giving me the facial of a lifetime. That's all I gotta say."

"It's probably clogging your pores," Jace says straight-faced. Alyssa looks like she's going to throat-punch him.

"We can always try the new rope swing out, and you can rinse in the river."

Alyssa groans under her breath. She's not a fan of swimming in the river.

"It's your best bet if that shit bothers you." Ford jumps in.

Alyssa looks over at me, wondering if it's true. "Are you sure you secured that properly? It's not going to untie when I climb on?"

"I'm positive. That sucker isn't going anywhere."

"And that water is deep enough for me to jump into?"

"Sure is." I reassure her. "We do it all the time."

As she walks over to the tree, I can tell she has no idea what she's doing. "So how does this work exactly? How do I know when to let go?" she asks.

All three of us look at her like she just spoke a foreign language.

"You just jump on and let go when you're over the water," Jace states dryly.

Walking back over to the tree swing, I grip the bottom of the rope and hold it out to her. "Grip this as high as you can. Wrap your legs around it the way you would wrap your legs around my—"

"John!" Her eyes nearly pop from her head. All I see is blue.

Alyssa grits her jaw together, and the blush on her cheeks causes me to grin. She's lit up like a sparkler of embarrassment. She's adorable.

"I'm never sleeping with you again," she whispers under her breath for only me to hear.

That only makes my grin grow. The tone in Alyssa's soft voice doesn't match her brazen words.

"I love when you try to lie to me," I say.

"Here goes nothing," she mutters.

I step back as she scans the water. I can tell she's scared to jump. Most people are their first time.

Taking a deep breath, Alyssa tugs on the rope a few times to see if it's going anywhere. When she's satisfied it's not, she grips it a little higher, and then jumps. Alyssa swings out and way over the river. She let's go and her legs flail in the air. I chuckle, getting a kick out of watching her. She plugs her nose before she hits the water, making a big splash. She comes up smiling like she did when she rode the four-wheeler and we hit a pothole. I walk to the edge of the bank and help her out.

"That was so much fun, but it made my heart drop when I let go."

"You did great," I tell her. "You want to try it again?"

She hesitates, then nods. "Nothing is going to bite me in the water?"

"I highly doubt an otter will attack." I pause. "Maybe a snapping turtle. But I'd be more worried about snakes."

Her jaw drops. "Don't play around like that."

I chuckle. I don't tell her that I'm serious. Being a native Georgian, what's swimming beneath the water never crosses my mind. Sort of like people who grow up near the beach. They aren't thinking about sharks when they're swimming in the ocean.

"I'm next. Will you video tape me?" Jace asks.

Alyssa holds her phone as Jace swings into a double backflip. She yells in excitement, and Ford calls him a showoff. I catch the sounds of the tree splintering before he lands in the water. I glance up, but nothing seems like it's breaking.

Ford swings next, and Alyssa continues to record. He's a bit huskier than me and Jace. As he swings, the branch cracks and snaps, and it causes his body to jerk. I look up and my jaw drops. Ford holds the rope as the massive tree limb falls with him into the river. My stomach plummets. I hear a collective gasp, and we run to the bottom. Ford explodes at the surface, unscathed, and grinning like a fool.

I exhale a sigh of relief. Jace, Alyssa, and I wear a similar expression of dread.

"That was crazy! Did you get it on camera?" Ford says.

Alyssa nods. It's a small success despite the harm it could have caused.

Ford gets out, and we watch the video, laughing hysterically.

"And you said it wasn't going to break," Alyssa says, reminding me of my earlier words.

LATER THE NEXT EVENING, I PULL INTO ALYSSA'S EMPTY driveway, and she's out her front door before I can even park. She told me one night that my headlights are a dead giveaway and how she knows I'm there. Alyssa opens the truck door and slides in close to me with a massive smile.

"What? What's wrong?" she asks.

My mouth hangs open, eyeing her body. "I'm shocked. Where did you get a camo shirt from? I know that's not something you had in your closet."

"I ordered it a few weeks ago," she says like it's no biggie.

A massive smile lights up my face. "You bought that for me, didn't you?" She doesn't answer, but the look on her face says it all. My stomach tightens at the thought behind her actions. "You're wearing a camo shirt for me," I state, but she shakes her head in denial. I've never smiled so much with a girl before the way I do with Alyssa.

"I didn't buy it for you, I bought it to fit into your little town."

I continue smiling, not saying a word for a moment. "You are seriously the worst liar I've ever met."

She chuckles and shakes her head. "Whatever." She purses her lips together, fighting the laughter, because she knows I'm right. "Let's go."

I put the truck into gear. She definitely bought that shirt for me.

"I'm never wearing this shirt again. In fact, I'm going to burn it tonight at the bonfire."

I bark out a laugh. "Then what will you wear?"

She looks over at me and blinks. "Your shirt, of course."

"Fair enough. But I like the way it looks on you."

"Can I drive your truck?" she blurts out.

I gawk as if she just asked me for my left kidney. "What?"

"Can I drive your truck?" she repeats, enunciating each word.

I hesitate. "Right now?"

She nods.

I glance at the empty road ahead and let up on the accelerator. Giving up complete control of my truck isn't something I ever do, but I'll make an exception for Alyssa.

"Want to sit on my lap?" I ask. "Or I can pull over."

"I'll sit on your lap."

Alyssa gets as close as she can and climbs onto my lap, making sure not to make any sudden movements. Once she's on my lap, I let go of the wheel and place my hands on her hips as she takes over and drives. I widen my thighs to give her room.

"Want the gas too?" I ask, and she nods.

Coming to a stop sign, I lean back and watch Alyssa drive. My dick is growing hard with her plump ass on me. She reaches over and cranks the radio, wiggling back and forth in excitement.

"I'm so high up. I want a truck now."

"You can drive my truck anytime you want." I squeeze Alyssa's hips and slide my hand lower to where her shorts are cut off. I curve my fingers and stroke her skin.

"What are you doing?" she asks.

I lean up to kiss her neck. My fingers slide close to her pussy, and she involuntarily widens her legs.

"Johnny," she says, her voice raspy. "This isn't a good idea."

"How easy would it be to slip my fingers in you right now?" I whisper against her neck.

She pulls into the open field. My fingers graze her panties. I slip a finger under the elastic and push at her entrance, teasing her. My dick is straining under her ass. We haven't had sex since the day we first went mudding. I'm aching to be inside of her again.

Alyssa slaps my hand, and I pull away as she parks my truck. I look out the window and notice Jace and Ford standing together. Their mouths are hanging wide open and they're clutching their beers to their chests. They're going to give me shit for this.

"I want to fuck you in my truck one day," I whisper in her ear, and she shivers.

Once we settle, which takes all of three minutes, Jace thrusts a double shot of whiskey at me.

"Here, you need this." He passes one to Ford and Alyssa too. "It'll put some hair on your chest and replace your balls."

I flip him off.

"That was a good one," Ford says.

"You should just hand Alyssa the keys. She looks much better driving it," Jace says.

"She can drive it whenever she wants," I say, looking at her.

"Let's make a toast," Ford says. The four of us raise our glasses high. "Here's to the good times and one epic summer."

We clink our glasses together and throw the shot back. Alyssa cringes from the burn at the back of her throat.

"I'm pretty sure I'll be growing chest hair by the end of the night." She coughs, her eyes watering. "That's some strong stuff."

"Get used to it, blondie. It's what's on tap tonight," Jace says.

ALYSSA

AFTER THE ROUND OF SHOTS, WE SPLIT UP TO MINGLE.

Everyone's relaxed, laid back, and having a good time. Games are being played—cornhole, which I now recognize—and country music is blasting from trucks. In the center of it all is the bonfire blazing under the star-dotted sky.

I walk hand in hand with John. The whiskey is streaming through my veins, warming my blood and making me feel too good. John keeps me close and hardly takes his eyes off me. In fact, I don't see him even glance at another girl. This friends-with-benefits thing isn't such a bad idea after all. We both seem to enjoy the benefits without the commitment.

Hooting and hollering pull John and me toward a large crowd. I have no idea what's going on, but as we shimmy our way through to the front, we quickly discover what all the noise is about.

Jace is doing a body shot.

His shirt is gone, and his shorts hang extremely low on his flat stomach. A brunette girl rubs lemon on him from hip to hip and then sprinkles salt across his skin. She leans over with her tongue out. When they're done with the body shot, Jace tilts his head back and spots John. The crowd chants.

"Johnny Boy!" he yells, his eyes glossy.

"Jace, let me guess… you lost your shirt." John slaps his hand.

Jace grins.

"You can't be trusted to be alone anymore. How do you always lose your shirt?"

"The fuck if I know," he says. "But it's not like I need one while doing body shots. Hey, girl," he says when he spots me. "Ever done a body shot?"

"Can't say I have," I say.

"Ah, a body-shot virgin. Well, now's the perfect time to do it. I'm lubed up and ready to go."

"She's good, Jace," John answers, squeezing my hand.

"Come on, you got to let Alyssa try it out." He pushes.

"I'll let her try it out on me anytime." Heads turn, and I spot Chad. His eyes fall on me. I swallow thickly. I know John doesn't like it because his fingers tighten around mine.

"Hey, Chad," I say, trying to keep the peace.

"No need, Chad. She's got me." John speaks up.

"And if she doesn't want him, she's got me." Jace jokes.

"And me," Ford chimes in.

"Why doesn't she answer for herself." Chad challenges.

"I'm good," I say quickly. "Thanks, Chad." There is no reason to be rude to him. He is my friend, after all.

"Let's do this," Jace says, breaking the awkwardness. He rubs his hands together. "Who's next?"

"I'll go," John says.

Reaching behind his neck, John fists his shirt and pulls it off. Some women holler at him, and I don't like it. But I see why they do it. I bite my lip. I gaze down his body, and my mouth waters at the sight. He climbs up on the tailgate and lies back, his legs hanging off the edge. A trail of peach fuzz leads into his pants that I hadn't noticed before. Sarah comes forward to put the lemon and salt on him, but I step in.

"I got this," I say sharply.

I take the lemon and run it slowly across his waist, making sure to give him a good coating, and then I sprinkle the salt on him. A shot is handed to me, and I ask what it is.

"Tequila," Jace says as if I should've known.

"I raise the cup and take a deep breath before I tip it back and swallow it whole. I wince from the burning, disgusting taste, then I bend down and slip my tongue out. I run it as slow as I can from one hip to the other and under the lip of his boxers. When I'm finished, John pulls my face to his and kisses me hard, thrusting his tongue inside my mouth. He shares the salt with me. My heart hammers against my ribs. I forget that people are around and kiss him back with the same intensity.

"You did that shit on purpose," John says, breaking the kiss. I grin, my heavy-lidded eyes gleaming at him.

"That's what you get for working me up when I was driving your truck."

A huge smile breaks out on his face, and he kisses me one last time before standing up.

"Alyssa's turn!" Jace yells.

"I think I'll pass."

"Aw, come on," Jace begs. "Don't be a Debbie Downer."

I glance at John, who shrugs. "It's up to you," he says.

"Do it!" Ford yells.

"What the heck? You only live once, right?" I jump on the tailgate and lift my shirt to expose my stomach. Our eyes meet as John rubs lemon down the length of my stomach, then sprinkles the salt. My stomach dips.

"Ready?"

I nod. John throws the shot back and then trails his tongue along my skin. When he finishes licking all the salt off, he drags his lips along my jaw to my mouth, where he delves in and kisses me deep and slow. I can taste the cool liquor on his tongue. I cup the back of his head and press his mouth to mine. Our tongues thrash in and out. That body shot worked me up good, and now I want John. I wrap my arms around his shoulders and lean up. The people around us holler once more and we break the kiss.

"Never, ever, do a body shot again," John says, panting. "That tongue of yours is dangerous."

"I could say the same to you," I whisper.

"Somehow, somewhere, we're going to finish what we started tonight."

I bite my bottom lip and nod in agreement, breathing in a mixture of Georgia air, John's earthy scent, and the firewood burning. He helps me off the tailgate, and I slide down his body to find my footing.

Time passes by faster than I realize. The party is winding down and the crowd is thinning out. We've been hanging out with everyone well past midnight.

"Hey, guys, ready to head out?" John asks Ford and Jace as they walk up to us.

"I'm ready," Ford says.

"Are you okay to drive?" I ask Ford.

"Sure am. I haven't drunk anything in over an hour, and all I had was some beers. I didn't take body shots like you crazy kids. I was ready to head out anyway. I gotta help my pops on the farm tomorrow. It's been an epic night," Ford says, walking away. "See ya tomorrow."

"Jace?" I turn to look at him. "Are you okay to drive?"

He doesn't respond, but I don't think he heard me. I look at his glossy eyes as he stumbles toward John.

"You know you're my best friend, Johnny Boy, right?" Jace says to John.

John laughs. "Oh yeah? That so?"

"That so," Jace states, walking to his truck.

"Want to head to my house, and we can hang out back for a bit?" John asks.

Jace wiggles his eyebrows. "Sounds like a hot date."

I shake my head. "I swear, you two can't say anything without turning it into a sexual innuendo."

They high-five each other, and I laugh.

"You okay to drive, Jace? We can drive if you want."

Jace looks at me like he's insulted. "I got this, pretty girl." He jumps into his truck and spins out.

It was an epic night.

Summer nights in a small town have their appeal.

TWELVE

JOHN

I follow Jace as I drive my truck.

Alyssa sits in the passenger seat next to me. It's past midnight, and the pitch-black sky makes it hard to see more than twenty feet ahead. There's a nervous energy that fills the air.

Jace pulls off to the side and does a crazy eight in an empty field, then speeds up to get in front of me again. I can hear his laughter carry in the wind. I should have tried hard to convince him to ride with me or Ford, but telling Jace to do anything won't get me anywhere. Jace being wild is nothing new. Sometimes he just scares me.

Jace gains speed, the truck's muffler crackling in the air. He swerves in and out of the yellow lines, hitting the reflector lights each time. He must be drunker than I realized. I have no idea how much he had to drink tonight. I sit a little higher and glance down at the speedometer. We've never gone this fast, at least not that I can remember. I worry at his recklessness, but I also know that it's doubtful anyone else will be on the road this late.

"Babe, grab my phone. Call Jace and tell him to take it easy, would you? He's worrying me."

"Sure thing."

Alyssa's blond locks cover the side of her face as she finds his contact info. I watch as she tucks a piece of hair behind her ear and then raises the phone. Her creamy, soft skin glows from the moonlit sky, and her foot bounces rapidly on the dashboard.

Glancing back to the road, I see Jace's silhouette lean over. Shit, he must be reaching for his phone. He swerves sharply to avoid a line of bushes, causing the back of his truck to fishtail. He hits a pothole. The truck pulls abruptly to the right and nicks the passenger side bumper. The ping is loud, the crunch of metal making my stomach clench. My heart drops into the pit of my stomach as a shiver runs down my spine.

"Just hang up. I don't want him to crash," I tell Alyssa.

Jace straightens up. We're approaching a four-way stop, where I plan to flash my headlights to get his attention. I want Jace to ride with me. We can pick up his truck tomorrow. I can see for miles ahead that no one is coming. Jace can too. He revs the engine and rolls right through the stop sign as if it isn't there.

"He's scaring me," Alyssa says. She grabs my thigh in fear.

I watch with wide, panic-filled eyes as Jace's truck knicks a mailbox then collides with a small bush. He keeps going, and Alyssa gasps. My heart is in my throat. He attempts to straighten out his truck, but it's too late. Jace bumps into another bush, creating a domino effect in slow motion. Pieces from his truck fly off into the shoulder—a broken headlight, the side mirror. Alyssa drops her feet to sit up higher. She draws in an audible breath and leans forward, blindly reaching for me and squeezes my forearm. The horror in her grip mirrors what I feel inside. Tires screech as a cloud of dirt puffs up behind the truck. Mini rocks fly up in the air and hit my windshield. Jace fishtails, causing him to pull hard to the right. His truck catches a large bush, ripping the front bumper off. I hear a crunch as Jace's truck teeters on the edge of the road. There's a row of trees ahead he's about to plow through if he doesn't stop his games.

Alyssa starts speaking, but I don't hear what she's saying.

I think about what's ahead of Jace, and my stomach drops. There's a fork in the road. I panic, wanting to flash my bright lights but not doing it because I don't want to distract Jace further. I shoot a quick prayer up to the big guy, hoping Jace remembers to turn the wheel in his intoxicated haze.

Jace's truck knicks the metal sign.

Time slows, yet it moves so fast.

Alyssa digs her nails into my thigh.

Air seizes in my lungs, and my mouth parts in shock. "Oh my God. Oh my God," I chant to myself.

His tires screech. The smell of burning rubber immediately fills the air, and the sound of metal crunching nearly stops my heart. I watch in horror as Jace's truck collides with a massive dogwood tree that's been in South Fork for as long as I can remember. The sound is deafening. I feel like I can't breathe. The truck is bent in an unnatural shape.

Pulling to a halt, I throw the gearshift into park, switch on the high beams for light, and fling the door open. I run at full speed toward my best friend and scream to Alyssa to call an ambulance. Smoke begins to flow out from under the hood. My stomach curls at the sudden thoughts running through my head. I need to get Jace out immediately.

"Johnny!"

Glancing over my shoulder, I see Alyssa climb out of the cab. She's running toward me.

"Get your ass back in the truck, Alyssa!" I yell.

Coming up to Jace's truck, I see the back passenger tire is twisted backward and the windshield is cracked into a million bloody pieces. The front of the truck is crushed like a soda can. I check the cab window and see the back of Jace's head. Bile climbs to the back of my throat. His head is sandwiched between the door and the steering wheel, his body hunched over, and his eyes closed as he lies unconscious against the driver's side door.

"Jace! Jace! Can you hear me?" I yell, running to the other side. "Fuck, man! Open your eyes! Jace!"

I reach for the handle and jiggle it until I can open it. Grunting, I reach for Jace's beltloops and yank, trying to shimmy him out. I give him a shake and yell his name, but he's not going anywhere and he's not waking up. Jace is stuck, and not only that, he's also dead weight. With a hard heave, I yank Jace and he's finally released. His head rolls onto my arm as I catch his limp body. Something sharp digs into my forearm, but it doesn't register in my mind as I carry him. Carefully, I place him on the grass. I hear Alyssa's frantic screams and pray she doesn't come any closer. I don't want her to see Jace like this.

"Come on, buddy. I sure could use some help right now," I mutter as a tear rolls down my cheek. "Jace, are you there? Jace? Do you hear me?" I tap on his chest, but nothing. Not a grunt or groan or even a huff of air.

I reach to check his pulse, but my hands are shaking and my heart is pounding so loud in my ears that I can't tell if he has one. I cup the sides of his neck as I desperately search for a sign he's alive. I grab the collar of his shirt and rip it in half. I watch for the telltale sign of a breathing chest, but I'm too frantic to spot it.

"Fuck," I murmur. "Please… Fuckin' answer me."

In the distance, red lights flicker and the sirens scream, but they don't register as I stare down at the bloody face of my best friend.

"Save him, Johnny," Alyssa cries.

Pinching Jace's nose and tilting his jaw, I breathe air into his mouth. "Come on, Jace. Come back to us. I need you," I beg. I layer my hands together and press up and down under his breastbone, feeling his ribs crunch under the necessary force.

Nothing.

"Come on, Jace. Wake up!"

Two heavy gulps of air and thirty hand compressions later and still nothing.

"Fuck, man." My voice cracks, and my eyes tear up. "Wake the fuck up and open your damn eyes. Please!"

I take two more heavy gulps of air and perform another set of hand compressions.

Nothing.

"Look at me! Wake up, Jace!" I begin shaking him. I yell and scream, pulling him, anything for him to open his eyes.

"Move back!" the paramedic orders.

Someone cups their hands under my armpits and yanks

me to the other side of the street. I sit across from the scene, watching the paramedic frantically try to resuscitate Jace.

"Alyssa." My voice cracks. Alyssa crashes into me. She squeezes my neck tightly.

Mud fights, bonfires, family gatherings, Christmas parties, endless nights of laughter, girls and more girls. It all plays in my mind like a giant blurry movie.

Jace and I in second grade on the playground.

Our mothers forcing us to join Cub Scouts, where we learned CPR. I never thought I'd have to use it on my best friend.

Food fights in the cafeteria.

Getting purposely kicked out of Cub Scouts.

Sleepovers.

Entering sixth grade, thinking we were hot shit.

Meeting Ford.

Entering high school together.

Sneaking out of the house.

Freshman pep rally. Cheerleaders.

Prom.

High school graduation.

College.

Too many events pass before my eyes, so many memories that I can't sort out.

We're so close. He's like my brother.

I DON'T KNOW HOW OR WHEN WE GOT TO THE HOSPITAL. Alyssa drove. She followed the ambulance and called

Jace's mom on the way. She found her number in my cell phone. I was too in shock to do anything.

I glance around. The pictures on the walls of sunny, lake-side images are lies. Cold and stiff leather blue chairs connected at the legs take up most of the space in the waiting room. A muted television hangs in the corner, subtitles running across the lower screen. Fake smiles dazzle the nurses' faces when they make eye contact, but I can see right through them. It's such a deceiving environment that it makes my skin crawl.

Alyssa sits next to me. She squeezes my hand, giving me support, but I don't have the strength to return it. I'm in a daze.

No one in the hospital can be thinking of days with endless sun. Their moments are full of gray skies and open-ended questions.

Seconds tick by, turning to minutes, turning to hours.

If I had blinked my eyes, it would have been over. And thinking back on it, I wish I had because the images replaying in my head will forever be seared into my brain. I'd do anything to erase them.

I don't understand how this happened.

Letting go of Alyssa's hand, I bend forward. My elbows dig into my knees while I cup my face. I pray. I beg for a miracle. I barter to cut a few years of my life shorter to spare Jace.

A doctor in blue scrubs strides forward. Specs of blood coat his uniform, and he looks exhausted. Shaking off the goose bumps, I stand as he stops before me.

"Evening. I'm Dr. Ortega. Are you the ones who were with Jace McConnell tonight?"

"Yes, sir."

"Are you family?"

"Not by blood, but he's like a brother to me."

His eyes skate around the room. "Are his parents here tonight?"

"His mom is on her way. Is Jace going to be okay?"

The doctor rolls his lips between his teeth, flattening them. His gaze wavers to the floor. "I'm sorry, but I must speak with his mother first."

"Just tell me if he's alive."

Sympathy weighs heavily in his tired eyes, and I fear the worst. The waiting room grows small, my vision turning into a long, narrow tunnel. I begin breathing heavily, emotions rolling up and taking over. Tears well in my eyes. This can't be happening.

The sound of sliding doors draws my attention. Maryanne, Jace's mom, rushes toward me, her eyes filled with desperation.

"John! Have you heard anything?"

I shake my head. "No. The doctor won't tell me anything because I'm not blood related." I turn to look back at him. "This is his mother."

"How is he?" she asks frantically.

"How about we take a seat somewhere private?" the doctor says.

"Just give me something." She begins shaking her head hysterically.

Clearing his throat, Dr. Ortega nods. "When Jace was brought in, he was covered in so much blood that we didn't know where it was coming from. After running some diagnostic tests, we were able to tell the bleeding was coming from multiple places in his body, one being his chest and the other his brain. He must have hit the windshield."

"The windshield was cracked when I got to him," I say quietly.

Dr. Ortega nods slowly. "Jace had two emergency surgeries. By some God-given miracle, he's breathing and in recovery. We had to place him in a medically induced coma to bring down the swelling, and we implanted a device into his skull to monitor the pressure on his brain. It should be able to come out in about two days, hopefully. After that, the ventilator can be removed, but it all depends on your son. Every patient is different. The fact that he is alive right now is almost unheard of. If he wakes up from this, he'll have a long road of recovery ahead of him. I suggest calling family and loved ones and letting them know of his condition. Your son needs rest, and until he's out of ICU, I'd rather he not have many visitors."

Maryanne is distraught. "You're looking at his family, Doctor," she says quietly. "His father took off once Jace was born, and we never saw him again. It's always been just me and him." A small sob escapes her. "Can I see him?" she asks, her voice heightened with hope.

"You can, but you can only stay fifteen minutes. I'm sure you'll want to stay in the hospital, so I'll ensure you have some blankets in the waiting room."

She thanks the doctor and then grabs my hand. "Come on, John."

The doctor places a hand on Maryanne's arm. "I need to advise you that aside from the implantation, your son is bandaged and hooked to a few devices. Prepare yourself, and please, don't touch anything."

We both nod.

Taking a deep breath, I exhale and crack my neck. I'm jittery, and my heart is pounding against my ribs so hard I feel like it's going to jump out. The walk to Jace's room feels never-ending. My anxiety is making me lightheaded. I can only imagine what the woman next to me feels.

Stopping in front of the door, the doctor turns to both of us. "Remember, you only have fifteen minutes. No more."

Nothing could have prepared me for what I was about to see.

THIRTEEN

JOHN

I don't want to go home, so Alyssa drives us back to her house instead.

She undresses me and leads me to the shower, where she cleans Jace's blood off me while I stand there in a trance. Luckily her mom is working, so she isn't here to question us.

The horrific memory of seeing Jace in the ICU fills my mind. Dried blood was matted in his hair. There were bruises already marring his skin. He was nearly unrecognizable. The fear of losing him hit me hard.

I shake my head free of the images. We're now in Alyssa's room. She's lying balled up on her bed. Her fists are propped under her chin, and her swollen blue eyes are void of any light. She chews on her bottom lip. She's been by my side the entire time, holding me up quietly and squeezing my hand, letting me know she's there for me.

When I walked out of Jace's room and saw Alyssa waiting for me, relief coursed through my body. I released a tense breath and my heart swelled at the sight of her. I don't know what I would have done if she hadn't been there tonight. I think I love her for it.

"Alyssa," I say, and her sad eyes look up at me. "I need you," I croak.

My voice is a broken whisper that carries through the air. Agony claws at my chest. Tonight was a wake-up call.

I kneel on Alyssa's bed and crawl over to her. She immediately wraps her arms around my shoulders and hugs me to her. I crumble on top of her and nestle my head into the curve of her shoulder. She breathes under me, and I realize I needed to feel her intake of breath.

"Have faith, John. Try. I know it's hard, but have faith in Jace."

"I'm trying, Alyssa, trust me, I'm trying." My voice breaks. "It's just so hard. I can't lose him."

Rising on my elbows, I peer down into her watery blue eyes. "I need to feel you. I need to feel all of you, Alyssa. Make me feel alive, because right now, I feel like I'm dying inside. It hurts. Make me forget."

She nods.

Wispy blond strands surround her beautiful face. I'm lucky to have Alyssa. I'm not going to take things for granted anymore. In the blink of an eye, everything could be gone.

I close the distance, grazing her supple lips with my needy ones. She sighs into my mouth. Her legs spread and my body comes alive. Her lips, so soft and willing, open to caress mine. I lift the hem of her black tank top over her head and drop it to the mattress. I take a moment to appreciate the sight before me.

"Alyssa," I whisper with need. I palm her breasts, my thumb circling her nipples as I loom over her. I slide my hands up her creamy skin, over her collarbone, and through her silky hair. I press a hard, bruising kiss to her lips. Alyssa moans into my mouth, and her hips undulate against mine. Threading her fingers through my damp hair, she squeezes her thighs around my hips, and I press my cock into her.

"Take these off," she demands, pulling at my shorts.

Alyssa slides my basketball shorts down my hips and then removes her panties. I moan at the feel of her heated skin against mine. She widens her thighs, and my cock slides against her pussy. She can't control her body as it unwinds. Moisture pools between her legs and makes me crave her more. Our kisses are feverish, quick, and wild. Untamed. We're both in a state of desperate need. She curves a leg over my backside and digs her heel into me. She wants me as bad as I want her.

My cock slides against her entrance. Her hips roll up, the crown of my head sliding up and down her pussy. Alyssa's pussy drips as she groans into my mouth again. She bites down on my lip, and I fist her hair while she rubs herself on me. She grips my shoulders as my cock presses into her opening. Our movements become frantic. I surge inside her pussy, and we moan in unison at the connection. She's so warm that it spreads across my body and causes me to shiver. Alyssa groans, her hips pushing into mine. She stretches to accommodate me and kisses me so deeply I lose all train of thought. We're both in pain dealing with our own suffering. Tonight we need to feel alive. I work my hips in and out of her at a slow but hard pace.

"More," I groan against her lips. She obliges.

Alyssa begins thrusting her hips, taking every inch of me as she can. Her fingers dig into my skin, sliding down my rigid back in a gripping tightness. The pleasure overrides everything and I drown in it. I pump into her, unable to control myself.

"Damn, baby. You feel so good. I don't want this to end," I say between strokes.

"I feel the same way."

I take her mouth aggressively, seizing her lips in a savage kiss. I fist her thick blond mane as I continue with deep strokes.

"John." She breathes against my lips. "I'm close."

"Not yet. Only when I say. Got it? I need this to last."

Alyssa nods her head feverishly. "You feel so good. I don't know how I'm going to hold on."

Grabbing both of her wrists, I press them into the mattress above her head. She moans loudly in response and thrusts her hips hard against mine. Her back bows as we pound against one another. The walls of Alyssa's pussy tighten around my cock and it only brings me higher. I continue my long, deep strokes. I should move quicker, but the buildup between us makes it that much better. I don't want to rush it.

"Johnny," she moans.

I thrust twice more. "Come with me. Come…"

I hit deep inside and it sets off her orgasm. She comes with me, and it only makes the pleasure that much better. Our bodies use each other's. We can't get enough.

"Johnny. Oh my! Johnny, don't stop."

"I won't, baby," I murmur as I unload inside of her. God, she feels so good. My cock is so hard that I hope I'm not hurting her, but I can't stop. Not until every drop is wrung from my body.

I continue thrusting inside of her until our orgasms

subside. I roll over and pull out, taking Alyssa into the crook of my arm. We both breathe heavily, our bodies coated in a light sheen of sweat. I've never gone without a condom before, and now I don't know if I can ever use one again with Alyssa. She feels divine.

"I love you, you know," I blurt out between pants. Alyssa stills. "You don't have to say it back, but I wanted you to know, in case anything ever happens, that I love you."

FOURTEEN

JOHN

What is that saying? It's five o'clock somewhere? That's precisely what I'm thinking as I crack open a beer and flick the cap onto the grass. I take a long, hard pull on it.

I snuck out of Alyssa's house this morning and headed straight to Whiskey River. She looked so peaceful sleeping that I didn't want to disturb her. I woke Ford up, though; and he met me at the river. I wanted to be close to Jace in a place that I knew he loved. I'd love nothing more than to find a punching bag and beat the shit out of it. I'm sinking inside. My chest burns with each breath I take. The only way to erase the pain is to drink it away.

I replay the entire night for Ford. He sits stone-faced staring at the ground while I explain in detail how Jace's truck looked wrapped around the tree. I tell him how I saw Jace lying in the hospital bed all banged up. Since then, we've been completely drunk and pissed off about life.

"I can't believe what happened. It's unreal," Ford states in disbelief before chugging another beer.

"This feels weird not having Jace here," I say.

I look down at my ringing phone and silence it again. This is the fourth time Alyssa has called me in the past hour, but I don't have it in me to talk to her right now. It's wrong after the way she was there for me, but I'm not right in the head at the moment either.

Stupidly, I told her I loved her last night. I meant what I said, but maybe I shouldn't have said it at all. I was obviously deep in my emotions and not thinking clearly. She was barely cool being friends with benefits. Why I thought she'd be okay with me saying those three little words is beyond me.

I'm devastated over last night. I stand up and throw my empty beer bottle, watching it smash into a million pieces covering the ground. I grab another and go to throw it, but I trip over a tree stump and fall to the ground. Rage fires through me. That little slipup only fuels my anger. Grabbing the sides of my head, I bend down and then whip my head back.

"Fuck!" I yell as loud as I can and squeeze my eyes shut. My heart is pounding so hard. I need to go see Jace. I look around for my keys but can't remember where I put them.

"What are you looking for?" Ford asks.

"My keys."

"What for? Where do you think you're going?" Ford says and places a hand on my shoulder.

"Don't touch me," I snarl, shoving him away.

"You just drank a shitload of beer with me," Ford reminds me. "You're not going anywhere yet."

"Don't tell me what the fuck to do. I need to go see Jace."

"Like hell you are." Ford pushes at my shoulder, trying to get my attention. "Just wait a few hours, then go."

"I can't. I need to go now." Feeling my empty pockets, I curse under my breath. "Where the fuck are my keys?"

"Do you want to end up like Jace, you stupid asshole?" Ford yells in my face. "Just wait a bit, then we'll go together."

My head snaps up, my eyes blazing with fire. "Back off. Now!"

Ford steps in my path. "Or what?"

"Or I'll force you out of my way. I'm in no mood right now."

"You think I'm not feeling it too? It's killing me right now knowing my best friend is holed up in a hospital bed, struggling for his life. It's not just about you."

"You didn't see what I did," I spit. "You didn't watch his truck wrap around a tree. You didn't pull Jace's body from the car. You didn't see all the machines monitoring every breath he takes! I did. I saw it all. It's seared into my fucking brain."

Lifting up the cooler, I find my keys. Snatching them up, I say, "Thank fuck." Before I can take another step, Ford yanks the keys from my hands. Fire speeds through my veins, heat rising to my face. I see red. My body shuts down. I have one thought, and Ford isn't going to stop me from doing it. Friend or not.

"Give them back," I growl.

"No."

"Ford," I warn.

"John."

My heartbeat pounds in my ears. I take two steps then spin around and swing my fist at him. Ford is quick and leans back so I only nick his face, which only infuriates me even more. The alcohol stimulates my anger. I swing again, and this time I miss entirely. I stumble past him. Ford shoves me to the ground, presses a knee to my back, and pushes the side of my face down into the dirt.

"What are you doing?" Alyssa yells, running up. Where the hell did she come from?

"Get away, Alyssa. John is fucked up right now," Ford says.

"Not too fucked up to get a swing on you."

Alyssa kneels down on her knees and leans over. "Johnny, are you okay?" she asks, brushing my hair away from my eyes. "Ford!" She shoves his shoulder. "Get off of him!"

Ford struggles to keep me down. "Only if he promises not to swing at me again."

"Johnny, please don't swing at him," she begs.

"Fine." I grit my teeth. "But tell him to give me my damn keys back."

Alyssa looks at Ford, and he answers the silent question in her eyes. "He had a shit ton of beer and wanted to drive. I said no and took his keys."

"I can drive him where he needs to go. I have my mom's car."

When Ford eases off me, I quickly stand up, brushing the dirt from my clothes. Alyssa places her hand on my arm, but I shrug it off. She swallows and looks at me.

"Go home, Alyssa."

"I'm not going anywhere. I've been trying to call you all morning. Did you get my messages?"

"I did."

"And?"

"And I didn't feel like talking to you. Still don't."

"Johnny," she says, her voice full of sadness.

"What?" I snap.

"Let me help you. I'll drive you wherever you want."

I stubbornly shake my head. "Just go home. I don't feel like seeing you right now."

Alyssa pulls back. "What's gotten into you?"

"Let me think. My friend is hanging on by a thread. Does that answer your question? I'm leaving. Going to see Jace." I stomp off.

"Johnny," she yells, running for me. She grabs my arm to stop me, but I pull away. "Get the hell away from me."

"I know you're hurting, but you don't have to take your frustration out on us."

Hurting isn't the right word. It's more like I'm dying inside.

Spinning around, I lock eyes with Alyssa and glare at her. She flinches. I need to get as far away as possible because I don't trust myself with her right now. I might say "I love you" like an asshole again, so I think of the meanest thing I can say to make her leave. No one is going to stop me from seeing Jace.

"Why don't you go hang out with that white trash friend you like so much and leave me alone."

Alyssa tilts her head to the side. Pursing her lips together, she says, "Who?"

"That degenerate, Chad. You guys are perfect for each other. You're the kind of easy he likes."

Alyssa sucks in a breath. "You don't mean that."

"Every. Word. Didn't take me long to get inside you, did it? It shouldn't take Chad long either. He's a sloppy seconds kind of guy."

"I know you don't mean it. You're just saying that because your emotions are all over the place. Remember what you said last night at my house? That's how I know you don't mean it."

I grit my molars. "Yeah, well, it was all a lie. I wasn't thinking clearly. Every word I said was a lie. Chad can have you since I'm done with you," I say, throwing open my truck door. "Get out of my way."

"Take it back." Alyssa's voice cracks. She shoves me, and I fall against the side of my truck. I feel like shit for making her upset, but I need to get out of here. "You said you loved me."

My eyes lower. I growl under my breath. I feel like an even bigger asshole now for saying that. I meant every word, which hurts even more.

"Alyssa," Ford says, grabbing her forearm. "Just let him go."

"Yeah, let me go and be the asshole I am," I say with a bite.

I jump in the truck and slam the door. I look at Alyssa one last time before I peel out.

I OPEN MY EYES AND LOOK AT THE WINDOW, TRYING TO figure out what time it is. I can tell behind the closed blinds the sun is going down. I lift my wrist and try to make out the blurry numbers.

"You looked cold. I had the nurse get a blanket for you."

I turn to Maryanne. "Thank you."

She sits in the chair next to me, disappointment written

122

on her face. Her drawn face hurls me back to the present. I clench my eyes, feeling the anguish fill me again.

"I'm sorry I came the way I did... Thank you for letting me see him."

How I made it to the hospital in one piece is beyond me. I was drunk when I got in the truck and gunned it. I had a one-track mind, and nothing was going to stop me. Looking back on it, shame layers over me like a coat of embarrassment. I never should have gotten behind the wheel.

She rubs my hand. Her frown makes my stomach tighten. "I know where your heart is. I just don't like knowing you drove drunk, considering..." She trails off.

"Considering that's what put Jace in the hospital." I finish for her.

She doesn't respond.

When I stumbled into the hospital earlier, I begged the nurse to let me into Jace's room, but she refused. Maryanne saw the condition I was in and took pity on me. I got fifteen minutes. But I wasn't ready to go home. I marched to the ICU waiting room and connected some chairs to make a bed. After seeing him again, I didn't like the feeling it gave me in the pit of my stomach. Those fifteen minutes were the shortest and longest minutes of my life. Jace lay there connected to life support while I sat there quietly as tears rolled down my cheeks.

"Have the doctors said anything yet?" I ask.

She nods, staring ahead like she's stuck in a trance. "His blood and oxygen levels are back to normal, but we still won't know about his brain activity. They said the surgeries he had look good, so now we play the waiting game." Maryanne pauses for a minute. Her jaw trembles.

A knot forms in my throat. "They said there's a good chance he won't have any brain activity. They'll wait another day or two until the swelling goes down in his brain to wake him up. Once they do, another test will be done, and we'll know then."

Maryanne paces back and forth in the cold, sterile room. I can only imagine what is running through her head. I sit still, watching her. Do I go to her? Do I say something? I'm so torn. I don't know what to do. I watch as she nervously wrings her fingers together. She turns to look at me, and I exhale a heavy breath. I let the tears I was holding in stream down my cheeks. Maryanne is a second mother to me, so crying in front of her is okay.

"When do I get to see him again?" I ask.

Her face softens. "You can go ahead now."

I right my clothes and take a deep breath before I walk down to Jace's room. I'm a mess, and I smell like a brewery, but I don't give a shit. I need my best friend.

Walking in, the room is dark, cold, lifeless. The blinds are drawn shut and the machines are beeping.

My knees shake as I walk over to Jace's bedside, and I crumble at the sight of him once more.

FIFTEEN

JOHN

The past four days have been a haze when I finally get the call I've been waiting for.

Maryanne doesn't say much, only that I need to come to the hospital. There's been news. I haven't been back to the hospital since the last update. I wanted to be there, but I also wanted Jace to heal.

I've spiraled into a depression over the accident. I consume drink after drink, saying "fuck you" to the world, and wallow in pity. Every time an image appears in my mind, I take a sip. The alcohol has given me the effect I was searching for—numbness. There was one point I couldn't even think straight enough to think of Jace.

Then there is Alyssa. I fucking miss her. The ache in the center of my chest proves it. I don't want to think about her either, but I'm consumed with thoughts that I drunk-dial her every night. She refuses all my calls and messages. I'm not surprised. I deserve it. I haven't spoken to her since the day at the river, but knowing she's been with Chad makes me see red.

And how do I know she's been with that dick?

She updated her social media status two days ago. That only made me drink more. I need to apologize to her and plan to later today.

I sit up to get out of bed but immediately regret it. My head throbs and my bedroom spins. Nausea churns in my stomach. I rub my eyes. I need to make a few calls, one being to Alyssa again, but first, I'm going to Maryanne. My heart races a mile a minute because I don't know what to expect. Will I walk in to find Jace with his eyes open? Will he be talking? Making a joke?

I take a quick shower and put on some fresh clothes. I grab a protein bar and a bottle of water and then leave. Pulling into the hospital twenty minutes later, I park my truck and head straight for the nurses' station to sign in. Anticipation is bubbling in my stomach. I'm wound up and nervous as hell, unsure of what to expect. I shake out my hands and crack my neck as I walk toward his room.

Gripping the doorknob, I take a deep breath and push inside. And what I see shakes me to the core.

I take three steps and still. My heart drops into my gut.

Jace's eyes are closed, and he's still hooked up to breathing tubes. Maryanne is crying at his bedside with red, puffy eyes.

Cold dread washes over me. I begin to shake. My heart pounds against my chest, racing so hard that I think I'm going to have a heart attack. Fear rattles my bones.

This can't be happening.

Maryanne stands and shakes her head as she walks over to me.

"Don't. Don't say it." My voice cracks. I shake my head furiously.

"There's no brain activity," she says quietly, skipping the pleasantries. Tears stream down her blotchy face. "There's nothing else that can be done."

Blood drains from my face. I feel like I'm going to faint. My eyes dart to where my best friend is lying.

"What?" I whisper. I'm struggling to breathe. Knots are forming in the back of my throat. "That can't be."

"The doctors performed an EEG. We've been waiting, but…" She's silent for a moment. "Nothing, John. There's nothing there." She cries quietly. "I've been waiting for some miracle, but the test shows no activity whatsoever."

Disbelief hits me hard. "Maybe he needs more time."

She shakes her head. "If there was some activity in his brain, then yes, but there's not. He's only alive because he's been on life support."

No brain activity?

My chest is splitting in two.

My stunned gaze meets hers, and I know what she's going to say next. The sorrow in her eyes suffocates me. I begin shaking my head quickly.

"I…" She struggles with words. "I have to take him off life support."

No.

Chills run down my spine. I grab my stomach as nausea rolls through me. No. Just, no. I begin shaking my head frantically. She's wrong. The doctors are wrong. Everyone is wrong. They need to give him more time. It's not Jace's time to go.

"He needs more time. Give him more time."

She shakes her head. "It won't help," she says sadly, tears streaming down her face.

"You don't know that. He could have a miracle. He hasn't had enough time!"

She begins to sob uncontrollably, and I suddenly feel like an asshole. I pull her into my arms, and she sobs on me.

"Don't do this, Maryanne. Don't. Please."

"Oh, John, honey. " She shakes her head. "I don't have a choice."

Angry tears blur my vision. "So that's it? You're just going to pull the plug on your son? You're just going to end it like that? Give him time! Don't do this. I can't lose him!"

She pulls back to look at me, and I nearly fall over at the heartbreak in her eyes. "No mother wants to make this decision. No mother wants to bury her child. Do you understand how hard this is for me?" She chokes. "I'd give my life in a second if it would bring him back. This is the last thing I would ever want to do." She glances away, unable to look me in the eyes. I called you in so you could say goodbye to Jace."

I grab the sides of my pounding head. Tears drip down my face. "Does anyone else know?"

"Ford already came and left. I figured at the funeral, if anyone else…"

Maryanne pulls a crumpled tissue from her pocket and dabs her eyes. Her jaw quivers so hard she flattens her lips to stifle the cry. She pats my arm, trying to console me.

"I'm going to get some coffee in the cafeteria. Take all the time you need."

I nod, unable to find the right words. "When… When are you doing it?" I ask. My throat is raw.

"After you leave."

I frown. "Alone?"

She nods.

"Absolutely not," I enunciate each letter. Hot tears rim my eyelids. "I won't allow it. I'll be here with you."

No way will I allow her to be alone while Jace takes his last breath. It will haunt her for the rest of her life. I'll stay by her side, because when Jace leaves this world, a part of her is going to die too. She's going to need someone.

Her shoulders drop. "John—"

"You're not doing this alone. I'll be here with you."

Tears are running down my cheeks. She nods and then leaves. I turn to look at the bed and have to drag my legs to take me there. It's just me and Jace in our final moments together. I look at him in disbelief. The ventilator is still hooked to his mouth. White tape runs down the sides of his face to hold it in place. Guilt eats away at me. God, what was I thinking letting him drive? Aching sorrow rips through my chest. I never should have let him get behind the wheel. That one reckless night of fun turned into a lifelong nightmare.

I place my hands on top of Jace's. His fingers are cold. There's some dried blood under his nails still. Tears are pouring out of me, and I can barely catch my breath. I have so many things I want to say that I don't know where to begin.

"It's not supposed to be this way," I whisper. "What the fuck am I going to do without you? Give me a sign, anything, that you're still here."

He doesn't move. His eyelids are still. His fingers are stiff.

I'm so angry inside. I'm shaking from seething so

hard. There's an old tale that says souls don't leave earth until they're told to. If that is true, then I see it as my responsibility to tell Jace that he needs to move on to his next chapter. I really don't want to tell my best friend to leave this world, but for his mom I will.

Leaning down, I get close to his ear. "Don't hang on. Go fast for your mama, Jace." My throat is quivering. My forehead hits his shoulder, and I cry so hard my whole body shakes. Inhaling deeply until my lungs burn, I pick my head up and exhale. "This isn't our last goodbye."

I STAY WITH MARYANNE UNTIL JACE TAKES HIS LAST breath. It doesn't take long, which makes me wonder if the tale really is true. When the machine flatlines, my whole world changes. Nothing will be the same.

Maryanne is too distraught to drive and needs consoling. My mom picks her up and plans to stay with her overnight. I'm glad I was with Maryanne until the end. She needed me. Jace would have done the same thing if the roles were reversed.

I sit in my truck and stare straight ahead at the rows of cars. I'm still at the hospital. Where do I go? What do I do? I'm in a fog. I feel lost, confused, and angry. Empty. There's only one person I want to be with, and she wants nothing to do with me.

I need her. Fuck, I need her so bad. I need her goodness and smart mouth. I need to be near her to breathe her in. I need to touch her to know that she is alive. I just lost my best friend. I need my girl. Pulling out my phone, I send her a text message.

Me: I need you. Please, Alyssa. I need you so bad right now. Meet me somewhere.

I stare at my phone, praying she'll respond. Seconds feel like minutes. When I see the little bubble indicating she's responding, I breathe a sigh of relief.

Babe: Where?

I think for a moment.

Me: Whiskey River.

Babe: Okay.

Turning the ignition, I leave the hospital and go straight to the river. My mind can't process anything else. I can't even put the radio on. My body is exhausted. I feel stripped of life.

What the fuck happened?

To get to Whiskey River, I have no choice but to pass the place that took Jace's life. Chills skate down my arms. I slow my truck down and look out of the window. Everything slams into me like it just happened. I shake my head and grip the steering wheel until my knuckles are white, trying to ease the tightness that's consuming me.

When I reach the river, I back my truck up under a tree and look around. Alyssa hasn't gotten here yet.

Getting out, I walk to the edge of the water. I pick up a rock and throw it as hard as I can across the river. I watch as it makes a splash and then sinks to the bottom. I bend down and grab another, then another, and throw those. I yell a string of curse words over and over.

Jace is dead.

I bend over and let out a loud howl of anguish and pain. I reach for the ground to stop myself from falling over. God, it hurts. It hurts so bad.

I hear branches breaking behind me. I look over my shoulder and see Alyssa. She tilts her head and locks eyes with me. She came.

"Alyssa." Her name comes out as a broken whisper. My mouth forms a tight, thin line. I shake my head, unable to get the words out. "Jace," I say.

"I know," she says and rushes for me. She wraps her arms around my shoulders and holds me tight as I sob into her neck. I can't control the tears and let it all out. I'm shaking, nearly convulsing, but Alyssa doesn't let go. She holds on to me.

"Jace is gone," I cry. "Jace is gone…"

Alyssa hugs me tighter. I hear her sniffles and feel the vibrations on her back. Jace was her friend too. Finding the strength, I take a deep breath and pick Alyssa up. Her legs automatically wrap around my waist. I walk to my truck, pull down the tailgate, and place her butt on it. I'm drowning in a sea of emotion I don't know how to make sense of.

Alyssa grips my jaw and smashes her lips to mine before I can process another thought. I don't fight to stifle a groan. I let it all out. Her warm body is what I need to feel alive. I kiss her lips, my tongue tangling with hers. I savor every second of her and commit it to memory.

In this moment I realize how completely in love with Alyssa Winters I am.

ALYSSA

JOHN PULLS BACK AND LOOKS AT ME.

His eyes are puffy and swollen. I wipe away the wetness that pools under them, then dry my thumbs on my shorts. A sad, small smile plagues his mouth. I lean in to kiss it away.

"Jace is gone," he repeats quietly, brushing a strand of hair from my face.

"Ford called and told me," I say. My chin quivers as I fight to hold the tears in. I don't tell him that Ford also gave me an update on John's mental state and to please respond to him when he texts me. "Want to talk about it?"

"What's there to talk about."

I place a hand on his chest, feeling his heart beat. "I think it would help if you did."

A breeze causes the branches to sway through the trees. I get a glimpse of the emotions running across his face, but John isn't looking into my eyes. He's staring at my shoulder. Like he can't make eye contact with me. His hands skim up my arms and land on the sides of my neck. I shiver at the touch of his fingers. He gently tilts my head back. Our eyes meet… and my heart breaks.

John is drowning inside. His eyes say it all. Gone is the vibrant ivy green that I've come to love, and in its wake is a deep, melancholy hue. I'm hurting too, but I can't pretend to know what this is like for him. I wish I could kiss his pain away.

John presses his forehead to mine, and I breathe him in. He heaves a heavy sigh. He doesn't say anything but doesn't need to. I can feel in his trembling hands how devastatingly hard this is for him.

"I'm sorry for what I said to you, Alyssa." John's voice is barely above a whisper. I pinch my eyes shut. "It was wrong of me. I shouldn't have said it."

"It's okay."

He shakes his head adamantly. "It's not. I fucked up, and I'm sorry." He pauses. "Do you need to be home soon?" he asks. I shake my head. I can tell he hopes I don't have to.

"Let's stay here tonight," I suggest. Relief fills his eyes.

John walks to the passenger door and retrieves a towel he has in the back. He lays it out on the truck bed. I scoot to one side and he sits on the other. Hooking my arm through his, I rest my head on his shoulder. Our relationship has been rocky the last few weeks, but we're nearly best friends without the label. He's been there for me. I want to be there for him.

A little while passes as we lie there listening to the crickets in the stillness of the night. It's peaceful even in the turmoil. He's suffering and if being in his arms is what brings him even an ounce of solace, then I'll stay here all night with him.

"Maryanne took Jace off life support tonight. I stood there and watched as the doctors did it. She didn't want me there, but I couldn't just leave her to do it on her own." His voice crackles. John squeezes his eyes shut like he's trying to erase the memory from his brain.

"That's because you have a good heart, Johnny. He would have done the same for you."

"How can a parent have the strength to do that?" John

says in utter disbelief. "I can't imagine being in her position."

"We aren't given what we can't handle. Not that any parent should have to do that," I say.

John looks at me and the pain in his eyes slices through my heart.

"You're my rock, my other half. I don't know what I'd do without you." He pauses, and I can hear the swallow in his throat. "I love you, Alyssa," he says quietly.

John places a soft kiss on the side of my head. He needs me more than ever tonight, and I plan to give myself to him in every way.

SIXTEEN

ALYSSA

The summer days are long as they pass.

I've sent countless texts to John, but he has yet to respond. I've called him so many times that it's starting to look pathetic. I want to help him, be there in the wake of losing his best friend. I know he's hurting, but I can't give him what he needs when he disregards me the way that he does.

Jace was my friend too. I wasn't as close with him as John was, but my eyes are swollen from crying, and my heart feels ripped in two. I'm reeling from his loss. So much has happened in the time that I've moved to South Fork. I never could have anticipated any of it. I don't regret a single moment. The moments that I did get to spend with Jace will stay with me forever.

"Why the long face?"

I look over my shoulder at Chad as I wipe the bar top with an old wet rag that smells like bleach. He must know that Jace died, right?

"Just a lot on my mind," I say softly.

137

Chad grabs a rag. "Here, let me help you."

"You don't have to do that. Go home. Your shift is over."

He shrugs. "I know I don't. I want to."

Chad helps with the rest of the tables and stays until I finish. Today I worked a double, and even though I'm exhausted, I'm too wired to sleep. There's too much on my mind.

"Want to talk about it?" Chad asks, dropping the rag in the bucket.

I shake my head. "Not really."

"Have any plans after work?"

A sad laugh rolls off my lips. "No."

"How about I pick up a bottle and we head back to my place? You look like you could use a drink."

I chew my lip and nod. I really wish John would answer me. I'd much rather hang out with him.

"What's your poison?" he asks.

"I'll take anything at this point."

"That bad?"

I look away. For me, yes. "Let me grab my tips. I kind of want to get cleaned up before I come over. I smell like a fast-food joint."

"Want to get washed up at my place? I'll give you some clothes."

"Yeah, that would be great, actually."

"Meet me out front, and you can follow me," he says, and I nod.

Chad only lives a couple of blocks over from my house. He decides on tequila. I'm not crazy about liquor, but at this point, I don't care. I just want to get drunk and forget about Johnny for the night.

After parking my mom's car, I follow him to the front door. Chad pushes it open and escorts me in. He flips the lights on, and I look around. The apartment is small and bare but relatively clean. No pictures are mounted on the walls, and there is only a couch, coffee table, and a flat-screen television in the living room.

"Is your dad home?"

He chuckles. "I don't live with my dad."

"Oh. I didn't know that."

"Yeah, we don't see eye to eye on many things, so I was out once I turned eighteen."

Curious, I ask, "How do you afford to live on your own?"

Chad drops his keys and the black plastic bag holding the tequila onto a small, round wood table in the kitchen.

"A one-bedroom isn't all that expensive on this side of town, and everything is included in my rent. If I'm not in school, I work. I have nothing else to do."

Chad uncaps the bottle and pulls out two tall, slender shot glasses from a cabinet. "A shot before you get cleaned up?"

"Yeah, that sounds good." He hands me the glass. I can smell the potency of the seemingly innocent looking liquid. I shiver before I even taste it. Chad sees my reaction and laughs.

"Not a big tequila fan?"

"Not really. Hard liquor isn't my thing, but sometimes beer isn't enough, you know?"

He nods with a smirk. "I suggest taking the whole shot in one. Tequila is more of an acquired taste."

I hold up the glass and look at it. This tequila looks brown, and not something intended for shots.

"It's a double," he says. "Ready?"

"Ready as I'll ever be."

"Bottoms up." Chad clinks his glass against mine.

I take a deep breath then take the whole shot. I almost gag as soon as it hits the back of my throat. I bring the back of my hand to my mouth. My eyes water, and I shake it off. The last time I had a shot of tequila was with John at the bonfire. It wasn't bad then, but I'd already had a few shots of whiskey before that, so maybe that helped. I cringe from the impact and swallow hard.

Chad laughs at my response to the shot. "That bad?"

"No," I lie. My nostrils burn. "I'm just not used to it. You drink this stuff all the time?"

He nods and begins pouring another. I need a few minutes before I have my second.

"Want to show me to the bathroom? I can smell the kitchen on me and want to wash it away."

Chad grabs me a pair of boxer shorts and a black Metallica shirt before showing me to the bathroom. I close the door and turn on the shower. Steam fills the room as I strip out of my clothes. Stepping under the water, I lean against the shower wall and close my eyes. Tears roll down my cheeks as I think about Jace. His death has left a mark on my heart despite not knowing him very long. He was the life of the party and so much fun to be around. I wish I had more time with him. Jace had become a good friend in such a short period of time. Now he's a memory.

I step out of the shower and towel-dry my hair. The tequila is already hitting my bloodstream and helping to ease the tension in my neck. Exhaling a tired breath, I slip on Chad's oversized clothes, then I wipe the foggy mirror with my hand and look at myself. I touch the puffiness under my bloodshot eyes and stare at my blank reflection. I want one night where I don't think about John or cry from losing Jace. A part of me feels selfish for wanting that.

Back in the living room, I watch Chad throw a dart and make it close to the target. Two more shot glasses wait on the table nearby. Walking over, I grab one, tip it back, and then hand the other to Chad without saying anything. It burns going down, but it's not as bad this time. I want to forget, not feel anything, and this will do just that. Chad rakes his gaze down my body as he takes the shot from me. He gives me a crooked grin, then slams it back.

"Let's go." He waves at me. "You're going to play."

Shaking my head, I say, "I have no aim." I can barely play cornhole. Throwing a pointy dart is going to be worse.

Chad hooks his arm around my waist and pulls me to stand before him. He picks up my hand and positions the dart between my fingers.

"Look at the center," he whispers near my neck. "Focus on it. Take a deep breath and throw. It's easy."

I swallow hard. The stubble on his jaw grazes my face, causing goose bumps to coat my skin. I follow Chad's directions and fling the dart. It bounces off the wall and hits the floor. I giggle, and Chad gives my hip a squeeze.

"You weren't even close," Chad says. "And it didn't even stick to the wall." He bends down to pick up the dart. "Try again. This time put a little oomph into it."

He hands me three darts. I bite my lip and launch one after another. This time they stick to the wall.

Humor fills his eyes. "I don't understand how you're so far from the target."

"I told you I have no aim!" I laugh.

Chad grabs the darts, closes his eyes, and shoots all three off, hitting the board.

"Show off."

He grins, and my eyes wander to his lip ring. My gaze lingers. The second shot is beginning to affect me, and I like the feeling it gives.

"Every time you miss, you have to take a shot."

"I'll get really drunk, and my aim will be even worse."

"I can't imagine it could get any worse."

Pursing my lips together, I grab the darts and focus on the board's colors. I shoot each one, my body angling forward from the power I add to the throw. This time I hit closer to the board, but they don't stick. Chad picks up the darts and walks behind me. He wraps an arm around my waist and yanks me to his chest. He doesn't let go. I can feel the hardness of his body pressed against me. My heart is pumping faster. Heat courses through my veins when he picks up my hand, puts the dart in it, and holds on. He pulls back, my hand going with his, and flings it. I lean forward from the force, and my hips press into his.

"Next time you miss, you take a shot."

I roll my bottom lip and nod.

Naturally, I miss my next shot.

"I'm determined to get this." I huff as Chad pours more tequila. I bring it to my lips and pause. "This isn't fair. You never miss."

He smirks. "I'll take one with you each time."

"Good," I say, and down the shot when an idea forms in my head. "No more darts. Let's arm wrestle."

Chad pulls out a cigarette. "I'll beat you in two seconds flat."

"You know"—I prop my hands on my hips—"you're supposed to let me win."

"Because you're a girl? That's not how it works in the real world, baby. When you want something, you gotta take it."

I'm pretty drunk and don't acknowledge him calling me baby or the fact that he made a creepy comment about taking what he wants. I pull out a chair and sit with my arm poised and ready. Chad shrugs and sits down, placing his cigarette in the ashtray.

"You ready to lose?" I taunt. A slow smile spreads across his face, and I stare at his lip ring again. That thing is sexy as hell. My cheeks flush as Chad cups my hand with his. I meet his gaze.

"On the count of three." I nod.

"One… Two… Three."

That's all it takes for Chad to win. Three seconds. The back of my hand presses into the tabletop.

"Hey! I wasn't ready!" I lie, and he laughs. Chad takes another inhale of his cigarette and then puts it down. I swipe it and take a puff for myself. I'm not a smoker, but I'm not a tequila drinker either. Inhaling, the smoke makes me instantly lightheaded. It heightens my drunk high, and I become really intoxicated. I wasn't expecting that.

"Well…" I draw out. "I think I'm high. And really drunk."

"From a cigarette?"

I nod. I don't know why, but I find his comment funny. "Okay. One more time, but I get to use two hands."

His mouth drops open. "That's cheating!"

"You gotta give me something!"

"Fine. One game, and you get two hands. If you don't win, two more shots."

They taste like water at this point. "You're so bad," I say, my words slurring.

"You have no idea, baby. Now let's do this." Chad puts his hand up, and I cup it with both of mine. He says, "On my count. One… Two…"

I put everything into winning. Chad's knuckles turn white. I start slipping off the chair as I lean to the side and try to pull his hand down. Just when I'm about to hit the table, he swings to the other side, presses my hand down, and wins. I fall off the chair and come face-to-face with his carpet.

"Oh crap." I laugh from the floor.

"You're a mess," Chad says, hooking an arm around my waist.

"A hot mess is the correct term."

He lifts me up, but I forget to use my legs and fall back down. I'm a mess for sure.

"Now I know what that saying means."

"What saying?" he asks, lifting me up again. He props me against the wall next to the table and uses his body to hold me there.

"One tequila, two tequila, three tequila floor."

"That really does apply to you," he says.

Chad doesn't take his eyes off me as he pinches his cigarette between two fingers and takes a drag. He blows the smoke out from the corner of his mouth and then brings the cigarette to my lips. I don't know why, but I find the move unbelievably hot. I inhale and blow it out, purposely hitting his face.

Tilting his head to the side, he says quietly, "Who knew you were so much fun, Alyssa?"

I shrug with a coy smile and reach for the shot glass. I drink half of it and give the other half to Chad.

He shakes his head. "Take it all."

"I'm really drunk."

"So am I, but I always finish what I start." His eyes darken. I find myself falling into them. I tip the shot back, and he gestures to the other one.

"No more. You take that one. I can't feel my legs."

Chad grins and drinks it.

"If you're really drunk and can't feel your legs, I'm thinking we're gonna have a slumber party." He winks.

"I think you're right," I say.

It would be irresponsible to drive in this condition. I won't take the chance. Thank goodness Mom doesn't work in the morning, so I don't have to worry about her needing the car.

"Can't imagine lover boy knows you're here."

I shake my head. "I haven't spoken to him lately. You know about Jace, right?"

Chad nods, but no sympathy is shown in his eyes. "It's unfortunate."

"Yeah."

Chad licks his lips, and I watch, mesmerized by his lip ring and movement. He threads his fingers through the back of my head and tips my face to meet his. He's so close that I can smell the tequila coming off his breath. He leans in and doesn't hesitate to kiss me. He thrusts tongue into my mouth, and our tongues tangle with one another's. I let him, because the truth is, I've wanted to kiss him since I met him. His kisses are different. He doesn't ask. He takes and demands. He tugs on my hair, causing a flash of desire to pool in my belly.

Reaching down, he grips my thighs and picks me up. I wrap my legs around his waist and lock my ankles. He rolls his hips into mine. I moan at the pressure. His movements aren't light, and I like that. He's rough with his kisses, and his touch is abrasive. He's touching me everywhere, all at once. My body is climbing with hot desire, and I want more. His palms glide up my thighs, and his fingers skim my pussy. He breaches my entrance, and I clench around him from the intrusion, both liking it but hurting. He rubs my pussy until I'm wet and grinding against him. My back bows, and he breaks the kiss. Chad pulls his fingers out and puts them in his mouth, his eyes never leaving mine.

My cheeks flush. A slow grin dances across his face. Before I can process what is happening, Chad pulls me off the wall and has me in his room and on his bed in seconds. He licks my neck, biting the curve of my shoulder, and I shiver. His hands go to my breasts, and he groans as he pushes his hips back and forth into me. His cock is rock hard and feels good rubbing against my pussy. My legs tighten around his waist, and he pushes his cock into me again. I try to stifle my moans but fail. My head is spinning. I'm wound up and turned on, and as much as my body is on fire and begging for release, I'm not trying to have sex with Chad.

I place my palms against his chest and turn my head to the side, breathing heavily. Chad grabs both my wrists and places them above my head.

"I …" I breathe, seeing triple of Chad. "I think we should stop."

"I'll be the one to decide."

"No. I don't want to."

"You don't get to work me up only to say stop." He kisses me again, and I lose my train of thought. My wrists are pinned to the bed as he slips his other hand into the boxers and runs his fingers along my slit. Fuck, it feels good. I can't close my legs since Chad is on top of me.

"I don't..." I say between kisses and squirm under him.

"Shh... You want this," he insists.

"I... No... I don't want..."

"Yes, you do."

He thrusts two fingers inside my pussy. My hips come off the bed, and my back arches as the searing pleasure washes over my traitorous body.

"Chad—"

He kisses me to shut me up as his fingers pump in and out. I whimper.

"See? I knew you'd like it."

His thumb circles my clit too well. I try to speak, but he muffles my sounds with his mouth.

Why did I have to drink so much? I'm having trouble forming words. My heart pounds, and the room spins. I want him to stop, but he won't. Chad applies more pressure to my wrists while his other hand finger fucks me. I struggle to move. I don't want this, yet I feel an orgasm climbing, and it's hard to stop it from happening. I open my eyes as wide as possible and focus on the ceiling.

"Chad. Stop."

He ignores me and keeps tormenting my body. He bites my neck, licking it and then biting again. My blood is rising, the impending orgasm getting closer, and I don't know what I want anymore.

LUCIA FRANCO

"I said stop," I beg.

"I know you want this, baby. You've wanted my cock inside that sweet pussy of yours ever since we met."

I squeeze my eyes shut, fighting off the orgasm.

"I... I..."

I can't get the words out as my release tears through me so hard I shudder under him. I thrust my pussy into his hand and grind on him. I can't stop the pleasure overriding my thoughts and let my body coast. He continues rubbing my clit until he wrings every bit of my orgasm from me. My hips move against his fingers, and I wish they didn't.

"Yeah... That's it. I knew you wanted it. Give it to me," he mutters near my ear.

Chad lets go of my wrists and stands on his knees. He flips me over, causing my head to spin. I'm a slow-moving pile of mush. I hear a zipper, and my body jerks back. My heart drops. Something isn't right. I don't know what, only that I want it to stop. My mind fades, darkness taking me under. I can barely hold myself up. Chad grabs me by the waist, and I hear him talk to himself before my world turns black.

MY HEAD IS POUNDING AS I OPEN MY EYES. I THINK I'M still drunk, and I'm nauseous to the core. I sit up too quickly, and the room spins. I lie back down, trying to fight off the bile rising to my throat. I look for a clock to see what the time is. I'm too disoriented and puzzled to care and flop down. I roll over to see Chad sleeping. He's passed out.

Last night was fun. We played darts, and I tried to arm wrestle him, but what happened after that?

My head pounds even more trying to remember how we ended up in his bed. I remember falling, giggling, him kissing me, me kissing him back, but the rest is a complete blank.

This is the first time I've blacked out. I have no idea what happened.

Something about last night isn't sitting right with me. Maybe it's the aftereffect from the bottle of tequila I chugged with Chad. I scissor my legs and feel a sting between my thighs. Frowning, I pause. I move my legs again, seeing if the sting is still there, and sure enough, it is.

Did we have sex last night? No. My clothes are still on, and even though I lusted after Chad when we first met, I don't want to sleep with him. I don't like him like that, especially after being with Johnny. Despite John's refusal to speak to me, he owns my heart. I just haven't told him.

I go back to sleep, deciding to figure it out later once my head stops pulsating.

SEVENTEEN

JOHN

I stare at the fresh lump of dirt in a daze.

The burial was today.

Five days ago, I watched my best friend be taken off life support. I saw him take his last breath, and my head has been in a fucked-up place ever since.

Five days ago is also the last time I spoke to Alyssa. That night in the back of my truck with her was one of the best and worst nights of my life. It took me to both heaven and hell. We went our separate ways after we left Whiskey River. She's made numerous attempts to get in touch with me again, but I don't want to talk to her. I don't want to talk to anyone. Not my parents, or my brother, Luke. I haven't even spoken to Ford. But judging by his disheveled appearance at the funeral service, we are on the same page. I've been drowning in memories, and I could tell he's been too. The only time I've spoken to anyone was to help Maryanne with the funeral arrangements. I fought my own tears so I could listen to her sobs. I'm missing my best friend, but she is missing her only child.

Nothing and no one can repair the brokenness I feel inside. I've descended deeper into depression, and it's no one's fault but mine.

I grab a beer from my truck and crack it open. I take a long, hard pull and sit in the grass next to where Jace is buried, trying to make sense of this moment. No one is here but me. When Alyssa showed up at the funeral, I couldn't talk to her. There were dark circles under her puffy eyes, and she looked pale. I kept my focus glued to the coffin for the duration of the service. Watching your best friend be lowered into the ground does shit to your head.

I tilt my head back and take in the deep blush and warm orange sunset, and stare. My chin quivers. Tears fill my eyes once more. Is heaven real? Is Jace up there looking down at me? Is he making fun of my suit and tie, saying I look stuffy? Or is he sitting beside me, drinking a beer, and I don't know it? I gulp hard and clench my eyes shut.

I drop my head between my bent knees as my beer dangles from one hand. The fresh scent of cut grass floods my senses. I inhale, absorbing the earthy soil into my lungs, and exhale a ragged breath. My chest is so tight. All I see is Jace when I close my eyes. I need to stop thinking about him. But if I don't think about him, then I'll forget about him, and I can't do that.

Bringing the longneck bottle to my lips, I take a long swig of beer, thinking this must be some sort of fucked-up nightmare and not my reality. I feel his absence everywhere I look.

I pick up a handful of dirt and watch it sift through my fingers. A part of me died with Jace that day.

I raise my beer and tip it over the dirt, pouring out Jace a drink.

I decide that I'm going to get obliterated tonight.

I SPEND THE DAYS FOLLOWING JACE'S BURIAL BY MYSELF, getting drunk on his memory. I'll stay in the cemetery for hours, listening to country music. The damn songs cut deep, especially while drinking.

Alyssa has been nonexistent during this time, but that's because of me. I have no idea what she is doing, and sometimes I don't even care. She has finally stopped reaching out, but that doesn't mean I'm not thinking about her. Alyssa has become my best friend, my other half, the one I reach for. I desperately need her, but I've pushed her away. I've probably ruined anything we had by now. At least I know what we had was real and it wasn't all in my head. I've seen the look in her eyes, the desire, the lust. It mirrored my own. The way I'm craving her says it was real. I miss her smile, her blond hair falling over her shoulders when she laughs, and the way her eyes sparkle when she tests my patience.

Reaching into my plastic bag, I take out the last beer I have and a red plastic cup. I pop the top and pour some liquid into it, then place the cup next to Jace's tombstone.

"Thought you could use a drink. Figured we could have one together." I take a sip of the beer and fight the fucking tears again. "I just wanted you to know that I'm still thinking about you, buddy. Miss ya, man. Everyone misses you." I shake my head, trying to blink away the emotion. The pressure in my chest is all-consuming. I feel like I'm suffocating. "I thought you might be lonely out here all by yourself, which is why I've been sitting here every night with you." I sniffle. "Why did you have to go? You're here, but you're not. It's so strange because I can feel your spirit around me. Sometimes I ask myself if you're really dead. It was supposed to be me and you until the end. I can't believe I don't have you by my side anymore." Tears stain my cheeks. "I'm not ready, man. I'm not ready to say goodbye. I just can't. Because if I do, then this shit is real, and you are gone. So I won't say goodbye. I just won't." Bringing the beer back to my mouth, I realize the bottle is empty. I eye Jace's cup and reach for it. "Not gonna drink it? That's cool. I'll drink it for you. Bottoms up." Extending my arm, I tip the cup over and pour a line of beer out for Jace, then I drink the rest of the contents. Stumbling to my feet, I stand up, and I'm drunker than I realize. Nevertheless, I'm ready to go home. "I'll never forget you. Never," I whisper.

Placing a hand on the side of my truck to steady myself, I take a deep breath before I pull open the driver's side door and climb in. It takes me a few tries to get the key in the ignition and pull out. I roll down my window and drop an arm out. Nothing feels as good as when I ride with the windows down and the music blaring. I'm beginning to understand how Luke feels about music. It calms my nerves and allows me to escape the madness in my head.

I drive down the dark road encased by old trees. I look for the yellow dotted line, but it's more complicated tonight. I frown. When did two lines appear? And why are they moving? Which one should I drive next to when they're swerving in and out of each other? I slap my face then sit up straighter. I'm almost home. I can't wait to hit the sheets. Hopefully, everyone's asleep when I get there. I'm not in the mood to talk. I'm exhausted. Yawning, I stretch my arms and arch my back, thinking about how appealing my bed sounds right now.

I blink and my heart jumps into my throat. Gasping, I slam on the brakes and my truck fishtails as I try to avoid hitting the deer that appeared out of nowhere. It must've been walking across the street and I didn't see it. The tires screech, and I pull to a jerking stop. My jaw drops. The deer gallops away into the field.

Throwing open the door, I jump out and try to catch my breath. I'm shaking from head to toe, and I'm nauseous. The scent of burned rubber permeates the air. It wakes me right up. I pace the ground and stop in front of the truck. I place my hands on the warm hood and bend over, emptying my stomach. Nothing but liquid comes up.

When I'm back inside the truck, I take out my cell and text Alyssa.

> Me: I'm sorry for everything. I miss you. I still want you. I need to feel you. I hate that I hurt you. I hate myself for hurting you. I know I fucked up, and I'm sorry. I will fix this. I promise.

Lying in bed, I watch the ceiling fan spin in circles. My life flashed before my eyes tonight, and it scared the shit out of me. I should have never driven drunk again. It was dumb and reckless. I could've killed someone. I have my entire life ahead of me, and I don't want to cut it short because of my stupidity. I could wake up tomorrow and be dead. I'm not ready to die.

I decide that I'm going to make a change. I don't like how I've been acting or what I'm becoming. Tomorrow, I'll tell my father I'm ready to follow in his footsteps and join the Marines.

I've been given one life to live, and I will live it to its fullest. For me, and for Jace.

EIGHTEEN
JOHN

three months later

The night I came close to meeting Jace at the golden gates was an awakening.

I can't believe I had let myself stoop so low. It was careless and selfish of me. I was drowning my grief and sorrow in alcohol, the worst possible thing I could've done. It scared the shit out of me, but isn't that how life works? It takes a life-altering event to wake up. If you're lucky enough. Losing Jace made me realize how short life is.

Other than my family, no one knows I enlisted in the Marines. I'm not good at goodbyes, but it's what I had to do. The first couple of weeks were absolute torment. They hit me harder than I expected. Boot camp chewed up the weak and spit them out. I was broken down, sore, and ached for weeks in places I didn't even know I had muscles. I was mentally drained then pieced back together. I have a month of combat training left, and then two months of aviation training. After that, I'm not sure.

For the next ten days, I'll be home. I plan to spend as much time as I can with my family. I also plan to fix other parts of my life that I royally screwed up. I left Alyssa high and dry. It was wrong of me. I should have told her I was leaving, but I also should have responded to her texts too. A part of me feels like I used her, and that's not who I am. I hope she forgives me. I miss her so much and will do anything to make things right with her. She's been my strength through all of this.

I also want to check in on Maryanne and see how Ford is doing. My town will never feel the same with Jace gone, but it's where my family and my life are. As Luke says, it's time to face the music.

Stepping into the airport after a cramped flight, happiness fills me at the sight of both my parents. Dropping my bag, I give Mom a hug first. Visibly seeing her puts me at ease. They weren't able to attend my boot camp graduation because she had a flare-up. Her multiple sclerosis has a mind of its own. I've seen how the disease has affected her over the years and the toll it has taken on her. Staying in bed was the best thing for her.

"Alright, Ma, it was only boot camp. You can let go now."

"I know. I'm just so happy to see you. I can't believe how much you've changed."

Pulling back, I grin. I've filled out and gained muscle. "I'm glad to be back for a couple of weeks."

Dad says, "Glad to see you, Son."

He reaches down for my bag. The three of us walk to Dad's car. Mom asks me a million and one questions on the ride home.

"How's Luke doing?" I ask. "I haven't seen him in so long."

"He's in town with Livy," Mom says. "I wish he would ask her to marry him already."

Dad chuckles. I shake my head. I'm in no rush to get married.

Luke has been head over heels in love with Olivia King since childhood. She's like a member of the family. But dreams took them on separate paths, and Luke suffered for years without her.

Once I'm settled in at home, I change into running shorts and a navy-blue shirt with "Marine" printed on the front. I grab my sneakers and go downstairs. I need to stretch my legs out and go for a run.

"Heading out already?" Dad asks.

"I'm just going for a run. I'll be back in a bit."

"Your brother is coming over with Livy later to see you for dinner."

I smile to myself. "Looking forward to seeing them."

I'm out the door. There's nothing like running. It frees my mind and releases stress stored in my muscles. Running is also the ideal medication for mending a broken heart. During boot camp, the recruits were forced to run miles and miles each day, so I built up a pretty good stamina. I pump my legs with nothing surrounding me but the wind at my back and rolling land. South Fork might be a little hole-in-the-wall town, but it's my home. I love the nostalgia it gives, the old dirt roads, all the land between the houses. I can see why Luke is always coming back. There's nothing like home.

Breathe in, breathe out.

Turning around the corner, I take the street that leads to

Alyssa's house. I had no intention of going there, yet it's the direction I'm pulled in. My body is still like a magnet to hers after all these months. I figured I'd see her at some point, but it seems I need her now.

Which means passing Jace's accident site.

I pace myself but nothing can prepare me. My heartbeat is loud in my ears and my throat feels swollen. I'm filled with more and more dread the closer I get. It's hard to face the truth. Jace's death is still fresh, and it hurts like hell. Deep down, I'm angry.

I sprint to the other side of the road. Fake, white flowers are stapled to a cross that holds a circular sign in the center. Tipping my head back, I read the bold block letters.

DRIVE SAFELY
IN LOVING MEMORY OF
JACE McCONNELL

I take a deep breath and rub at the ache in my chest. This is all that is left of Jace.

I don't understand how this is supposed to get easier. All those people who say death gets easier with time are full of shit. I stare in disbelief. I still can't believe this was his fate. Jace was too young. He hadn't lived yet. He was a good guy. But I guess death doesn't care about morals. When it's your time, it's your time to go.

Why was it his time? Did Jace even have a chance to really live? I'm left with so many unanswered questions. Losing a loved one is a bleak sorrow that can only be understood by experience.

"Miss ya, man."

I turn around and book it toward Alyssa's house. A burn settles in my thighs, but I push past it and keep going. I think about what I will say to her. If she'll even talk to me after the way I treated her. I squint seeing long blond hair blowing in the wind. For a minute, I think it's Alyssa, but that isn't Alyssa's address, so it can't be her.

I kick my legs harder, ignoring the fire running through them. The girl closes the door to the mailbox and flips through the mail. I'm having déjà vu. This is just like how I met Alyssa. My legs slow of their own accord when I'm a couple of feet away. The girl picks up her head and freezes.

It is Alyssa.

She looks stunned. Her eyes are two large circles as she watches me close the distance. Her mouth parts like she's seen a ghost. She wraps a protective arm around her stomach and straightens her back. My gaze drifts lower and I frown. Creases form between my eyes. I wish I was seeing things, or I could say that the heat got to me, but I can't.

I step closer. She draws in an audible breath when I'm inches away. I reach out and gently place my hands on the sides of her growing belly. She holds still. I want to be pissed. I want to be fucking mad and yell at her for not telling me. Surprisingly, I'm not any of those things. Not when my child is growing inside of her.

My gaze lifts to hers. Alyssa's teeth are digging into her bottom lip. Unshed tears are about to spill over. I pull away, and she flinches at the sudden movement.

"Did I hurt you?"

"No," she says quietly, looking at the ground.

"Whose place is this?"

161

She hesitates, and I don't like the taste it leaves in my mouth. When she finally looks in my eyes, she says defiantly, "Chad lives here."

Silence hangs between us. Dread curls in my stomach. "What are you doing here?" I ask.

She visibly swallows and the dread spoils. "I live here now."

I take a step back in shock and spin in a circle, clasping my hands behind my head. Alyssa is living with Chad. This is the worst type of news to come home to. I look toward the run-down apartment complex she's living in, feeling the irritation seethe inside of me. How could she shack up with him?

"How far along are you?" I ask.

She rubs her belly. "I'm about four months."

"Is everything okay with the pregnancy?"

"Yes. The baby is healthy."

I bob my head, taking in the shock of the century. There are so many things I want to say and ask. My mind is a muddled mess. I don't know where to start. I think back to the training I had at boot camp to not panic under duress and apply it to this moment. I don't want to blow up on Alyssa, but she's pregnant, and she didn't tell me.

"It seems we have a lot to catch up on. Are you free in the next couple of days. We need to talk, but I'm not doing that inside his place."

"I should be able to get away," she says.

"I don't know why you're with Chad or care to know, but I plan to be there for him. Chad isn't playing daddy with my kid."

Alyssa swallows and looks away, shaking her head.

"It's not that easy. Chad's been there for me since the beginning," she says.

"Doesn't matter. I'll pay back whatever money he's spent. But he better not try and play house with my kid."

She studies me for a moment then drops a bombshell on me. "Chad thinks the baby is his."

I rear back, stunned. "Four months ago you were with me," I say. But she shakes her head, and my heart drops into my gut. I watch as Alyssa nervously chews the corner of her bottom lip.

"I was also with him."

I feel so betrayed. I'm not sure a long run will help this situation.

"You slept with him when you were with me?" I ask, my voice low and accusatory.

Alyssa averts her gaze to something behind me. She's embarrassed to look at me while I'm struggling to remain calm and collected. How could she have done that to me? We weren't officially dating, but the stark knowledge that she slept with Chad is like a knife to my heart. I thought I meant more to her than that.

I step back. "Why?" My voice cracks. "When?"

"Around the time you started calling me a white trash piece of shit," she says with no remorse and looks at me again.

Fuck. I knew that was a low blow.

I tore her down with words that can never be taken back. I want to apologize for what I said and how I behaved, but I didn't cause her to have sex with Chad.

"So it's possible that it's not my baby." I pause. "How could you?" I whisper. "Did you sleep with him to get back at me?"

She shakes her head, hurt slashed across her face. "No. It's not like that. And anyway, I don't owe you an explanation. I thought you were done with me. You closed off and pushed me away. What was I supposed to do?"

I could never be done with her.

I go off. "My best friend is dead. He fucking died, Alyssa. You were not supposed to run and fuck Chad." My voice shakes, my eyes watering. "That night was the worst night of my life. I made a few mistakes but... Fuck."

Alyssa fights back her tears. "It wasn't planned. I didn't do it to hurt you." Protectively rubbing her belly, she says, "For what it's worth, I'm ninety-nine percent sure this baby is yours."

I huff, shaking my head. "Ninety-nine percent... Can you come over later instead?"

"I can't tonight," she says with a shaky voice. My eyes narrow at her sudden change in tone. Swallowing, she says, "I'll call you when I get up."

I nod suspiciously. "What's going on? Is everything okay?"

"Yup. Fine," she replies quickly. "I just need to start dinner. I'll talk to you tomorrow and then we'll talk." She pauses, then says, "It's good to see you."

Alyssa waves goodbye and turns around. The bright blue eyes that once held so much spark are gone. That isn't the Alyssa I know and love.

She walks up the driveway. I'd never guess from behind that she's pregnant. She seems so tiny and frail. The oversized shirt she's wearing could be a dress on her. A gust of wind blows by and causes the back to flare into the air. It's only for a split second, but I see a black-and-blue welt across the back of her left thigh.

I PUSH THE FRONT DOOR OPEN TO MY PARENTS' HOME, AND it slams into the wall, leaving a hole from the doorknob.

"Whoa!" my father says, coming around the corner. "What the hell is going on?"

I'm huffing hard, my chest tight with each breath of air. I ran home as fast as I could, not stopping to take a break. All the control I learned over the past three months has gone out the window. Everything makes sense now. Now I know why Alyssa doesn't want me to call her. I know why she looked so skittish.

Motherfucking Chad.

Somewhere deep down, I pray it isn't true. Pray that Chad isn't using his fists on her. Because so help me God, I will kill him. Consequences be dammed.

"What's troubling you?"

"Alyssa," I say through gritted teeth. "I saw Alyssa. She is pregnant, and she has a huge black-and-blue bruise across the back of her leg. I think Chad is abusing her."

"Whoa. Slow it down, Son. You can't just throw heavy words around like that."

I'm frantic and panicking inside. "Something was off with her. She was acting different."

"Let's not jump to conclusions. Talk to her. See what you can find out. Did you see any other marks on her?"

I shake my head.

"You said she's pregnant?"

"Yes."

Dad is quiet.

"Is it yours?" He stares at me. "I know you're worked

up right now, but let's consider who's at the center. Alyssa. You can't be jumping down her throat or stressin' her out. I know you're upset and angry, but carrying a baby takes a lot from a woman's body. Their emotions are all out of whack. Lord knows I watched your mother go through it enough. Be easy on her."

Dad is right. I need to simmer down. But how can I? If Alyssa is being physically abused, I won't be able to function knowing she's in Chad's home and under his hand. This is my fault. I should've never ignored her.

"First things first," Dad says, "let's not tell your mother about this just yet. Talk to Alyssa, then we'll decide from there."

I nod. Dad is right. Mom doesn't need the extra stress. She's doing well on her new medication, and I don't want to tire her out.

"If Alyssa is pregnant with your child, we will be happy to help her while you're training. We'll treat her like our own and take care of her until your placement is sorted out."

I swallow. I only hope I can be half the man my father is one day.

"Thanks, Dad. I really appreciate that. So, how long do I have to wait to see if it is my kid?"

I'm absolutely clueless about anything related to pregnancy or babies. Google is about to become my best friend.

Best friend…

Jace. At this moment, I wish Jace were here to talk about this. I need my friend right about now more than ever.

"What am I supposed to do? I'm twenty-one years old."

Dad reaches across the table and rests his hand on my shoulder. He doesn't say anything.

I haven't craved a beer in months, and I suddenly want one.

Instead, I will take a steaming hot shower to calm my nerves and then call Ford.

NINETEEN

ALYSSA

I thought if I went to bed early, it would help ease the thoughts weighing on me. If I'm asleep, I don't have to think about it.

Instead, it backfires on me.

I tossed and turned all night long. I couldn't sleep with the knowledge that John is back in town. My heart does this little summersault at the thought of seeing him again. I'll have to sneak off at the right time to see John. There's a point in the day Chad is so busy with work that he can't talk on the phone. He won't know if I'm gone. The last thing I want to deal with is Chad and his rapid mood swings. I don't know what mood he'll be in when he walks through the door each day after work. Some days, he'll come in smiling, hugging me, and kissing my neck. On other days, he'll come in with a scowl, hating everyone around him, including me. Those days, I know to stay quiet and do whatever Chad demands. The last thing I want is to make him angry.

Last night when Chad walked through the door, I was

like a ball rolling on the edge of a building. I was skittish, worried he'd notice a change in me. There's no way he'd find out I saw John, but that didn't stop making me feel like I did something wrong. I managed to cook dinner and have it plated. I waited on him hand and foot and gave him what he wanted. If he was happy, then all was good in the world.

Turning onto my side, I curl into a ball and readjust my pillow. I pull the blanket up to my chest and glance at the clock. Chad turns over and nestles his nose in my hair.

"Mornin'," he says groggily, nudging me with his obvious erection.

My eyes close, and I grimace. I bite into my bottom lip to stifle the sound. I'm not in the mood to have sex this early in the morning, especially after a restless night of sleep, but that doesn't matter to Chad. When he wants it, he gets it, since he pays all the bills. Just the other day he said it's my duty to fuck him.

It's not my duty.

However, it's my way of paying my share, so I just roll over and put on my fake face. It doesn't take him long to orgasm, and thankfully, the sex is over in ten minutes. Still, it's ten minutes too long.

Sitting up, I wrap the sheet around my chest and watch Chad dash around the room. He's always late for work, and it's never his fault.

Nothing is ever his fault.

"Damn it, Alyssa. Haven't you done any laundry lately? I can't find any clean work jeans." Walking out of the closet, he says, "They're still in the hamper."

Unease works through me. My fingers are jittery. I should have thrown a load into the washing machine yesterday, but my leg was still aching from the day he took his belt off and hit me with the metal buckle. Plus, I didn't want to do anything for him. Now, I regret my defiance.

"I work so you can stay home. I dropped out of college for you. All you have to do is make sure my fuckin' clothes are clean. Can't you even do that?" he growls.

I swallow. I dropped out of college too, but I don't say that.

"I'll make sure they're all done today. I promise," I say.

Chad walks around the bed and leans down into my face. "You will make sure all my clothes are cleaned and put away by the time I get home from work. You ain't got nothin' else to do but sit on your fat ass all damn day. The least you can do is make sure my clothes are clean. Do you understand me?"

I nod my head furiously. "I do. It will be done, Chad. I wasn't feeling well, and my leg was still hurting."

His lips lift into a sneer. "Fuck up again, and I'll make the other leg hurt too. Don't try using that pregnancy as an excuse around here."

My eyes widen. "I wouldn't do that."

"Good." He leans down and smashes his lips to mine. He pulls back and shoves me. I fall back onto the bed, and the back of my head hits the wooden headboard. I flinch, squeezing my eyes shut.

Fuck, that hurt.

The sheet I'm holding drops from my chest and exposes my enlarged breasts. Chad's eyes turn dark, his tongue slipping from his mouth to lick his lips.

"Damn, you are so beautiful. Even fat and pregnant," he mutters, staring at my chest. He readjusts his pants, and I pray he doesn't demand sex again.

171

His eyes soften. I lie there in silent panic over his next move. His knee indents the mattress as he crawls over me.

"I'm sorry, baby. I didn't mean to yell at you," he says, using the sheet to wipe my tears away. "Forgive me?" He pleads with puppy dog eyes.

I pull my hand away from my throbbing head and gently cup his stubbly face. I bring my mouth to his.

"Of course, baby." I whisper my lie so easily and kiss him like I mean it.

"See you later."

I breathe a sigh of relief when the door clicks shut.

The following nine hours are the highlight of my day.

TWENTY

JOHN

W hen I offered to pick Alyssa up earlier, she declined, saying she'd rather walk because she needed the exercise. I should've ignored her plea and picked her up, but the tone in her voice was louder than her words, so I listened.

The wait is making me antsy.

Alyssa was supposed to be here seven minutes ago. Unable to sit still any longer, I grab my keys and head to my truck. I back out and begin driving in the direction of Chad's apartment. I find her walking in jeans a half mile up the road. I pull up next to her and roll down the window. Relief fills her eyes as she pulls the door open and plops down onto the leather seat. She wipes the beaded sweat from her forehead and looks over at me. My brows knit together.

"Thank you," she says.

"Why the hell are you wearing jeans in this heat? Are you out of your mind?"

Alyssa flinches. "Nothing else fits me right now. I'm in between sizes, so I wear what I can."

I nod, feeling guilty for laying into her. My eyes scan the length of her swollen belly. I still can't get over the fact that she's pregnant. I was up all night long thinking about it. Reaching over, I take Alyssa's hand and lace our fingers together. I run circles on the inside of her palm with my thumb. I want to argue with her and say that she should've just called me so she didn't have to walk in the heat, but I don't. We drive for a minute when she scoots closer and rests her head on my shoulder.

I put the truck into park and then get out to open Alyssa's door.

"How long do you have with me?" I ask.

"Not long. Maybe two hours at most."

"Are you hungry? Thirsty?"

She nods. "I can always eat."

In the kitchen, I pull out a chair at the island for Alyssa. She walks over, and even with the sadness around her eyes, her skin is glowing, and her hair looks like silk. I have the urge to run my fingers through it. My gaze drifts lower. Either she's wearing a push-up bra or her boobs grew because my mouth begins to water at the sight of her creamy, plump skin.

I reach for two plates in the cabinet and then pull out some cold cuts and condiments. I slap a couple of sandwiches together and hand her one. Alyssa digs in before I do. Seeing her eat like this makes me feel good for some reason.

"You just devoured that in record time," I say, sliding her a glass of sweet tea. She blushes. "Hey," I say, "don't be shy about it. You're eating for two, remember?"

Alyssa takes a sip. "How could I forget? I'm getting fatter by the minute."

My eyes darken. "You're not fat, Alyssa. You're pregnant."

Alyssa nods and then eats the last bite of her crust. When we're finished, I pile the dishes into the sink.

"Should we just get straight to it since our time is limited?" I ask.

Alyssa takes a deep breath and looks down. "Can I say something first?"

I nod. I wasn't sure where to begin anyway, so I let her take the lead.

"When Jace got in the accident, I tried to be understanding. I knew you were in a dark place, but you kept pushing me away." She swallows. "I didn't run to Chad; he was just there. I never meant to sleep with him. I knew that would hurt you, so I didn't want to." Looking at the ceiling, Alyssa blows out a breath.

"Then why did you?" I bite out. "I told you from the beginning that Chad was no good. Did you think I was lying?"

Alyssa shakes her head and shrugs her shoulders at the same time. "You were right. I know he's no good now, but at first, he was the opposite," she says quietly. "He was my friend."

"So you just spread your legs for anyone? Is that it? Do you always stoop that low?"

I grind my back molars together. There goes my self-control.

"Stop," she says quietly.

"No. Don't tell me to stop. You fucked another guy while you were with me."

"We weren't together, Johnny. We were just friends, remember? I didn't technically cheat on you."

I rear back. "That's how you saw us? Just friends? I can't believe this. You knew we were a hell of a lot more than that. Don't deny it."

"We weren't exclusive. We were on and off."

I shake my head. "There was no on and off with us. We were always on. If I take your hand, kiss you in public, and fuck you, is that not enough?"

"This is why I said from the beginning friends with benefits was a stupid idea. Look where it got us."

I huff, closing my eyes when it hits me. "How many other guys did you fuck while we were 'unofficial'?" I ask. Unofficial, my ass. "And why the hell didn't you use protection?"

Hurt crosses through her blue eyes. "There was no one else other than Chad. I swear. And as for protection, I assumed we had at first. Finding out I was pregnant was a shock since you were the only one I didn't use protection with," she says. Then pauses. "I don't remember it all."

My forehead bunches together. I squint at her, confused. "What do you mean you don't remember it all?"

"I got drunk."

It's all she says.

"And? He can't put a condom on?" When she doesn't respond, I say, "So you're with him, I take it? Officially dating him? You wouldn't date me, but you'll date that scum?" The gaze in her eyes crushes me. My gut twists into a pretzel.

"When did you first sleep with him?"

"I don't remember the exact date, but it was after work

one night. Around the time when Jace died. It sort of just continued after that."

I'm trying not to resent her for hooking up with Chad while my friend was dying. In her defense, she did try to contact me, so I have no right to be angry.

My knee bounces nervously. "What are you going to do if the kid is mine? Stay with him?"

"I don't know. I really don't."

My brows shoot up to my hairline. A storm is brewing inside of me. I'm trying in vain to keep my emotions under control, but it's a struggle.

"You don't know?" I repeat in disbelief. "If that baby is mine, I'll tell you what you're going to do. You'll leave his piece of shit ass and come back to me." I pause. "Unless you love him."

"I could never love him," she says quickly.

Now there's fire behind her blue eyes. If Alyssa had said she loved him, I don't know what I would have done.

"But if you don't love Chad, why are you living with him?"

She looks down. "It's complicated. My mom kicked me out when I found out I was pregnant. I had nowhere to go."

I bite my tongue despite the many things I want to say. How could her mother do that to her?

"I'm going to ask you a question, and for both our sakes, you better tell me the truth." Alyssa's eyebrows furrow. "How did you get that bruise on your leg?"

She averts her gaze and stares at the floor once again. "I fell."

She's lying. I know she is.

"I know you didn't fall. What could you have fallen on

to get that mark? Is that why you're wearing jeans today? To cover up the bruise?"

"I fell," she repeats.

"Alyssa," I plead gently, looking into her sullen blue eyes. "If he's hurting you, please tell me. I'll get you help immediately."

"You don't get to ask me questions after you disappeared, John. That's not how it works."

"Yes, the fuck it does if you're being abused and possibly carrying my baby."

"What does it matter to you?" she yells. "You're going to leave again anyway." Alyssa scoots off the barstool and paces the kitchen floor. She rubs circles on her belly. "How long will you be gone this time?"

"I have combat training for the next month in South Carolina. Then after that, I'll start aviation training for two months. I may get a break in between. I just don't know when."

"Exactly. I have to do what works for me right now."

"But it's not what's best for you," I retort. She shrugs her shoulders. "Does he even know you're here?"

"No," rolls off her lips. "He'd be furious to know I'm here."

"Can I see you tomorrow?"

She looks at me with wide eyes. "I don't know. It's hard for me to get away."

"Can you try?"

She nods. "I'll try. Just don't call me. I'll call you after Chad goes to work, okay?"

It's not what I want, but I'll take what I can get. "Let me drive you back home. I'll stop a few blocks away so no one can say anything. There's no way I'm letting you walk in this heat."

Alyssa nods, agreeing with me. Not realizing what I'm doing before it's too late, I lean forward and kiss her forehead. She leans into me, and I automatically wrap my arms around her back.

"I hate that you left me," she murmurs against my chest. "But I understand why you did."

"Me too. I thought about you every day. It's what kept me going." I kiss the top of her head and ask, "How long does it take to find out the DNA?"

"A few tests can be performed now, but they're invasive. I'd rather wait until the baby is born."

I pull back to look down at her. "What do you mean invasive? Like it could hurt you and the baby?" I ask. Alyssa nods.

"The chance of a miscarriage is high, so it's not usually recommended. I heard there's a newer test out, but I don't know anything about it."

"I don't want to take any chances with you or the baby. I'll talk to Livy, Luke's girlfriend. She's a doctor. She may be able to help. Find the resources for us. This isn't her field of medicine, but it can't hurt to ask."

Recognition dawns in her eyes. "She's the one he writes music about."

"You remember?"

She nods, her jaw quivering. We walk back to my truck, and I open the passenger door for her.

"We'll figure this out. It might take some time, but we will."

Walking around to the driver's side, I pull the door open

with a little too much strength. I have no clue how I'm going to figure any of this out, but I'm going to try my damndest. This isn't where our story ends. I refuse to believe that.

"If this baby isn't mine, will you stay with Chad?"

A tear slips down her cheek as she meets my gaze. "I don't have anywhere else to go."

TWENTY-ONE

ALYSSA

M y life is a colossal mess.

I've had a lot of time to sit and think since I can't do anything else.

I should be starting my third year of college, meeting new friends, attending parties, and having the time of my life.

But nope. Here I am, unhappy, pregnant, and so, so alone in a small town.

I rub my growing tummy, thinking about how in two short weeks I get to find out the baby's sex. It's the one thing I'm looking forward to. Chad doesn't want to know or seem to care. But I do. He doesn't even seem to want to know me at times.

Chad. I sigh inwardly. He's the typical bad boy you're supposed to stay away from, and I stupidly fell for him. He is edgy and reckless, attractive, and beckons girls with a sideways glance. Underneath that hard exterior is a man with a chip on his shoulder big enough to cover the state of Georgia.

Glancing at the clock, I groan. It's close to dinner time. The last thing I want to do is make dinner for Chad. He seems to either love what I cook or hate it with a passion. It is rare I do much right.

My lower back has been aching all day. Reaching into the pantry, I take out a box of pasta and a jar of tomato sauce. Which I regret the moment Chad walks in the front door.

"What's that smell?" he asks with a scowl.

Playing nicely, I walk up and kiss his scruffy cheek. The stale stench of Marlboro cigarettes makes me cringe. "Pasta," I say with a faux smile. "I put some garlic bread in the oven too."

Chad glances down at me with almost hostile eyes. I flinch, my smile fading. What have I done wrong now?

"You don't want pasta?"

"Meat. I need some meat, girl. You didn't cook any meat?"

"I didn't, but I can see if we have some in the freezer and cook it up quickly in the sauce."

My heart pounds. Please, dear God, let me have something.

Chad works his jaw back and forth. "That's going to take too damn long. I want to eat when I walk in, not an hour later."

"Next time, I'll have some protein for you. I'm sorry, Chad," I say earnestly, "I didn't know, but it won't happen again. I promise. I just want to make you happy."

A happy Chad means a happy hand.

That's what I tell myself, at least.

"I'll let it slide this time, but don't let it happen again. Got it?"

I nod my head vehemently. I won't make the mistake again.

He pulls me into a half, lazy hug and kisses the side of my head. I should be pushing him away, but instead I wrap my arms around his shoulders and nestle my face in his neck. I don't love him, but he doesn't need to know that.

"I know I'm a mean asshole sometimes, but I don't mean it."

"I know you don't," I whisper softly.

I'M UTTERLY DISGUSTED WITH MYSELF.

I've become just like my mother, and I hate myself for it. She's the one person in my life that I did not want to turn out like.

Chad reminds me daily that I'm his problem now, forced to take care of me because my lousy mother didn't want me. His words not mine. I don't understand why he acts the way he does when I cater to his every need.

"Alyssa!" he yells. "Where the hell are my work clothes?"

I hear him mutter "bitch" under his breath, and it pisses me off.

"Please stop calling me names. I don't deserve it. You can ask me without calling me a bitch."

"Shut the fuck up and find my pants," he sneers, a cigarette bouncing on his lip. "I'm gonna be late for work because of you."

I find the items he was looking for. They were right in front of his face. "I don't have to stay with you, you know. I can leave. I don't deserve to be called names."

He perks up. "Oh yeah? Do you think you can take my kid and run? Where ya gonna go? No one wants a fat bitch with stretch marks. You got no one. You're stuck with me."

"I'm not fat," I say in defense. "I'm tired of you saying that."

I remember what John said at his house that day, telling me that I'm not fat, that I'm pregnant. I replay the words constantly in my head. They give me courage when I feel so low.

Chad takes three long strides and stands in front of my face. He grips my arm hard, and I wince, leaning away. Pinching the cigarette between his fingers, he exhales the smoke in my face. I gag, turning my head, and he takes the opportunity to press the hot cherry into my skin. I jump, screaming, as he burns me. I try to pull away. His musty breath invades my senses, and I feel my stomach churn. I yank and tug, but he holds me in place.

"Thinking about running? Cause I got plenty more where this came from."

I shake my head rapidly as tears stream down my cheeks. "No," I say quietly. "Please stop."

"That's what I thought, whore," he says, then shoves me until I stumble back and fall on my butt. I stay there until he storms out of the house and leaves for work.

Chad's upbringing is partially to blame for his ways. People don't act the way he does unless they're exposed to it. One night, Chad told me about his childhood, his absentee mom, and how his alcoholic father took his anger and frustration out on him for his mother leaving them. His father blames Chad, telling him he is unlovable and nobody wants him. Maybe it's my hormones acting crazy, but everything is starting to make sense. I actually feel bad for him. He grew up in a world of violence and without any love. No child should ever be made to feel that way, and I am going to make damn sure mine doesn't. Chad is an adult and ultimately knows right from wrong, which is why I don't put all the blame on his father.

It's also why I'm packing my stuff and leaving. History repeats itself. The next time, he could hit my stomach. Or what if he got angry and hit my child?

That's a risk I'm not willing to take.

I wait for his beat-up truck to peel out of the parking spot and then I sprint to my room. Heart pounding, I stick what I can in my old school backpack. Material possessions can be replaced, but my life cannot.

Today is the last time he will have the chance to hurt me.

Today, I'm no longer weak.

TWENTY-TWO
ALYSSA

I t takes me fifteen minutes.

I weave in and out of backyards, ducking behind cars, and run as fast as possible. It's more like power walking because of my growing belly, but I do it. I'm finally free.

Slowing down, I try to catch my breath while I walk. I pray John's family doesn't turn me away. I'm taking a huge chance on them opening their doors to me and hope it doesn't backfire.

Removing my sunglasses, I tuck them into the front of my shirt and wipe the sweat from my nose and from under my eyes. I wipe back the loose strands of hair that stick to the sides of my face. Emotions take over as I step onto the driveway. Looking at the ground, my blurry eyes try to make out the tiny pebbles. This is my only chance. If they turn me away, I'll ask if they can give me a ride to a shelter. But I can't go back to Chad, and I won't.

Taking a deep breath, I exhale and adjust the backpack. The straps are digging into my shoulders, the weight causing me to arch my back even more. I'm sweating everywhere and in dire need of air conditioning. I feel sick from how hard my heart is pounding. Raising my fist, I bring my hand down to the door and knock. A few seconds later, the bolt is turning, and the door is opening. I suck in a breath when a pair of aged green eyes stare at me in recognition.

"Alyssa?"

"Can you help me, please?" I beg.

John's mom, Diane, ushers me inside and takes me straight to her kitchen. Without asking, she hands me a glass of water. I finish it quickly and she refills it.

Placing the glass on the counter, I lick my lips. "I know you probably have many questions for me, and I'm sorry for showing up the way I did, but I had to get out."

She shakes her head empathetically. "Don't apologize. I'm glad you came here. What's going on? You know that John isn't here, right?"

I nod. "I know he's at training camp. He doesn't know what's going on. I didn't tell him. Will you promise to not tell him just yet?"

Diane's eyes soften. Her eyes drift to my stomach then back up to meet mine. "I won't say a word, but he'll have to know sooner or later that you're pregnant. I won't keep that from him."

"He already knows, Mrs. Jackson," I state quietly, looking at the floor.

"He does? And he didn't tell me? And he still enlisted and left you here all alone? I know I raised him better than that." Her voice rises with each question.

"In Johnny's defense, he didn't know I was pregnant until he came home after graduation."

"Hmm." She studies me. "Please don't take offense to this, but is the baby his?"

Shame washes over me. If my cheeks weren't red from the heat, they are now. I'm not going to lie because all that does is cause more problems.

"Honestly, I don't know. I'm ninety percent sure it's his. It's either Johnny's or Chad's. Chad Jones."

"Is that where you came from? Chad's?"

I nod. "My mom threw me out when I found out I was pregnant. Johnny was gone, and I had nowhere else to go."

"Oh, honey. I'm so sorry to hear that. You can come here any time," she says sincerely. "Tell me what brings you here. What can I do to help?"

I really didn't have a plan once I left. All I knew was that I had to get out. I release a long sigh and glance up at the popcorn ceiling.

I stand on shaky knees. It feels like I'm baring my soul as I remove my jacket, but it must be done. It's only fair that I show her the same consideration she's shown me. I pull at the sleeves and slide it off, feeling ten times better from the cool air hitting my arms. I hang the sweaty jacket over the barstool, and Diane hisses. Shame fills me and my gaze drops straight to the floor, unable to make eye contact with her.

"I need a place to stay," I whisper.

When Diane says nothing, I peek up and see unshed tears in her eyes. She can't seem to tear her wide eyes from me. Diane reaches out and gently runs the tips of her fingers down my arm, touching each bruise and fingerprint that Chad has left. She mutters something inaudible under her breath, then touches the faded yellowish bruise under my eye.

"He's been doing this for some time now, hasn't he?" I nod, my lips a firm, thin line. "Do you have the same marks on your stomach?"

"No," I say. "He's never hit me there. It's like he knows where to hurt me and where not to. These marks are a few days old. I don't even remember what I did to deserve them—"

"You don't deserve them, ever. No one deserves this, Alyssa. Nothing warrants this kind of behavior."

"His favorite is getting the back of my legs with his belt buckle. He says it's what his father used to do to him. John saw the bruise when he was here, but I lied when he asked me about it." Hurt crosses Diane's eyes at my last comment, and I quickly add, "I had to lie. I didn't want him running to my defense, because it's something he would have done."

"You are not to go back to him. Do you understand me? I will not allow it. You'll stay here, and we'll figure something out." The tone of her voice makes me burst into tears. Diane pulls me into a hug. I drop my head on her shoulder and months of pent-up emotion pour out of me. I can't stop crying.

The front door slams, and I hear, "Di? Where you at?"

Diane dries my tears with the pad of her thumbs. "I'm in here!" she yells. I quickly reach for my jacket, worried about what Mr. Jackson will say, but Diane stops me. "No, don't hide it."

Putting my trust in her, I agree despite my racing heart.

"I brought you your favorite—" John's dad, Clark, halts when he sees Diane and me standing in the kitchen. "What in good heavens?" He drops the tulips on the counter and rushes over to us. He puts his hands on his hips. His face turns beet red. "Who did this to you?"

"Chad Jones."

Clark swears under his breath. "Does he know you're here?"

My heart begins to hammer in my chest. "No, he doesn't know."

"We need to go to the police," he suggests, and I feel nauseous at the thought.

"The police?"

"He's not going to get away with this. He'll continue beating on women until someone stops him."

I swallow back the lump in my throat.

Pulling out a barstool, Clark sits down. "You can stay in John's room for as long as you like. We're not expecting him back just yet. But for that to happen, I want you to go to the police and report what's been going on. We won't stand by and watch Chad get away with what he's done to you."

Panic fills me. The pressure to report him clogs my throat. My chest lifts and falls quickly.

"I'll be there with you, honey," Diane says, patting my hand to comfort me. "I'll be by your side, so you have nothing to worry about. If you don't report him, you'll be living in fear every day, and I'm sure that's not something you want for you or your baby." I shake my head in agreement. Diane's lips flatten. "Then it needs to be done. Now."

My heart stops. "Right now?"

"If he comes home and finds you gone, he's going to be livid. Better to protect yourself now rather than later."

Diane may be small, but she isn't one to argue with. I nod.

"Let the police take pictures while the bruises are still fresh," Clark says, and stands.

THE TREES TURN BLURRY AS I STARE AT THEM FROM THE back seat of Clark's car. We're on our way back to their house from the police station.

I had to strip down to my underwear for the female officer to take photos since there were welts on my legs. She suggested going to the hospital for an internal exam and even insisted on one, but I refused. That damage had already been done and healed. I didn't think anything would show.

It was unnerving, but I know I did the right thing. My heart was racing the entire time. The police officer commended me for walking away so early on. Once a hitter, always a hitter, she said. I gave a lengthy statement and proceeded with pressing charges. I learned that Chad will be charged with felony domestic violence, a crime that could be served for up to three years and a fine. I pray Chad will get the maximum sentence allowed. That would be three years of freedom for me.

"Alyssa?" Clark says.

I sit up higher. "Yes?"

"Tomorrow, we'll call the police station to get an update. Once we know Chad's been arrested, we'll get all your belongings. For now, you can use whatever we have. Sound good?"

"Yes. Thank you. For everything."

I don't have much, but it would be nice to get what I do have.

"You're welcome. We're happy that you trusted us enough to come to us."

I swipe away the lone tear that falls from the corner of my eye.

I let out a breath that isn't tense.

Today is the first day of my new life. I'm going to do my best to heal the wounds in my heart and make a fresh start.

TWENTY-THREE

ALYSSA

I t's been two days since I went to the police station.

I turn off the ignition to the car John's parents loaned me and look up at Chad's apartment, dreading what I have to do. I'm glad I skipped breakfast. My stomach is in knots despite Clark confirming Chad's arrest. Taking a deep breath, I open the car door and walk up to the front steps, feeling unease twist my nerves. I was going to forfeit the few things I had and not come back here, but it sort of felt like him winning, and I didn't like that. He's already taken so much from me.

My heart hammers in my throat as I slide the key into the lock. I pause and my brows knit together. Leaning in, I place my ear to the door and listen quietly while holding my breath. I swear I heard a sound. It must be in my head, but I wait for another moment to pass, then I turn the key. My nerves are getting to me. Paranoia is a bitch.

As I'm pulling the key out, the door is yanked open, and I fall forward on my knees. A meaty hand wraps around my arm, dragging me up and shoving me into the wall. The back of my head bounces against it, and I recoil, wincing in pain.

"Thought you could get away from me? Thought you could steal my kid and take off?"

Dread fills me. My gaze meets Chad's, and I'm terrified. The disgusting odor of stale cigarettes and beer on his breath makes me sick. His face is bright red with anger. He raises his fist and aims it toward me. I put my hands up to cover myself and yell out. Chad punches the wall by my head. I jump out of my skin. The cracking sound of drywall frightens me. Specks of dust fall onto my shoulder and sprinkle to the floor.

How is he home? He shouldn't be home.

"I… I…" I can't form words into a sentence.

"You got another thing coming if you think you can take off so easily. That's my kid, you bitch."

Anger fills me from the name calling. "It may not be yours," I spit out, finding the courage deep down.

Chad rears back. He's eerily quiet as realization forms in his maniacal eyes. He squeezes his grip on my upper arm. I try not to wince so he doesn't see that it hurts me.

"I should have known you lied to me about fucking him too. You were so easy to get in bed, just like his one girlfriend. You were no challenge after a few shots of tequila."

"That night," I whisper, "I blacked out. But when I woke up, I had a feeling something happened. I would've never thought …" I can't say what's in my mind. The thought makes me too sick.

Chad's snicker makes my skin crawl. While I had willingly slept with him in the days following, and used protection, that drunken night left me wondering. I figured the condom had a hole in it. I was just too scared to bring it up. Something told me he'd lie anyway.

"All I had to do was work you up and slide right in. So simple. You were a good fuck until you had to get pregnant and fat—"

"I'm not fat!" I scream in his face.

Digging deep, I shove Chad away from me. He stumbles back but quickly finds his footing. A sneer spreads across his face, and my heart drops into my stomach. Before I realize what he's doing, Chad backhands me across the face. I fall to the side and gasp, but his tug on my arm prevents me from hitting the floor. His nails dig into my arm once more and he shakes me.

"This is for thinking you can get rid of me so fast." He punches the side of my stomach, and I feel a crack. I gasp so hard that I lose my breath and my legs give out.

Chad drags me back up. I can't even cry. The pain is so intense it leaves me speechless. For a split second, I think I'm glad Chad hit my ribs and not my stomach. My ribs might fracture or break, but my baby can be saved.

"This is for dragging me along, making me think it was my kid."

He backhands me across the face again, the other side this time. A metallic taste fills my mouth. I never told him I slept with Johnny. I didn't want him to know.

"This is for having me arrested, you fucking whore."

He knees me right in the center of my thigh, and I huff out a breath of agony. My face is stinging from his hand.

"And this is for screwing up my life," he roars before swinging his fist around and punching me in the temple.

My vision blurs as I crumple to the floor. A dirty boot comes at my legs. I can't fight him off, so I curl into a ball to protect my stomach. Chad picks me up by my hair and I cry out, reaching for his wrist, hoping he'll release the pressure on my head. My feet shuffle across the worn carpet as he drags me into his room and throws me to the floor. I fall in a heap. I look over my shoulder, hair matting my tear-stained face. Chad slams the door shut, locking it behind him before he stalks over to me.

One thought crosses my mind before my eyes close: Please let my baby be okay.

Low, hush voices cause me to stir. My face is pulsating, and my eyes are swollen. I groan in pain, my throat sore and dry. A faint beeping sound plays in the background. Confusion swirls in my head, and it causes the pain to intensify.

"Shh…" I hear and relax immediately.

Somewhere in the back of my mind, I know that voice. I know I'm safe and drift back to sleep.

I take a deep breath and exhale, waking up again. Bright fluorescent lights cause a stabbing pain in my head. I turn away and spot a dirty-blond buzzed head sleeping next to me. The rest of his body is in a chair. Johnny.

Frowning, I take in my surroundings. Everything is hazy. IVs are hooked up to the top of my hand, and gauze bandages are wrapped haphazardly on my arms.

How in the…

I gasp so deeply that my lungs burn. My baby!

I reach for my stomach, shuffling the blankets off me and lifting the hospital gown to bear my belly. My heart is in my throat, and tears clog my eyes. Please... Please...

I run my hands over my stretched skin. I don't see any bruising, but that doesn't mean there isn't any internally. Chad hit me a few times near my ribs, but I blocked most of them. My emotions take over and my jaw burns as it quivers. Hot tears stream down my cheeks. I cover my face with my hands and cry quietly. I thank God I'm okay, but I pray my baby is too.

Suddenly, it's all too much. The past and present slam into me, and I break down. My chest aches from holding everything in, from the abuse I've endured, the fear I've lived in, my mother rejecting me, and everything that has happened since moving to South Fork. The bed shifts next to me, and the next thing I know, John is trying to pull me into a hug.

"It's okay. The baby is okay," he says. I lean forward, needing him, and gasp. Pain shoots through my side and stops me instantly. "Your ribs are fractured. Move slow," he says.

I nod, my jaw trembling. "Chad nailed me in the ribs. Once I blacked out, I don't know what he did to me."

"You blacked out?"

I nod. "From the pain, I think. He hit me so hard I saw black, and that was it. I woke up in here."

"I'm going to kill him," he mumbles, and I shake my head.

"Please don't do anything to retaliate. He's not worth it."

Anger ignites around him, but I'm not scared. I know it's directed toward Chad.

"He won't get away with what he did," John says.

I squeeze his hand. "He won't. I already filed charges against him."

It moves me deeply how much he wants to defend my honor, but I can't let him do that. He has too much to lose.

"What are you doing here?" I ask. "I thought you were training and couldn't come home for a few months."

John scoots the chair closer to the bed. He cups his hands around mine and brings it to his mouth. Leaning down, he kisses our fingers but doesn't lift his head.

"That's not for you to worry about. All that matters is that I'm here."

"But I don't want you to be kicked out. Please tell me that's not what happened."

"I love that you're concerned about my placement, but it's nothing to worry about. I took an emergency leave. Everything is okay. I won't be kicked out."

I release a heavy breath and nod. "Will you call a doctor in, please?" John stands, but I grab his wrist. "Wait. Is my mom here?"

His lips form a thin, flat line. My heart sinks. I already have my answer before he says it.

"No, I'm sorry. She didn't come."

My shoulders sag, and I nod to myself. Am I such a disappointment?

A man who looks way too young to be a doctor walks in. His black hair is slicked back, and his eyes are a deep, dark brown. He's medium height, wearing green scrubs under a white lab coat.

"Hello, Ms. Winters," he says, holding a bunch of folders to his chest. "I'm glad to see you're awake and talking. I'm Dr. Cahill."

I give him a weak smile.

"We did an ultrasound the moment you came in and have monitored the baby's heartbeat the entire time. You're fortunate the baby is thriving considering the state you arrived in." He drops his chin to his chest, one brow rising.

I don't remember being transported to the hospital. I don't remember much at all. Tears rim my eyes.

He walks over, places the folders on the rolling table next to me, and leans in to examine my face. His fingers press on my temples and around my eyes. I draw in a hiss. Between the light he's shining in my eyes and the pressure he's applying, it's causing my stomach to churn.

"Lift your gown, please," Dr. Cahill requests as he pulls on a pair of latex gloves.

He presses three fingers to my ribs, and searing pain ricochets throughout my body. I cinch my eyes shut and struggle for breath as I pull away. He reaches around to my other side and follows the same motions. I feel no pain. He pulls my gown back into place then removes his gloves.

"Your ribs are fractured. You have a mild concussion. There are contusions on your head and around your body. I'm putting you on bed rest until your ribs are healed. You must follow up with your OB/GYN once released." I nod. Dr. Cahill grabs his files. "If you need anything, page the nurses' station, and they'll call me. You should be able to leave in a day."

"Thank you," I say softly.

He gives me a tight, firm smile and leaves. The door closes with a swish. John's eyes connect with mine as he walks back over to me.

"How long are you here for?" I ask.

"Not long. Three more days. I leave Sunday night."

Sitting down, John leans over and rests his elbows on his knees. His hands are clasped together as he stares at the floor. "Why didn't you tell me it was so bad?"

The disappointment in his voice hurts my heart. I turn my head away and stare at the closed drapes.

"I couldn't," I answer quietly. "You have no idea what it was like. I couldn't pull you into the fire after what you went through with Jace. Then you'd just enlisted, and I wasn't going to mess that up for you."

"He could have killed you. Do you have no regard for your life or your unborn child's life?"

"I left, didn't I?" I retort.

"You left too late."

My shoulders sag, and my eyes are heavy. I'm too depleted of energy to argue.

"John, I can't do this right now."

"Did you think about me at all? About the devastation I would've suffered if something had happened to you? You saw how Jace's death affected me," he says, placing a flat hand on his chest. "It damn near destroyed me. I have still not fully recovered from that, and I don't think I could handle it if something happened to you." John lets out a loud sigh and lowers his voice. "Alyssa, when I got the call from my dad, I was sick to my stomach. I couldn't think straight. I raced down here as fast as possible to be by your side, praying and wishing you'd be okay." A lone tear drips down my cheek. John notices. "I'm sorry for making you cry. That's not what I want."

"It's okay," I whisper, wiping the tear away.

"No, it's not okay to make you cry. I don't want to hurt you, Alyssa. It's the last thing I want. I'm just frustrated with how things turned out." Grabbing a tissue, John sits on the edge of the bed and blots my tears away. "You look exhausted. Why don't you get some rest?"

John leans over and kisses my forehead. He turns to walk away, but I grab his wrist to stop him.

"Please don't go just yet. I don't want to be alone. Will you stay with me?"

John nods and my shoulders drop. I need him. He makes me feel safe.

I lift my hips up and scoot over. Pain shoots through my ribs and into my chest, but I hold it in.

"I don't want to hurt you."

"You won't."

John takes his shoes off and climbs into bed. Lifting his arm, he wraps it around my shoulders and holds me closer. I rest my head on his chest, sighing as I do, and wrap my arm around him. My whole body goes lax as I soften against him. For the first time in months, I can fully unwind without an ounce of fear. I'm safe and at ease because of John. Releasing an exhausted sigh, I feel myself sinking back to sleep.

John is the one person I can rely on through thick and thin. I feel it in my heart. If only I had followed my intuitions from the beginning, perhaps I wouldn't be in the predicament I'm in now.

TWENTY-FOUR

ALYSSA

"You can stay in here with me," I say, getting under the comforter on John's bed. "There's no reason why we can't share a bed."

I was released from the hospital the following day and went straight to John's house. He's been taking care of me ever since.

"No, I can't."

"Why not?" I push.

His hard eyes bore into me. My eyes drift away, and I scoot under the sheets. I thought it was because he didn't want to hurt me since I'm a little roughed up, but not wanting to sleep next to me is a different story. It hurts hearing him deny me when I crave his contact. Especially now. John will be leaving soon, and the thought of him gone again puts a gaping hole in my chest. I need to toughen up, but I'm struggling. My hormones are all over the place. I miss my mom. I'm staying at another man's house, again. I'm stressed to the max, unsure where to go

205

or what to do. The one person I want next to me doesn't want to be near me.

"How are your ribs?" John asks, standing in front of his bed. "Do you have a headache or anything?"

"I'm fine."

A tick works in John's jaw. "If something hurts, I need to know. You have black and blues on your face that makeup can't even cover up, and your ribs are pretty fucked up."

I say nothing. The bruises are still fresh, and my body aches, but I don't complain.

"Fine," he says.

His sudden change in attitude puzzles me. "What are you doing?" I ask.

"I'm going for a run."

Turning away, I close my eyes and fight back the tears that are threatening to spill over. My body sinks into the mattress. John's bed feels like I'm lying on clouds.

I STIR AT THE SOUND OF THE DOOR OPENING. I'M A LIGHT sleeper these days after living with Chad. I look over my shoulder and see John standing in front of his dresser. He's in a pair of shorts, and he's unaware that I'm watching him. My mouth runs dry seeing all his muscle and beauty. Joining the military gave him muscles overnight. I badly want to reach out and run my hand down his back. I want those strong arms wrapped around me, making me feel safe and wanted. I turn away and curl on my side when I feel the bed dip and an arm slip under my pillow. John's other arm folds over my stomach as he scoots behind me.

His body is so warm and inviting that I release a soft sigh and relax. He softly kisses my shoulder. I nuzzle against him.

"Hey," he says.

"What are you doing here? You didn't seem too keen on talking to me before."

"I had a lot on my mind."

I roll onto my back to look at him, but he doesn't look at me. I don't like the sad tone in his voice.

"Want to talk about it?" I ask.

He ignores my question and looks at my stomach. The blankets have slipped down. I'm wearing a white tank top with no bra and a pair of basketball shorts he loaned me.

"May I?"

I take a deep breath and nod. I'm not used to anyone wanting to touch my stomach, but John's asking melts my heart. Cautiously, he rests his palm on my protruding belly. His movements are slow, tentative, like he doesn't want to bring me pain.

"It's okay. You can push a little."

I place my hand over his to show how far he can press. As I do, a kick pushes through, and John abruptly pulls his hand away. I chuckle at the look of shock on his face.

"Whoa. Does he always kick like that?"

"That was nothing. He's only getting warmed up." A timid smile tips my lips. Reaching for John's hand, I place it back on my stomach. We both wait for another kick.

"Wow. That's amazing," he says.

I watch his face as he touches my belly, his fingers exploring every inch. I love that he's curious. Chad never was. He couldn't stand to look at it. Without him having to ask, I lift my shirt and rest the hem just under my breasts.

"Alyssa," he whispers, taking in my growing stomach. "Does it hurt?"

I shake my head. "No, I don't really feel it growing. Some days my stomach itches, and that's how I know it's getting bigger, but typically, I don't feel anything."

"What does it feel like?"

I chuckle. "Like I swallowed a giant watermelon."

"A watermelon that kicks?" He jokes, a brow raised.

"I guess." I laugh.

"I've never really given pregnancy much thought until now." He pauses. "I think he's break dancing. He has better moves than me."

"Oh, yeah? He? Set on a boy?"

"You know it." The room is quiet while John feels the baby kick. "I spoke with my parents last night. They want you to stay here for as long as you like. So do I. I'll send money to help you with whatever you need, so you don't have to worry."

Tears form in my eyes. "I have some saved from working at Roxie's Chad didn't know about." I hate that I'm so emotional. "Why are they being so nice?"

"It's just who they are. My parents have big hearts. They love knowing that this could be their grandchild too." My jaw quivers. "Don't cry. You know how I hate to see you cry," he says, wiping away my tears.

"I can't help it. It's these stupid pregnancy hormones. I can't stay here without paying my way, and I don't want to stay once the baby is born. It wouldn't be fair to your parents to support us too."

Gently caressing my jaw, his voice lowers. "I'm sure you guys could come to some type of agreement."

"That's really nice of them. Eventually I'll need to figure something out."

"After Jace died, while I was at boot camp, I realized sweating the small stuff doesn't matter in the end. I decided that I was going to live each day like it was my last because tomorrow it could all be over. Everything will eventually work out. I'll be by your side to ensure it does. You have a place to stay with people who want you around. You only need to focus on recovering." John moves his palm around my stomach. "Have you thought about names?"

"Not much." I pause. "What would you name him?" I ask.

John purses his lips together. "Dexter. Dex."

"Dexter? Like that serial killer show?" I ask, appalled. "And call him Dex? Not a chance."

"Travis?"

"No way."

"What's wrong with Travis?"

I shrug. "I just hate that name. It's ugly. How about Albert?"

His face drops, and I chuckle. "Alyssa, don't you dare."

"You don't like it?"

"No, it sounds stupid. What about Mason?"

I pucker my lips together. "Mason, I could do, but then I'd always think of Mason jars, so I guess I can't."

"How about Dierks? Like the country singer. He's incredible."

"A country—" I stop and side-eye John. "No way am I naming my kid after some country singer I've never heard of."

"Kip?"

"Is that another country singer?"

His lips form a tight, thin line. He tries to hide his smile, but it's useless. A full-blown grin breaks out across his handsome face. John laughs, and says, "You should see your face."

He is provoking me. There is no way he can be serious.

"You want to name my kid after a country singer?" I say, horrified. "Since I'm carrying him for nine months, I should be able to pick the name." I pause when a thought hits me. "What if his name is Jace?"

John grabs my wrist and holds it to his chest. He laces our fingers together. He doesn't respond, but he doesn't need to. I can hear his pain without him needing to talk about it. The silence brings peace. I squeeze our fingers together and turn toward him. John puts his other arm behind my head so I can lie on his chest. He cuddles me to him and then trails the tips of his fingers down the side of my stomach, to my hip, and glides them across my butt. I scissor my legs, trying to play it off as if I'm just moving into a new position, but the truth is, his touch lights a fire inside of me. I clench my thighs together and pull in a deep breath. A groan reverberates from his throat.

"Feel good?" he asks.

"Yes," I whisper. I shouldn't want his touch right now, but I do. I crave it.

"Do you want me to stop?" he asks hoarsely.

"No."

After another minute of silence passes, he tips my chin so I have to look at him. "I shouldn't ask this, but can I kiss you right now? I really need to."

I don't give him an answer. I close the distance with my lips and our tongues collide in a frenzy. He slides his hand around my neck and threads his fingers through my hair. A soft sigh escapes him, and I love the way it sounds. John deepens the kiss, his tongue stroking mine so good and slow I feel it in my pussy. Just as we're getting started, he abruptly breaks the kiss.

"We need to stop. If I keep touching you, I'll want to fuck you. And now is not the time."

My heart crumbles, but I agree with him. Sex is what got me into this mess to begin with.

I roll onto my back, and John adjusts his bulge. He kisses the side of my head near my temple before getting up and walking out of his room.

TWENTY-FIVE

ALYSSA

J ohn didn't come home the following weekend.

Or the weekend after that.

Or the next.

The last time I saw him was when he came home two months ago after the attack. Since then he's been so busy with training that he spends his weekends catching up on sleep.

I miss John fiercely. His absence is all around me. It's not easy being surrounded by his loving parents while living in his room.

Lying back on the bed, I rub my belly while I elevate my feet. At nine months pregnant, my stomach grows daily, and my back is bending at an ungodly angle. As much as I enjoy being pregnant, I can't wait to hold my baby in my arms.

I agreed to not move out once the baby is born. John didn't like the idea of me being alone, and his parents wanted to help. They said it would be too much too soon for me to handle. I'm worried about being alone with a newborn. As much as I read about babies and what to expect, I know nothing can prepare me for what it will actually be like. Having parents around to help is a blessing I won't take for granted.

My stomach tightens in a way I've never felt before. I clench up and hold my breath. The pain lasts for a couple of seconds and then releases. This is new, and it startles me. A few more minutes pass without pain, and I relax again. I've been so tired lately that I start to nod off to sleep when I catch the faint sound of vibration.

I reach for my phone and read the screen. *Yours Truly.* I smile, thinking back to when John added the contact name for himself. It feels like many moons ago.

Yawning, I answer. "Hello?"

"Hey, baby."

I smile, hearing the drawl in his voice. And because he called me baby.

"Hey, yourself."

"Were you sleeping?" he asks.

"Not really…just nodding off a little. What's up?"

"Want me to call you back tomorrow?"

"No, it's fine. What's going on?"

"I was thinking about you. I wanted to hear the sound of your voice."

I smile even though he can't see me. "When do you think I'll be able to see you again?"

"About another few weeks, before I go to my new station."

I bite my lip. I hope he isn't placed far away or in another country. "Where's that? Do you know yet?"

"My base will be MCAS Beaufort, South Carolina."

"What does MCAS mean?" I ask.

"Marine Corps Air Station."

"Oh. I should've figured that out." I laugh. "Are you looking forward to it?"

"Yeah, I am, actually. I can't wait to see what's in store for me."

"You're so—" I gasp and clutch my stomach. I forget what I'm saying because the pain is so intense. "Shit."

"Alyssa? What's wrong?"

"Nothing," I say between clenched teeth. "Nothing is wrong."

"Don't lie to me. What just happened?"

"My stomach… It's weird… I've never felt this before… It's tightening up and squeezing together."

"Is it contractions?"

I pause and then release a loud sigh. "Okay… It's gone. I don't know what it is. But I'd know if I had a contraction, right? I've heard they can't be mistaken for anything else."

"I don't know. How long does it last?" he asks next.

"Just a few seconds."

"Well, if it happens again—"

"Oh shoot. It's doing it again."

"For the love of God," he says, his voice rough, "go get my mother."

A few seconds pass, and I exhale. "It's gone. I'm okay."

"Are you sure?"

"Yeah, I'm okay. I'll get your mom if it happens again."

We talk for a couple of minutes more before John hangs up. I love that he called me because he was thinking about me. I begin to doze off when a sharp, shooting pain runs through my body and startles me again. I hold my stomach and hold my breath at the same time.

215

Dear God. Now, this has to be a contraction. If not, then I'm dying.

The pain is excruciating. It's like a burning ball of fire when it tightens. As my stomach slowly begins to relax, I exhale. Before I can process what just happened, another one rips right through me. I turn on my side and curl up into a ball, wishing away the pain. These are definitely contractions. They have to be.

I get out of bed, holding the bottom of my stomach, and walk to Diane's bedroom. I tap on the door lightly and whisper, "Diane? Diane?"

Diane wakes up immediately. "Alyssa? Everything okay?"

I push the door ajar. "I think I'm in labor."

After ruffling blankets and the sound of footsteps, Diane is standing in front of me. The woman always looks so well put together, even just rolling out of bed. "Go get your hospital bag, and I'll grab the keys and wake Clark."

"Okay."

Panic sets in, and another contraction sweeps through me. I'm barely able to walk back to John's room. I palm my stomach, hold my breath, and count the seconds until it's gone.

Can I do this? Be in labor?

I've waited nine months for this moment, and I'm suddenly terrified. All the reading and preparation I did during my pregnancy goes out the window as I sit stone-faced on John's bed. My mind is running a mile a minute, and I don't know what to do.

Diane pops her head into the room. "You—What are you doing? Get your stuff. Let's go. Where are your things? I'll get them for you."

"In the closet."

She shuffles over and picks up my bag. Walking back to me, she places her hand in mine. "Let's get going, honey. The hospital is a good twenty minutes away."

I follow Diane out of the room to where Clark is standing. He takes the hospital bag from Diane. "Remember to breathe, okay? I used to tell Di that because she would forget."

I nod.

The three of us rush out to the car. Diane opens the door for me while Clark gets behind the steering wheel. Thankfully we aren't too far from the nearest hospital. Ten minutes into the drive, I have another contraction, this time stronger.

"Remember to breathe. I know it feels better to hold your breath, but you can't, okay? Just breathe."

"I am," I say through gritted teeth. I'm beginning to sweat.

Diane chuckles. "I used to hate when Clark would tell me to breathe. I felt like he was saying to just relax. And that is the worst thing to say to a pregnant woman. Or any woman."

"You would forget with each delivery," Clark says.

"Do you want to call your mother?" Diane asks.

"No," I say softly.

We arrive at the hospital, and everything happens so quickly.

A little less than two hours later, I'm holding my daughter. The ultrasound had been wrong.

I'm holding a baby girl in my arms, and all I want to do is cry happy tears. I'm elated, full of joy, so ecstatic that I can't make sense of my emotions. All I can do is smile at her little flushed face and kiss her button nose.

Labor wasn't easy. I feel like a semi-truck hit me. My entire body is sore and aching, and I can hardly keep my eyes open. I feel like I could sleep for a week straight. Diane stayed by my side the whole time. She asked numerous times if I wanted to call my mom, but I refused. Mom didn't come around after the attack, so I assumed she wouldn't for the birth of my child. I didn't want that negativity while bringing a life into this world anyway. Diane had been my rock through the entire pregnancy. I couldn't imagine going through labor without her.

"Have you picked a name for her?" Diane asks, smiling.

"I'm thinking Brooke Elyse. What do you think?"

Her eyes shine with tears. I notice that her jaw quivers. "I think it's a beautiful name. Perfect."

I beam. "Do you want to hold her?"

Diane's face lights up. "Hand that precious baby over to Grandma."

My smile falters, and I bite my lip. What if Brooke isn't her granddaughter? Would she still say that?

"I know what you're thinking," she says, gently rocking Brooke Elyse. "Regardless of who the father is, I will always be Grandma, if you'll allow it. Wipe that frown off your face. You just had a healthy baby girl."

Tears fall from my eyes.

Diane returns the smile. "Get some rest. Lord knows you're gonna need it. I'll make sure she's put to sleep."

"Thank you, Diane, for everything."

A DAY LATER, I'M ON MY WAY HOME FROM THE HOSPITAL.

I'm sitting in the back seat with Brooke Elyse, watching her suck her thumb. She's so tiny in the blue train-themed car seat. Little ringlets poke out from her bonnet. Mom told me once that I was born with a head of hair, so that's where I assume Brooke gets it from.

"You doing okay, sweetie?"

I smile from ear to ear. "I am. Just really happy."

When we pull into the driveway, I unbuckle Brooke and nestle her to my chest as I walk up to the house. I hold her tight and close to me, afraid that I may drop her. Not that I would, it's just that she's so fragile and small.

Diane contacted John's person in charge and sent word on the birth. She spoke to John briefly, but she didn't mention Brooke's name, just that I had the baby. I asked her to keep that to herself because I want to be the one to tell him. Diane said John would call once I got settled in later. I'm eager to hear his voice. I haven't spoken to John yet, but that's because I barely have the energy to keep my eyes open. The delivery exhausted me. I'm overwhelmed, but I can't sleep because I keep checking on Brooke to ensure she's breathing when she sleeps. Diane said all new mothers do that and that it's totally normal. It was a relief to hear that.

Time passes quickly with a newborn, and before I know it, my cell phone is ringing. Excitement washes through me. I sit on the bed with my phone propped on the dresser and swipe to answer.

"Hey, beautiful," John says as his face fills the screen. He is all smiles.

Our eyes meet and butterflies fill my stomach.

"Hey," I say, biting my bottom lip.

"It's so nice to hear your voice. You look good."

Heat blossoms through my cheeks. "Thanks. I feel like a swollen Oompa Loompa. I'm sore from pushing a ten-pounder out. It hurts to sit."

John chuckles. "You've never looked better."

"Liar," I say playfully. "If you saw me in person, you'd say otherwise." I don't tell him I wear a diaper to help with the bleeding or that my stomach is puffy and soft.

"Not a chance. How are you feeling?"

I stare into his eyes, wishing he were here, and shrug. "I'm feeling many things right now, but I think I'm good overall. Happy. Safe." I glance at my daughter and say, "I can't believe I have a baby now."

"I wish I could've been there for you."

I softly smile at him, longing to be near him. The way John cares melts my heart. I know he doesn't have the luxury of dropping everything and coming to the hospital. I have no doubt that he would've been there if he could.

"If it helps, your mom was by my side the entire time. I don't know how I could have done it without her."

I swallow thickly, thankful for her support when my own mother wouldn't give it to me. The moment my daughter was born, a protective coat fell over me. There isn't a thing I wouldn't do for her. How my mom could turn me away without a second thought hurts more than words can explain.

"I'm happy my mom was there for you, and you

weren't alone. Did you have an easy delivery? Mom was surprised at how fast it went."

"Wasn't too bad. Those pains I felt the night I was talking to you were, in fact, contractions. But the labor was over as quickly as it started. I didn't have to push too many times. Your mom kept reminding me to breathe." I chuckle.

John picks his head up. "Did you forget or something?"

"Kind of. I didn't realize I was doing it. The pain was so intense when the contractions hit that I held my breath, wishing them away. She said it happened to her too."

He looks overjoyed by what I'm telling him. "So where's my daughter? Show her to me. Mom took a video, but her hands must've been shaking because it's blurry. I didn't tell her that, though."

I draw in a breath for the big moment.

Brooke coos next to me, stirring awake. She wrestles blindly to put her fist in her mouth. Diane told me that means she's hungry. Gently, I pick her up and turn her around to face the phone screen. John analyzes my every move, watching intently.

"Aw, she's so tiny! She's like a little meatball," he says excitedly. I chuckle, agreeing. "What did you name her? Mom wouldn't tell me."

"Yeah, so about that," I begin, adjusting Brooke so she's cradled in my arms. "I couldn't believe it when they yelled, 'It's a girl,' after she came out. I demanded they show me. I was so sure she was a boy. I asked your mom not to tell you her name because I wanted to be the one to tell you."

"So I have a daughter," he whispers. I swear I see hearts form in his eyes. "I have a little girl."

Air seizes in my lungs. My chest is tight. I nod, holding back the tears. "You do," I say, my voice quiet. "A little girl."

John leans in close to the screen. He's quiet but awestruck. Seeing his expression makes me feel good inside. I'm already overwhelmed with emotion. I've been so anxious for this moment. Most men want boys, and I knew he was eager for one.

"I wish I could touch her," he says. I swallow thickly. "She has your blond hair. What did you name her?"

I meet his gaze and hold my breath. "Brooke Elyse."

One corner of John's mouth turns up. "Elyse is my mom's middle name."

"I know."

"You did it for her?" he asks hopefully.

"I did."

"I wish I could be there with you right now. I'm going to try to get an early leave. If I can't, give me about two weeks, then I'll have a small break and will be there."

"I'll be counting down the days."

John is quiet for a moment while he watches Brooke. I lay her down and remove the blanket, then I hold the camera above her so he can see her body. He laughs, smitten with her.

"Not that I want to ruin the moment, but when is the arraignment? Are you bringing Brooke with you?"

Dread fills my stomach. That impending day has been on my mind more often than I care to admit. I turn the camera back to face me.

"I got a letter in the mail from the courts while I was at the hospital." I shiver just thinking about it.

"What does it say? I can see if I can get down there for it."

I melt from how caring John is.

"I'm going to see if your mom will watch Brooke. I don't want to bring her around people, let alone near Chad."

Relief splashes across his face. "If I could get the early release approved for sooner, I would so I can be there with you, but I don't think I can. I hate for you to go alone. You can always ask my dad to step in. Maybe even Luke would."

I'm so lucky to have someone like John who cares about the safety of me and my baby. "Thanks. I'll keep that in mind." Changing the subject, I say, "All I have are boyish clothes for her. Everything is blue with trucks and fish."

"I don't think she cares, Alyssa." He laughs. "She'll be a tomboy in no time anyway. How old do you think she has to be to go on the four-wheeler?"

Happiness fills my face. I shake my head. "You're gonna introduce her to mudding too?"

"You know it," he says proudly. "I don't want to hang up, but I have to go. Send me some videos and pictures when you can. I can't always respond, but I'll try."

I nod, promising him I would.

"Give her a kiss for me. I have to go."

We hang up, and I quickly send a bunch of photos to him. We text for a few minutes before ending the connection.

I pray this bond between us stays.

TWENTY-SIX

ALYSSA

The first week of motherhood flies by so fast that I don't know what day it is when I wake up.

I'm delirious. My eyes burn from lack of sleep, and my body screams to stay in bed, but I have a bundle of joy that needs feeding. How I thought I could leave the Jackson home after Brooke was born is beyond me. I'm glad Diane and Clark talked me into staying. I wouldn't have been able to do it on my own. I'm grateful for them and their generosity.

I carefully swaddle Brooke to my breast and begin nursing. With a slight pinch, I feel my milk releasing. This is another thing I owe to Diane. She showed me how to breastfeed, something I desperately wanted for my child but didn't know where to start. As Brooke feeds, my eyes scan her milky skin, and I can't help but wonder who my daughter looks like. The thought crosses my mind several times a day. It's still too early to tell by looking at her, but it isn't too early for a paternity test. That could be done at any time. I'm just not ready for it.

Chad's arraignment is today. Even though Diane has her MS under control, flare-ups happen occasionally, and I don't want to be the cause of them. I didn't want to bring Brooke to the courthouse, but I was hesitant to ask Diane to babysit given her health. Clark pulled me aside earlier and said he hasn't seen Diane this cheerful since before the MS diagnosis and that it was a good thing I asked her to babysit. He also said he would prefer to stay home with his wife in case she needed him, and I agreed.

Pulling my sleeping daughter away, I gently lay her in the bassinet. I fix my shirt and stuff my breast back into my bra when I hear my cell phone vibrate.

> Yours Truly: Good luck today. Call me when you're done. I have a free morning.

My heart softens. I thought John would've forgotten about the hearing, but he didn't. I'm so lucky to have him. He could be out with friends, or he could have a girlfriend I don't know about, yet he sent me a text letting me know I was on his mind. He's so good to me.

Tears stream down my cheeks. I can't stop them from coming. I hiccup, fighting the little sounds from escaping my throat. Not wanting to wake Brooke, I grab a pillow, press my face into it and cry. I let it all out.

Suck it up. Suck. It. Up.

I force myself from the bed. I wipe the tears away with the hem of my shirt, grab the baby monitor, and walk to the bathroom. Crying a little each day has helped relieve the anxiety of being a new mom. I only have an hour before I need to be in court. The quicker I get this over with, the faster I can be home with my little girl.

Stepping out of the car, I lock it and drop the keys into my purse. I take a deep breath and exhale, trying to get my nerves under control as I make my way inside the building. My heart is pounding like it's about to jump out of my chest. My stomach is in knots, my palms sweaty, and my hands jittery. Will I see Chad? And if so, what will he say? I hope I don't have to see him.

"Where is family court?" I ask the police officer.

"Straight down the hallway, turn left, and then go straight. You'll see an officer. Sign in with him before heading into the courtroom."

"Thank you."

I do as the officer says and sit behind the prosecutor's desk. My heart continues to pound, my nerves are coiled tight. I have no idea what to expect. Anxiety is hitting me hard. I wish John were here.

The doors to my left open, and a shackled Chad comes in wearing a jumpsuit. My heart skips a beat, and a knot forms in my throat. Chad eyes me immediately. He takes a seat while keeping his eyes trained on me. If looks could kill, I'd be dead right now. I look away. He makes my skin crawl.

"How's my kid doing?" Chad yells across the room.

I stay faced forward.

"I know you hear me," he yells.

I continue to ignore him.

"Alyssa. How. Is. My. Kid?" he says slowly, drawing out each word. I can hear the irritation in his voice.

"Don't give into him. He wants a response from you," the prosecutor whispers over her shoulder at me.

"Now rise! The honorable Judge Galloway…"

I become tongue-tied the minute I see the judge enter. My stomach climbs into my throat, and I pray for the strength to get through this. I think about Brooke. I realize that my daughter needs me to be her voice, and that she isn't safe in a world Chad walks free in.

I SLAM THE CAR DOOR SHUT AND HOLD THE PHONE PRESSED to my ear. My hand is shaking. I'm out of breath for no reason other than the adrenaline rush hitting me.

"Hey, babe," John says.

"It's over." I exhale and repeat my words. "It's over. I'm done. Chad took the plea deal. I was so afraid he wouldn't. Actually, I didn't know what would happen, to be honest. I was just hoping the judge wouldn't release him."

"Thank God," John says.

"The state prosecutor handed me a card afterward. She said the attorney listed on it works closely with the Victim Assistance Program, and they take on cases like mine pro bono when children are involved. I'm going to give them a call when my nerves settle. She said it would be good to talk to them about child support and DNA testing."

"If he's going to jail, what do you need them for?"

"Custody."

"Oh," he says, his voice low. "That makes sense."

"I was shaking the entire time. I thought I was going to throw up. I don't know how I did it."

I don't tell him about how Chad was yelling.

"I'm so proud of you. You did it for yourself and Brooke. You know that, right?

I nod as if he's in front of me. If John wasn't hours away, I know he would take me in his arms and hold me tight. He would kiss away my fears and shower me with love.

"I can't believe it. I'm still in shock. My knees were rattling together. Have you ever had that happen where you can't control the shaking? It was so bad," I say.

"What's his sentence," John asks.

"Five years. It's the maximum sentence he could get."

"That's it! Then he's free?" John is enraged.

"Unfortunately, yeah. But hey, in five years, I plan to be hidden far away so well he'll never be able to find me."

"Alyssa, you can't live in fear for the rest of your life."

"I won't. I'm not going to. This just buys me time to figure things out."

John says, "Tell me about this custody thing. How can I help you?"

Tears form in my eyes, but I hold them back. "You'll have to give a saliva sample for the paternity test," I say hesitantly.

"That's no problem. Just tell me when and where."

I breathe loudly and close my eyes. "Thank you."

"For what?"

"I don't know. Everything? For agreeing to take a test. For letting me sleep in your room. For having such good parents. For being so good to me. For treating Brooke like she's definitely yours. It's nice to know I'm not alone."

"I'd do anything for you. I hope you know that."

I don't speak the thoughts on my mind, but I can't help but wonder if John will still feel this way if the results come back in favor of Chad. I feel sick to my stomach just thinking that.

"I'll be seeing you soon, okay? Only a couple more days before I get to hold my girls."

I sniffle quietly. "I can't wait."

"Give my girl a kiss. I gotta run."

TWENTY-SEVEN

ALYSSA

"Can I hold her?" John asks, standing over Brooke.

"Of course. Do you know how?"

He stalls. "Kind of. It's been a long time since I held my brothers. Can you show me?"

I smile, feeling my heart race. John takes a seat and looks up at me. The eagerness shining through his wide, green eyes makes me flustered. I shift my arms to show him what to do, and he watches intently.

"Now put your arms out like you're carrying a watermelon, and I'll place her in them. Make sure you hold her head up."

I kneel in front of John with Brooke in my arms. He arrived home only ten minutes ago and made a beeline for Brooke. She was wrapped up in a blanket, sleeping in her bassinet. He didn't even say hi to his parents. It was adorable and made me feel all mushy for him. I wish I had gotten his expression on camera when he saw Brooke for the first time in person. He looked at her with wonderment and so much love that it made my knees weak. Carefully, I place her in his arms. He's stiff, and it's cute.

"Hold her like you're running with a football, but support her neck. Otherwise, her head will flop," I say, and lift his elbow slightly. "See how she's elevated? Keep her like that."

Brooke sucks away at her thumb as he cradles her. I sit next to him, and he turns to look at me with a smile so big it causes my heart to pitter-patter. His eyes roam over my face like he can't tear his gaze away until they fall on my mouth.

He turns away, and I can breathe again. I get the urge he wants to kiss me, but maybe it's in my head.

"She's like a tiny cupcake I want to take a bite out of. Her curls are the icing, and the rest is the yummy, fluffy cupcake part. She's so precious," John says in awe. He looks at me. "I can't believe I'm holding our daughter."

My smile falters, and John notices. "Uh-uh. No more of that. She's mine. I know she is."

I glance down. Shame colors my cheeks. "I hope you're right," I say.

"I know I am."

"What makes you think so?"

John shrugs. "I don't know. Her hair, her eyes. It's a gut feeling I have."

"Her eyes are grayish blue, John. I hate to break it to you, but many babies are born with eyes that color." I pause. "Chad has brown eyes." I shiver just at the thought of him.

"Yeah, so I think if Brooke were Chad's, she would have been born with brown eyes since it's a dominant gene. Anything else would be green or blue coming from either parent if they both had those colors, right?"

I shrug. What John said makes sense, but the hell if I know. Thinking about Chad makes me think about the paternity and how nervous I am about it.

"I had the meeting with the attorney, but luckily, I was able to do it over the phone and didn't have to go to the courthouse. I haven't gone for the test yet."

"I'm not concerned with it, Alyssa. You have a lot on your plate right now. When you're ready, you're ready. "

"All I keep thinking about is how invasive the test will be and that it's humiliating that I don't know who her father is." My hands form into fists just thinking about him. I hate Chad for taking advantage of me. "I don't want to do it, but I know I have to."

Concern is written all over John's face. "I was thinking we could go together. It doesn't have to be now, but maybe when I come home next time. That way, you don't have to do it alone."

"Are you sure?" I ask, and he nods.

If Brooke is not John's, will his feelings toward me change? The thought slices through me.

"What are you thinking about?"

Our eyes meet. I chew on the inside of my cheek, fearful of the future. Brooke grunts, not whining, but like she's about to, and it saves me from admitting what's on my mind.

"Oh, shoot. She's fussing," John says.

"It's okay. Just give her the pacifier."

I rest my head on John's shoulder and lean on him.

"Does she sleep at night for you?" he asks.

"Heck no, but your mom has been a blessing. During the day, I'll take a nap and she'll watch Brooke."

John lightly bounces Brooke in his arms. His voice is low as he speaks. "So I was thinking, and I know this sounds crazy, but what if we got an apartment by my base? That way, I can be around more. There are places all around my base in South Carolina. The military will help pay for accommodations. We get major housing discounts."

I'm quiet. It's a lot to take in and not at all what I expected from John. I don't have a job, so I don't know how I'll pay for things. I'm worried about being alone with a newborn too. Diane and Clarke are my safety nets. John will be gone all day, and I'll be alone.

John continues, "I want you near me, and I'm willing to do what it takes. I miss having you around. I miss our friendship. I miss us." He looks deeply into my eyes, nearly pleading for me. "Will you at least think about it before you shoot it down? All I know is that after holding Brooke, I need to be near this little cupcake more than ever. I'll even have an extra set of keys made to my truck so you have a vehicle when you need one."

Considering the strife we have dealt with over the past year, our friendship has grown stronger than I could have ever hoped for. John is free to do anything he wants, yet he's with me as often as his training permits. He's been in Brooke's presence for less than an hour and already doesn't want to leave her. This is everything I could have ever hoped for, except there's that notion that he'll change his mind if the paternity comes back in Chad's favor.

When I think about it, the choice is an easy one. "Let's do it."

His eyes widen like he expected me to reject him. "Are you serious?"

"Yes. Nothing is holding me back here other than your parents. We'll have to make time to visit them. They're already attached to her." He studies my mouth. My heartbeat pumps faster. "I plan to get a job eventually, but I don't have a babysitter."

"We'll figure it out. You don't even have to work at first if you don't want to. But when you do, I can help care for Brooke."

"Why are you doing this?" I ask, my voice soft.

"Because Jace's death has shown me how little time on earth we have. I don't want to waste precious minutes that we'll never get back." He takes a breath, licks his lips, and swallows. "It's no secret how I feel about you. I'm still very much attracted to you as I was the first day we met, if not more seeing you as a mother. But I'm not really looking for that type of relationship right now, and something tells me you aren't either. We can take it slow and just be there for each other."

My strong, fearless Johnny. He's hard to resist. He makes me want to hold on to him and never let go. Brooke starts fussing again. We both immediately look at her.

"What's wrong with my little cupcake?" John coos. He turns to me. "What do I do?" he asks, and I chuckle. "Is she hungry?"

"She's always hungry," I say.

"Do you have a bottle I can give her?"

I nod. "I do. Let me get it ready for you."

I'm warming some breastmilk when I hear John from the kitchen.

"Baby girl, what's going on with you?" he says in a

baby voice. "Why are you so fussy for your mama? Got nothing to say?"

I return to the living room and hand John a warm bottle. He gently places the tip of the nipple at her mouth, and she opens. She begins eating immediately. John only has eyes for Brooke and it's the cutest thing. I don't understand his thinking or why he's so eager to help me when the chance of being her father is fifty-fifty. Most men, I assume, wouldn't want to put that kind of work in when it's not their kid, and they're not even dating. As much as I want to poke, I won't. I rest my head on his shoulder and snuggle in close. He leans over and drops a kiss on my head. I've missed John so much. Something as simple as watching him feeding my daughter is all it takes for me to let down my defenses.

"You're hard not to fall for, Johnny."

John turns to me and smiles. "Good."

I giggle and then say quietly, "That was the quickest she's ever gone to sleep."

"You look exhausted. Why don't you get some sleep too?"

My eyes are heavy. "I'm so tired."

John presses his lips together. "And that's why I'm here. Go get some sleep."

"Can I stay here? I miss being next to you," I say. He nods, his gaze softens. "Do you want me to put her down in the bassinet?"

John shakes his head. "Can I hold her while she sleeps?"

"If she's your daughter too, like you say, then you don't have to ask me." John's eyes shift between both of mine, then he nods once.

John sinks further into the couch and gets comfortable with Brooke in his hold. He wraps an arm along my shoulders and cozies up next to me.

"I have my two favorite girls right by my side."

TWENTY-EIGHT

JOHN

L ife moves quickly in the next few weeks.

As soon as Alyssa gave me the go, I spoke with my sergeant, who got me in touch with the right people. They helped me get housing accommodations for the three of us. The rent is low, and there's a grocery store that's significantly discounted nearby for the military. Once the housing papers were signed, I drove down the following weekend to move Alyssa and Brooke into our new place. Alyssa doesn't have much to her name, and Brooke is still so small with very few items that we were able to pack up my truck in a couple of hours and leave early the following day. I didn't want her to be left with figuring things out on her own, so I helped her unpack what she had, knowing that I would have training and not much time left for anything else in the next five days.

We don't sleep in the same bed, not that I'm against it, but I don't want to pressure her into anything she's uncomfortable with. Just because we live together doesn't mean it comes with stipulations. Although I wouldn't be against sex, I'm just not going to rush her into that.

Before we left Georgia, we took the paternity test. It was over before I could blink my eyes. The results won't be ready for two weeks and will be mailed to our new apartment. Since our mail is being rerouted, it could take a little longer. I'm anxious to read the results.

I hear Brooke giggling through the door as I insert my key. It makes me smile. That little girl makes me happier than I thought possible. Every day she looks different, yet all I see is Alyssa when I look at her.

Opening the front door to our apartment, I step inside to see Alyssa carrying Brooke while vacuuming. Her blond hair is wild and messy at the top of her head. I don't think she brushed it when she woke up. She's wearing an oversized white T-shirt and a tiny pair of shorts peeking out. She isn't wearing a stitch of makeup and yet she looks more beautiful than ever. Brooke's chubby arms flail as she bounces on her mother's hip. The door shuts with a click and Alyssa spins around as I walk toward them. I reach for Brooke and scoop her up.

"You're home," Alyssa says, surprised.

I nod while only having eyes for Brooke. "I got out early. Hey, cupcake. Did you miss me like I missed you?"

Brooke leans into me with a slobbery, wet mouth. Her mouth is wide open, and her tongue hangs out as she goes for my nose. I scrunch my face and huff out a laugh.

"Nice to see you too," I tell my daughter.

Alyssa chuckles. "That's Brooke's way of giving you kisses."

"I can see," I say, wiping my nose. Brooke does it

again, holding the sides of my face with her little hands. "Who taught her how to give kisses like that?"

"Could you imagine if people went around kissing like this?" Alyssa asks.

"No. That would be weird."

"She must've missed you," Alyssa says.

I tilt my head at Alyssa. "You okay? Are you sick? You look a little pale."

She shakes her head. "I'm good, just exhausted. I was getting ready to cook dinner. Are you hungry?"

Rubbing Brooke's back, I say, "I can always eat. Need help with anything?"

"Nope. I'm good. Just watch Brooke for me, please."

Sitting on the couch with Brooke in my lap, she goes straight for my dog tags. She plays with them in her hand, turning over and inspecting each before shoving them into her mouth like most things these days. I laugh, and she looks at me with vibrant, hopeful eyes. She babbles now, and while I have no idea what she's saying, I mimic her and she loves it. Brooke leans in and faceplants on my chest. I giggle at her, so she knows she isn't hurt and doesn't cry. I didn't know loving a child could happen at first glance, but it did with Brooke. I think I loved her while Alyssa was pregnant. Regardless of what the test results show, I've always seen her as my daughter, because her mother is mine. Even though Alyssa tries to fight what we have, I have the patience of a saint, so I'll wait until she sees what I see.

Bringing Brooke in close, I carry her to the kitchen. I heard pans clang together and then Alyssa curse, so I want to make sure she's okay. I smile to myself. It's cute watching her cook. Alyssa told me she learned how to cook from her mom. For some reason, it hits me in the chest, and I hope one day my daughter will be doing something I taught her too.

I lean against the doorframe and glance around. Mail is strewn across the counter, as well as a few empty baby bottles, a carton of fruit punch, and the diaper bag. Bold, black writing catches my eye. On one of the pieces of mail, there's a stamp on it that looks like it's official. My smile falters, and I stand a little taller to read the front of the envelope.

Alyssa turns and jumps when she notices me.

She grabs her chest. "You scared the crap out of me. How long were you there?

"Not long."

"Is something wrong? With Brooke?"

The corners of my mouth turn up, and I shake my head. Her shoulders relax. She's what I'd call a paranoid new mother.

"She's good," I say, reassuring her.

Alyssa's eyes travel the length of my body. Her mouth makes a small O. I'm still dressed in my cammies. I haven't even taken off my boots yet. I had a one-track mind when I walked in the door, and it was to see my girls. Even though she doesn't tell me she likes it when I wear my standard uniform, I know she does. Her facial expressions give her away.

I step into the kitchen, reach behind Alyssa, and turn off the stove with Brooke balancing on my stomach. "Burgers are done, babe."

Alyssa stares up at me with doe eyes. Her cheeks redden. It's cute that she's embarrassed. At least I know she still wants me.

"I just caught you checking me out."

She shakes her head adamantly. "No, I wasn't. You just scared me."

"Right," I drawl.

Alyssa rolls her eyes. My smile grows, and her cheeks get pinker. I know it's because she's flustered.

"Don't get ahead of yourself, country boy."

My eyes drift back to the mail. I'm suddenly anxious to know if it's the results. She notices and tenses.

"Is that the mail on the counter?" I ask.

"Yeah, I forgot to check the mail the last couple of days. I don't know how long the stuff has been there. Can you strap Brooke into the high chair, please?"

"Of course," I say. Alyssa follows me into the dining area. "Did you check to see if one is from the laboratory?"

ALYSSA

I'M CHEWING ON MY BOTTOM LIP. I DON'T NEED TO TURN around to know what Johnny is talking about. I saw him looking at it a few times.

"I think so. I haven't opened it yet. I was hoping you'd want to wait until the weekend to do it."

"Why didn't you tell me it came? Were you not going to? Or did you think I would forget?"

A stinging pain slashes through my chest, and my stomach tightens. My face falls. "How could you think I would do such a thing?"

He shrugs. "I don't, but I did expect you to tell me immediately that you got them."

John breathes heavily, an angry tick working in his jaw. I never want to hurt him, but I understand why he's upset. I knew I needed to tell him. I just didn't know how to say it. The whole situation is intimidating.

I lower my voice. "I thought I would show you on the weekend."

"This beautiful baby girl could be mine, and you were going to wait until it was the right time to go over the results?" he says.

"You're acting like I was never going to tell you. I wasn't going to hide it. If you want to do it right now, we will."

"I'd like to, yeah." It's all he says.

Tears burn the back of my eyes. I stroll past John, head for the kitchen, and swipe the envelope. My heart is racing. The back of my neck is clammy, and my stomach is churning. So many thoughts run through my head. I'm thinking of the worst-case scenario and working myself up into a panic attack.

I've never been so nervous in all my life.

"Ready?" I ask, walking back into the dining room.

John is sitting next to Brooke. He places a hand on mine. "I'm sorry for lashing out. I'm just eager to know the results. That paper won't change anything between us. The moment I saw Brooke, I was committed." He pauses. "I think it's when I saw your pregnant belly that made me realize my purpose."

A tear trickles down my cheek as my shaky hands flip over the envelope. I take a seat next to John and slip a finger underneath, slowly ripping the letter open. My stomach is doing backflips, and my mouth is drier than sandpaper. John doesn't look over my shoulder or breathe down my neck. He just sits stoically as I take my time.

I remove the paper from the envelope and flip the top half up, then the bottom half down. My pulse beats in my throat.

My whole body is trembling as I scan the paper fast and examine the chart. These results compare Brooke's DNA to all three of us. I sit motionless as I speed-read the three small paragraphs. Being that Chad is in jail, his mouth had already been swabbed. His DNA had been collected months ago.

I get to the bottom, and I suddenly feel like I'm on the Maury show, only this is real life, and somebody is about to get hurt.

"What does it say?" John asks.

My mouth moves, but nothing comes out. The paper slips through my fingers and floats to the floor.

"Alyssa?" John says softly.

I stand up and pace.

Reaching down, John picks up the results and reads them over.

TWENTY-NINE

JOHN

I don't need a paper to prove anything.

I know what I feel in my gut. I'm right where I'm supposed to be. Truthfully, I never intended to ask Alyssa for a paternity test, but I know she needed it for her peace of mind, and because she wanted to fight for full custody. The other night she told me she was going to do everything in her power to make sure Chad isn't ever alone with Brooke. But in order to do that, the court requires a DNA test. If I hadn't been so hardheaded, maybe we wouldn't be in this predicament. I feel like part of me is to blame. If I had answered her calls and text messages, then she would have never hung out with Chad.

Reaching down, I pick up the piece of paper she just dropped. I turn it over as Alyssa paces the floor, avoiding me. I haven't prepared myself to not be deemed Brooke's father. I didn't have to be part of her DNA to be a father.

I take a deep breath and begin reading. My gaze scans over the words. I read them again, and again. An icy coldness fills my veins. Seeing the percentage does something to me. It twists my gut backward like a cranking clock. I crumple the paper in my hand and clench my eyes shut. I hear Alyssa sniffling, but I can't bring myself to look at her. The devastation hits deep, and I feel a twinge of resentment. I'm sick to my stomach. There is no way this is right.

I'm not Brooke's biological father.

Fuck.

My chest feels like it's caving in.

I finally glance up. Alyssa looks at me. Tears pool in her eyes. The devastation I felt moments ago is nothing compared to the way she looks. I don't want to see her cry, but I'm too distraught over the results to console her.

This isn't fair.

I need to go for a run.

I reread the results again. I wanted Brooke to be mine so fucking bad. I might not have been present for her birth, but I've been there for everything else I could be. I've clothed her, fed her, sheltered them. I've been a father to her since before she was born.

"I'm sorry," Alyssa says, breaking my thoughts.

I make my way to where Brooke is sitting in her high chair. I look at this beautiful baby girl gnawing on her fist who has no idea what is going on in the world. I'm devastated. My stomach is in knots. I truly felt that I was her real father with every fiber in my body. Big blue eyes look up at me. Brooke reaches for me. She makes an open then closed fist and kicks her little legs until I'm reaching down to unbuckle her. I need to hold Brooke. I need to smell her baby powder skin, otherwise I think I'm going to break. Brooke is *my* daughter. I don't care what any paper says.

Removing the tray, I pick her up and hold her to my chest. Her chubby fingers reach for my tags. Once in her grip, she nestles in the crook of my neck, where she rests her head. I inhale her sweet scent and close my eyes to savor this moment. I press a gentle kiss to her forehead. I hear Alyssa's silent sobs and turn around. My chest aches at the sight of her. Tears stream down her rosy cheeks. Her eyes express the depth of her pain and remorse.

Possessiveness rolls through me like thunder.

I whisper, "Brooke is mine. I don't care what that paper says."

Alyssa bursts into tears. She lowers her eyes and says, "I'm sorry."

I kiss Brooke's curly hair and then place her in her bouncy baby chair. I don't know why Alyssa is apologizing. It's not like she had a choice in the matter when it comes to Chad.

"I can pay you back for everything," she says. "There's no reason for you to stick around now."

I stop her. It's like she hasn't heard a single thing I've been saying.

"I'm not going anywhere, Alyssa." I pause. "I'm not leaving. I just want to be part of her life. I care about that scumbag never getting his hands on her or you ever again."

Alyssa stares at me in disbelief. "Knowing that you're not her biological father, you could leave at any given moment. I can't risk that. It's not fair to Brooke. Me, I can handle it, but Brooke? She'll get attached easily, and I don't know if I can handle that."

I lower my voice so it's even and steady even though I feel like I'm about to blow up right now. "So you're saying that if I walked out of your life right now, you wouldn't care one bit? After everything?"

Fear fills her wide eyes. Her jaw bobs. "Of course I would care. Life would suck without my best friend. You're my other half."

"Then what's the real problem?" I ask. "Do you not trust me? I'm telling you I'm not going anywhere."

The effervescent blue in her eyes fades. "I'm scared, okay? I'm just scared." Alyssa turns and sits on the edge of the couch. "I just don't want you to walk out when times get tough, because there will be tough times. What if you have a girlfriend, and she suddenly becomes your priority? What if you get tired of playing house? What if you have a baby one day?" She licks her lips, and my gaze follows. "Do you see where I'm coming from now?"

I walk to where Alyssa is sitting and sit next to her. "Please don't shut me out. Just give me a chance. That's all I'm asking for, a chance. Let me show you that I'm not going anywhere. I promise I'll never shut you out again."

Fresh tears fill her eyes. Alyssa rolls her lips between her teeth and presses down. "I thought you were her father. I felt it in my bones, in my heart. Why did we have to go and get that stupid test done?" The tears begin to flow. "I wish we hadn't."

I stroke her cheeks and wrap an arm around her shoulders. "That paper won't stop me from caring for you. It should mean nothing to you."

"Johnny," she whispers. "I'm so scared. What if Chad fights for custody out of spite?"

"I won't let it happen. Trust me. I will fight until my last dying breath before I let that happen."

Alyssa turns to hug me. She buries her head against my

chest and quietly cries. She hugs me tight, and it breaks my heart.

"There's no other place I want to be but with you and Brooke. You won't ever be alone," I say.

"You should leave now. Get out while you can. It would be better if you did."

My brows knit together. "Better for whom? You or Me? I'm in too deep to get out now, babe."

A strangled cry escapes her throat. Alyssa cries so hard she can't stop to catch her breath. She turns her head up to face me and finally looks at me. Her puffy, red nose matches her bloodshot eyes.

"I'll tell you until you're sick of hearing me." I pause. "I'm not leaving you."

I thread my fingers through her tangled hair and tip her head further back. Her sadness envelops me. It pulls me under and forces me to feel her pain.

"Let me be there for you. Hold on to me," I say hoarsely.

Tension radiates beneath my fingertips, so I massage her scalp to alleviate any strain she's dealing with.

"Will you let me be there for you?" I ask.

"Why? Why do you want to so bad?"

"I don't know. I wish I could explain it. I really like you, and I just want to be with you. I want to be with Brooke."

My heart is starting to beat fast. I'm saying things I wasn't ready to say yet.

But maybe she should know. Then she'll see that I'm not going anywhere.

Alyssa studies my eyes. She nods subtly then scoots closer. Her gaze falls to my mouth, and I'm praying she'll kiss me. I haven't kissed her in months. It's been torture. She's been through a lot, so I've kept my hands to myself even though I don't want to.

Alyssa cups my jaw, her fingers splayed out on my cheek. She's lingering, and I'm seconds from closing the distance.

"Kiss me," I tell her, my voice low.

Her eyes snap to mine before she does. Her soft lips are like pillows and her scent surrounds me. My eyes close, and dear God, I've missed her. I don't wait for Alyssa to make the next move. I slide my tongue across the seam of her lips and press through. Her kiss releases endorphins into my blood. Her fingers glide down my neck, over my shoulders, and roam my chest. She strokes her tongue with mine, but then Alyssa abruptly breaks the kiss. Panting, her wild eyes take me in.

"Can we take it slow? Maybe focus on Brooke?"

Naturally, I want to balk at the question. But instead, I agree.

THIRTY

JOHN

Walking through the cold, sterile room makes my skin crawl.

I feel out of place. I'm already antsy to get out. I'm not a criminal. I may have screwed around in my youth and had to do community service at one point, but I don't belong here.

I spot my target. My eyes lower and narrow. Hatred for the man in front of me runs deep in my veins. Chad is the epitome of a piece of shit. I would love nothing more than to wipe him from the earth.

But unfortunately, that's illegal. And I really don't want to spend the rest of my days behind bars when Alyssa and Brooke need me.

After Alyssa fell asleep the other night, I went to work on my cell phone and started researching what it would require for her to gain full custody of Brooke. I know all of this law stuff is overwhelming for her on top of being a new mom, so I took it as my responsibility to help with it. My heart had been ripped in two reading the DNA results.

I took it harder than I thought I would. I knew she did too. Alyssa was devastated. Brooke is Chad's daughter, which means he still has rights to her. Luckily, with my brother being in the entertainment industry, he was able to help me find the right attorney the next day and draft up the proper paperwork.

I walk to where Chad is waiting for me and sit across from him at the stainless-steel table that's bolted to the cement floor. I place the folder I brought with me on the table. Chad eyes it. He looks rough around the edges, but I don't see any bruises.

"To what do I owe this pleasure?" he says.

"Your daughter," I reply, and his eyes lower. I knew this would grate under his skin. Good. He deserves it. "Alyssa wants full custody of Brooke, and I'm here to make it happen." I know the lab sent him a copy of the results as he's Brooke's biological father.

Chad's jaw flexes. "I don't see how this has anything to do with you since she is my kid."

"It has everything to do with me. Let's be honest. You don't give a shit about either one of them."

Chad cocks his head to the side. "You're not wrong."

Anger bubbles under my skin. I can't stand how callous he is. "Did you know that you're not even on the birth certificate? It says father unknown." His nostrils flare. Chad doesn't respond. I guess I hit a nerve. "Let me make you an offer you can't refuse."

"There's nothing you have that I want. I have what you want for once."

I shake my head. This guy is delusional. "Because you stole it. You had to take it to get it. We're not the same, and we never will be." Looking him dead straight in the eyes, I say, "How much money do you want?"

"Money? That's what you're going to give me? Please. You don't have two pots to piss in. Unless you ask your daddy and mommy to pay."

I give him a droll stare. I didn't ask my parents.

I asked Luke for help, who was willing to step in.

"How about ten?" I ask.

"Ten thousand?" he asks, and I nod. Chad contemplates the offer for a moment. "Talk to me."

I huff under my breath. I knew he would take the bait.

"What if I told you I would give you ten thousand dollars right this minute if you signed your parental rights over to Alyssa. She gets full custody. You can never contact Alyssa again or look for Brooke once she's an adult."

Chad's eyes narrow. "Twenty thousand, and the little bastard is hers."

I swallow thickly. Red-hot hate washes over me. Deep breaths. Deep. Breaths. I need to take five deep breaths, or else I'm going to lose it on this scum of the earth.

"Twenty-five thousand." I up it. Not that it would ever be enough to put a price on her. "Agree to it, and I'll call the bank when I leave here."

"How do I know you're not lying?"

"You don't. But at this point, what do you have to lose?"

Chad considers the offer for a few seconds. "What makes you think I don't want my kid after I get out?"

I huff. "You don't want your little bastard." I hate to use that word to describe my cupcake, but I have to in order to

255

stoop to Chad's level. "You didn't even want her to begin with. When I leave here, I'll have the money wired to your account. I can't do it in front of you because I can't bring a cell phone in."

"And you have the papers to sign over my rights? What about a paper where it says you'll pay me?"

I smirk inwardly. As if I'm not prepared.

"Not only do I have the custodial papers you need to sign to relinquish your rights as Brooke's father, but I also have two copies of my offer stating in return that you'll never contact her again or seek out Brooke. One for you, the other for me."

Chad is surprised. I can tell he wasn't expecting it. "Show me."

I produce two sheets of paper from my folder and fill in the amount before sliding them and the pen over to Chad.

"This states that I'm required to pay you twenty-five thousand dollars. I've already signed them. Sign both and keep a copy."

"Did you automatically think I would take your offer?" Chad asks while reading the papers over.

"No, but I came prepared."

Chad pauses. I watch him hesitate. The pen flickers between his fingers before he scribbles his name on both papers then slides one back to me.

I give him the custodial papers to sign next.

"Just so you know, I had already planned on signing custody papers before you arrived," he says as he signs any rights to Brooke away. "Alyssa can have the kid. One last thing I don't have to worry about when I get out. Five years will go by fast. It's a good thing I waited since you bought her off." Chad snickers like the little prick that he is.

I pause. "Just so you know, I was prepared to pay you even more. Not only that, but I didn't buy her off. The first paper states you are not allowed to be in the same city as Alyssa, and you're never to contact her or Brooke again. Read the fine print, asshole. I was protecting them, not buying them."

"Whatever you say." Chad stands. "Are we finished here?"

I scan all the places I needed Chad's signature. I stack the papers together and stand.

"We're done."

Chad salutes, then turns and walks shackled in the other direction. I release a strained breath once I see him walk through the door without so much as a glance back.

I'm glad it's over. I'm happy I came in Alyssa's stead. The last thing I want is for her to be in this nasty place.

THREE HOURS LATER, I'M PULLING INTO OUR neighborhood with a massive smile on my face. I can't wait to see Alyssa. She has no idea I did what I did, but I hope it doesn't upset her.

I turn off the ignition, grab the folder with the papers inside, and stroll toward the door. I devised a few different ways to tell her the great news the entire drive back. I step inside and see Alyssa playing with Brooke on the floor. They both look in my direction. Alyssa looks happy and it makes me feel good. The dark circles under her eyes are slowly disappearing. The puffiness from crying over the results is gone too. Brooke spots me and bounces on her butt. She clasps her hands together and begins babbling. This is the best part of my day.

I walk toward them and bend down to pick up Brooke and kiss her forehead.

"Why are you all smiles?" Alyssa asks, standing up.

"I have some good news for you."

"Is that so? Because I have good news for you too," she tells me.

My brows rise and Alyssa nods excitedly. "You want to go first?"

"I need Brooke to show you."

I hand Brooke to Alyssa, and she walks across the living room. Alyssa gets on her knees and gently places Brooke on all fours. She holds her by the waist to help her balance.

"Brooke," she says sweetly, "where's Johnny? Can you crawl to Johnny for Mama?"

My mouth drops open. I quickly place the folder on the back of the sofa and squat down with open arms.

"Is my little cupcake going to crawl to me for the first time?"

Brooke grunts between a whine and a happy cry as she stares at me. She picks up one chubby hand, places it in front of her, and then does it with the other. Alyssa slowly removes her hold and allows Brooke to crawl on her own. She's wobbly, crying and laughing simultaneously, trying to crawl to me while I wait with open arms.

"Come on, baby girl. Come to Johnny," I urge. Happiness spreads through me. She's two crawls away when she rocks back and forth. "Come on, you can do it." She edges closer at a snail's pace. A few laughs, and

Brooke reaches me. I scoop her up and hug her tight. I love the smell of her baby soft skin. Brooke rests her sweet face on my shoulder, and I'm overcome with emotions. I fight back the feelings burning in my chest. Being able to watch her crawl for the first time is something I will never forget.

I glance at Alyssa. She's beaming from ear to ear. I can feel her joy. It dawns on me that I can't remember the last time I saw her smile so big. I walk over to pull her into a side hug. I kiss the top of her head.

"Thank you for that," I say. "I really needed it."

Alyssa wraps both arms around my waist and squeezes. Tilting her head up, she smiles. "You're welcome. I've been working on it with her to surprise you."

"It means a lot to me. Thank you."

Alyssa shared Brooke's milestone. It's a big moment for both of us, and I only want to kiss her sweet lips because of it.

"So what surprise do you have for me?" she asks excitedly.

Dread overwhelms me.

"About that… Just know what I did was for you and Brooke." Her brows furrow. Happiness slips from her face. "It's nothing bad. I promise."

I walk back to the couch and pick up the folder. "I think we should sit for this."

Alyssa nods slowly, eyeing the folder wearily. "Let me put Brooke down for her nap, and I'll meet you back here."

I hand over the munchkin and wait on the couch. I'm scrolling through my cell phone when Alyssa walks in.

"That was quick," I say, surprised she's back in ten minutes.

"Brooke skipped her nap this morning. I could tell she was tired, but I kept her awake until you got home to see her crawl. I knew she'd go to sleep easily for her afternoon nap."

Alyssa sits down next to me, and I hand her the folder. "What is it?" she questions slowly.

My heart is thumping wildly in my chest. I crack my neck. Alyssa takes the papers out and begins reading them.

"They're custody papers. Chad signed over Brooke to you, relinquishing his rights."

Alyssa freezes, and her mouth parts. She lifts her head to look at me. Her brows bunch together. "What...? How...? I don't understand. How did you do this? And without me there?"

I explain the steps I took and that I contacted my brother. She listens to every word I say. She reads over the agreement where it states he can't be within a certain amount of feet of her or Brooke. I leave out the part where I paid Chad cash. She doesn't need to know he'd rather have money than see his daughter.

"The attorney told me that you didn't have to be there for Chad to sign the papers. I didn't think you were comfortable seeing him ever again, so I went to where he's incarcerated. He did it with no problem." I pause, swallowing. "She's all yours now, Alyssa," I say quietly.

Alyssa is speechless. All she does is stare at me.

"I-I don't..." she stammers. Tears well in her eyes, and her shoulders sag. Alyssa's jaw quivers as she says, "Thank you. I don't know what else to say other than thank you."

Overcome with emotion, Alyssa flings herself at me. She wraps her arms around my shoulders and quietly cries. Brooke is my everything. So is Alyssa. I hold her tight, running my hand in circles on her back. Nothing feels as good as having Alyssa in my arms.

"I'm sorry I went behind your back. I was worried you'd be mad."

She shakes her head on my chest and then sits up to look at me. "I'm glad you did it. You were right about not wanting to see him again." She pauses, looks down, then looks in my eyes again. "I can't believe you did this."

"I'd do anything for you, Alyssa. I hope you know that."

She nods and tears form in her eyes again. She sniffles. "It's like a weight has been lifted off my shoulders. I wanted full custody but didn't know where to start."

"Chad is scum. He is not a man. What he did to you is despicable. No real man ever raises a hand to a woman." I let her see the rage in my eyes, the anger and determination. "I wanted to make sure he never has the opportunity to come back into your lives again."

"I could never repay you," she whispers. "Thank you."

"We don't have to talk about it now, but I was thinking about it on my car ride back and couldn't figure it out. Were you seeing Chad while you were seeing me?"

Alyssa shakes her head adamantly. "It wasn't like that. I was never hooking up with him while I was with you. It started a few days before Jace's funeral. I think that's when Brooke was conceived too, but I'm not entirely positive since I'd been drinking. I drank a lot that night. Chad picked up some tequila after work and asked me to hang out. I was upset about Jace's condition. I was trying to be there for you, but you weren't letting me. So I figured why the heck not. Everything got really hazy after a handful of shots, and they hit me all at once. I'd never had tequila but once at the bonfire. Chad came on to me, I vaguely remember telling him no, but I don't remember much after that. I just remember waking up with a little pain, but I didn't think much of it and forgot. We started hanging out every night after and sort of just became a thing."

My jaw is locked tight. Rage rushes through my blood. Alyssa has just confirmed what I've suspected all along.

"So Brooke is the result of a rape."

She shakes her head vehemently. "Don't say that."

"Why? It's what happened. Chad raped you."

Alyssa's eyes widen. "Don't call it that. I never want my daughter to think that's why she was born. I never want her to feel like she's not wanted. Promise me you'll never tell a soul, including Brooke."

THIRTY-ONE

ALYSSA

"I t'll never leave this room. I won't tell anyone. You have my word."

My shoulders sag. "I don't know what I'm going to tell her when she's older, but I figured I'd bridge that gap when the time comes."

John bobs his head in agreement, and relief courses through me. My mother often made me feel like I was an accident and that she didn't really want me. I promised myself that when Brooke was born I would never treat her the way I was treated. It's hard to admit the truth when it hurts so much. Deep down, I know Chad took advantage of me.

John's eyes fall to my mouth. They linger. "It's killing me not to kiss you. I'll never push you, but make no mistake, I still want you."

It's been hard to keep my hands to myself living with him, and I don't want to fight it any longer.

"I want you too," I whisper.

John licks his lips as he stares at my mouth and moves

closer. I suck in a quiet breath when he lowers his lips to mine and moves them back and forth. Softly, he tugs on my bottom lip to nibble on it. I lean into John, pushing him into the couch, then I crawl onto his lap and straddle him. He plunges his tongue into my mouth and kisses me hard, letting out a moan that makes me melt inside. He palms my jaw, spreading his fingers out to cup my neck. His lips never leave mine. The passion brewing between us is electric. It always has been. I can't deny it because it would be silly to. I feel John down to my bones, and I know he feels the same way. Our connection has been strong since the day we met.

John's hands roam the length of my body until they settle on my hips. He gives me a tender squeeze. He sinks deeper into the sofa and takes me with him. His erection is clear as day, and I feel it push into me. My body softens, and my hips rock into his. Damn, I want him. It dawns on me that I haven't had sex since before Brooke was born.

Slowly, we kiss, moving in sync with each other. A little moan escapes me, and I feel his cock twitch. His mouth devours mine like it's his last day on earth. John rocks into me and groans. He moves a hand up to fist my hair, and our tongues dance dangerously on the edge. I can't get enough. I widen my legs, wanting to feel the heat between us.

But it isn't enough.

I need more.

I always need more when it comes to Johnny, and that's what keeps me holding back. I've always been so scared of getting attached and having to say goodbye. But things are different with us now.

"Don't," he begs when he feels my resistance.

I try not to pull away, but I'm not the same person I was before I got pregnant. I have stretch marks, and I'm not tight and as small as I once was.

Breaking the kiss, his wild eyes search mine as he says hoarsely, "I want you so bad."

I grab onto the back of his neck and devour his kiss. I need him as much as he needs me. He grips my hips. His hands roam and knead every inch of my backside like he's desperate to touch every part of me. Heat floods my pussy, and a groan escapes my lips. I fight hard to stifle my moans, but it's pointless. John's touch ignites a fire inside of me that I thought had long been extinguished. His fingers change tempo as they slip into my shorts and panties and graze my naked flesh.

"Johnny," I moan when he cups my ass right next to my sex.

A guttural groan vibrates in his chest. I love the way it sounds.

John stands up with me in his arms and takes us to my bedroom. He lays me down. My knees part, and then I snap them shut.

"Don't, baby. Let me see you."

I gulp. "It's hard for me, Johnny. My body isn't how it used to be."

"I know."

My eyes round in surprise. Before I can say anything, he shakes his head and says, "You're even better than before. Even when you were pregnant, I wanted you so fucking bad it hurt, but I knew you weren't in the right frame of mind, so I held off." He pauses. "It's a struggle to hold back." John places two hands on my knees and slowly spreads them open. "I want you," he repeats, looking into my eyes. "Alyssa, I want you." My heart pounds against my ribs at John's admission. His eyes are filled with arousal. "So. Fucking. Bad."

Tears well in my eyes. Sitting up, I reach for him. I cup his cheeks and whisper, "I don't want to push you away, but I'm petrified you'll leave. Tell me that I'm wrong. Fight against me. Push and shove and tell me that you'll be there no matter what I do. Just be there, Johnny. Even when I say no over and over. I know I'm stubborn, but I don't want to push you away." I tremble inside. My jaw quivers, and my eyes water. I swallow. "I need you to show me you'll always be there."

"Alyssa," he says as he kisses away my tears. His nose grazes my cheek, then along my jaw and back up so our lips touch. We hover in front of each other, breathless, waiting for the next move.

"I want you," I confess. My heart is racing. "Take me and do what you want."

Deep down, I know he will never truly hurt me the way Chad did.

"There's no going back once I start," he says. His voice sounds as rough as gravel.

"I don't want to go back once we start."

"Let me get the monitor and bring it into the room just in case Brooke wakes up."

My heart melts knowing Brooke is on John's mind. He grabs the monitor from the living room and places it on my dresser.

John tugs his shirt off as he walks to the bed and drops it to the floor. He's quick to remove his pants and shoes. His body is so defined now that I can't stop staring at it. I can't wait to run my hands over his muscles and feel his strength. His thumbs slip behind the elastic of his boxers and he pushes them down. I draw in a thick breath at the sight of his hard cock. He steps out of his boxers and palms his erection, stroking himself while watching me watch him.

John presses a knee onto the mattress and crawls over to me. He reaches for the hem of my shirt and tugs it over my head. I gulp hard. His eyes focus on my breasts before leaning in to take one into his mouth. My back arches, and my lips part. I cup the back of his head and urge him to continue. He flicks my nipple with his tongue and my clit throbs with desire. His fingers move teasingly across my lower stomach to the elastic of my shorts. He tugs them down swiftly, taking my panties at the same time, and tosses them to the side. My thighs widen as he places his body between them. His mouth searches for mine, and we both moan in unison at the connection. John's cock is warm and hard as steel as it presses against my pussy. Our tongues wrap around each other's as his cock slides up and down my wetness. His fingers thread through my hair and grip the back of my neck.

He thrusts his hips against mine and desire slams into me. I mimic his rhythm and find myself moving at the same tempo. It's sexy and hot. It's what I need.

"Johnny," I moan.

John slides down my body, his tongue leaving a trail of wetness on my stomach. I try to lean up on my elbows, but he pushes my chest down.

"Lie still," he orders.

I do as he says.

John spreads my legs open as wide as my hips will allow and stares at my pussy. Heat flames my cheeks. I hold my breath and squeeze my eyes shut. I'm exposed and baring it all to him in this position. It's erotic and freeing at the same time. He leans his head down and runs his tongue up my slit. Goose bumps break out over my arms as he does it again from bottom to top. I sigh, my body turning soft and pliant under him. John's tongue delves deeper, and my hips roll into his mouth. I fist the sheets as John laps at me. He pulls and manipulates my inner lips, sucking and licking all around. A shiver runs down my spine, and my thighs tighten around John's shoulders.

"Mmm, " I moan.

His finger enters me as his lips wrap around my clit. Pleasure ricochets through me and I gasp loudly. My hips buck off the bed and I grab John's head. It's been a while since I've had any kind of penetration. The tightness combined with his sinful mouth relaxes my body and feels so incredible. His finger is slowly stretching me out and making me drip with desire.

Picking his head up, he grins. "Just wait until I get inside of you."

"I don't have a condom," I tell him.

"You don't?"

"Well, no. I didn't need them since I wasn't sleeping with anyone."

"As much as I love hearing you're not fucking anyone else again because that would set me off, I figured you had some protection. Are you on birth control?"

I shake my head. "No. There was no reason to be on it yet." I pause, not wanting to stop this. "Do you think you could pull out in time?"

He nods yes. "I can always get you Plan B tomorrow morning too."

I like the sound of that and nod.

John rubs my clit in circles and teases my entrance. My hips lift again, signaling I need more from him. He rises up on his elbows and palms his cock at my entrance.

"I need you to look at me while I slide in, okay? Don't look anywhere else except for my eyes. See me, Alyssa. Only me," he says. John runs the tip of his cock up and down my opening. My knees fall back as he positions himself.

He pushes in just the tip, and I tense. John waits a moment. Once I relax, he pushes in a little more. His gaze never leaves mine. A heavy breath rolls off my lips. Pressure builds as he carefully pushes in further. I go to turn my head away, but he won't allow it. He grabs my chin and brings me back to him.

"Don't lose focus, Alyssa. Look at me. Look at my face and know it's Johnny above you."

I begin nodding frantically.

"Remember we've done this before."

And just like that, I feel everything inside me let go.

"Make love to me, Johnny. Make me forget it all."

"Don't gotta ask me twice."

John pulls out and then surges back in. I roll my hips to meet his and moan. I clench my thighs around his body, squeezing his cock. My nails dig into his back.

"Johnny." I pant. "You feel so good."

John grabs both of my wrists and traps them above my head. He thrusts deeper, faster, rolling his hips and hitting my clit simultaneously.

"More," I beg, and he obliges.

Leaning down, he draws my nipple into his mouth. My

back arches, and I cry out. He laps at each nipple until I'm writhing in desire under him.

"Close… So close," I groan. "Don't stop." I struggle in his hold, but John never loosens his grip. He makes love to my body effectively and efficiently until we reach the peak together.

"You ready?" He breathes against my mouth. I nod. "Open your eyes and look at me. See only me." My eyes are heavy with arousal. His hips pick up speed, pushing into me faster. I moan, back arched, eyes still open.

"I'm gonna go. I'm right there."

"Come." John kisses me hard. "Come with me."

The most intense orgasm I have ever experienced rocks through my body, sending me over the edge and bringing me higher than I've ever felt before, all while looking Johnny in the eyes. It's the most intimate thing I've ever done. John kisses me deeply. His cock twitches, and I feel him come undone inside of me. He lets out a long groan, and I love the sound of it.

"Did I hurt you?" he asks after a few moments.

A blush paints my cheeks. I shake my head. "It was a little painful at first, but that's because it was more my nerves than anything."

John smiles, and the dimple near his chin shows. I've missed his smile. "I didn't pull out," he says as he pulls out now. "I'll get the pill for you later."

I nod, thinking about how I need to find a new doctor so I can get on birth control. I should be angry he didn't pull out, but I'm not. I'm overwhelmed by how much chemistry we still have after all that we've been through.

Until then, it's Plan B for me.

I won't be having more kids any time soon.

THIRTY-TWO

JOHN

A faint, little cry stirs me awake.

I'm dog tired, and my eyes are dry as I turn over and reach for Alyssa, but she isn't there.

Sitting up, I look around the dark room but find it empty. The muffled cry resonates throughout the room again. I look to my right and see the monitor light up on Alyssa's dresser. Each time Brooke whimpers, red lights appear on the baby monitor.

"Shh, Mama's here, baby. Go back to sleep." Alyssa's voice comes through the small speaker.

I glance at the clock. Damn. It's three in the morning. It feels like we went to bed only a few hours ago. Rubbing my eyes, I get up and go find them.

Peeking into Brooke's room, I see Alyssa's back is to me as she rocks Brooke in her arms. Alyssa's blond hair is an untamed mess, like she was tossing and turning all night. Her T-shirt hangs down to her knees and one shoulder is bared. I squint my eyes and realize it's my shirt she's wearing. She must've put it on when she got up.

Alyssa sings softly to Brooke as she lulls her back to sleep. Watching them sends my heart soaring with so much love. Brooke's little arm is wrapped around Alyssa's side. Her tiny hand fists my shirt. Not wanting to interrupt them, I retreat back to the bedroom and wait for Alyssa to come back.

Fuck. What is it about Alyssa that gets my blood simmering with wanting her so bad? Lying in bed, I fold my arms behind my head and stare at the ceiling. I need to figure out a plan. I won't push her, but I want to be her man. The one she runs to.

Jace's death proved how short life is. Tomorrow we could wake up dead. We're given one chance at life, and I want to make the most of it.

Despite the grief, Alyssa is still the one I turn to. She's my light. My strength. My motivation.

And now Brooke is too.

Jace's death has forever changed me. I see life with a different set of eyes now. I will mourn my best friend until my last breath, but I have to keep trekking ahead. I won't let the sorrow suck me under again, even though some days I want it to. I have a reason to live, to fight.

ALYSSA

STANDING ON MY TIPTOES, I GENTLY PLACE BROOKE BACK into her crib. She rolls onto her side and sucks her thumb. I quietly step out of her nursery and close the door.

The hallway light allows me to see John splayed out on

the bed in nothing but his boxers. One leg is bent up while the other is cocked to the side. His arm is propped behind his head as he stares at the ceiling. My eyes roam his body. I bite my lip at what I see. I can't help it. I'm still so attracted to him. His boxers are low on his waist, but that isn't what catches my attention. It's the deep V that shapes his hips and dips into them. My mouth waters just looking at him. Stifling a groan, I feel my body coming to life as I remember what happened between us only a couple of hours earlier. John turns to look my way. I walk into the room, and he lifts the covers for me to climb into bed.

"Come on, sugar. Get into bed," he says. "Let me hold you."

John scoots behind me and wraps his arm around my stomach. He spoons me tight and nestles close. Inhaling, I draw him into my lungs and fall asleep in minutes, feeling safe and secure.

BRIGHT LIGHT STREAMS THROUGH MY BEDROOM WINDOW. Rolling over, I open my swollen, sleep-deprived eyes and glance at the clock. 7:12 a.m.

Then it hits me. Brooke. She didn't wake up again. Panic shoots through me. It's not like her to sleep through the second feeding. She usually wakes around six to have a bottle and then goes back to sleep. I can't stop the alarm that travels through my veins. I shoot out of bed and race to Brooke's room. Throwing open the door, I find she isn't in her crib. My heart drops into my stomach and nausea forms in my throat.

I sprint into the living room and stop dead in my

tracks. Chest heaving, my bones rattling from thinking the worst, I spot my daughter on Johnny's bare chest. She's curled up and sucking her thumb, a blanket covering them both. She's sleeping peacefully with John's tags clenched in her hand. She loves his tags. An empty baby bottle sits on the coffee table.

I'm overcome with emotion. She's in a deep sleep. John's hand looks so large on Brooke's small back. The air kicks on, and I see red lights in the corner of my eye. The baby monitor.

That's why I didn't hear Brooke wake. John must've taken it with him and put it next to the couch. I sniffle, and John's eyes open to meet mine. He presses a finger to his lips to silence me. I watch as John carefully sits up. He places both feet on the carpet and then scoots Brooke higher on his shoulder, draping the blanket over her. Pressing a hand to the back of Brooke's head and one under her butt, he stands in only his boxer shorts. Brooke is sound asleep as Johnny carries her to her room and places her in the crib.

I sit on the couch and lean forward to pick up the empty baby bottle. I wave it back and forth between my fingers, watching the leftover baby formula coat the inside. I always have formula on hand even though I nurse Brooke.

Last night was one of the most emotionally compelling nights of my life. Between Johnny getting Chad to sign over his parental rights, and then having sex again, it's a lot to take in. Now he's feeding Brooke and letting me sleep.

"Good morning, beautiful," John says, coming around the back of the couch. "Cupcake is sound asleep, which means you're all mine," he says, crawling over me. A smile tips my lips as I swivel and lie back. He lies on top of me and his erection presses into my lower stomach.

"Johnny," I say.

John groans, rolling his hips into mine. "When you say my name like that, it's hard for me to hold back from taking you. I love how you say it."

John grabs my lips with his in a no-surrender hold. He kisses me hard, and he kisses me good. He kisses me so I forget the world around me. I moan into his mouth and kiss him back with the same intensity.

Pulling away, he breathes against my mouth. John tips my chin up to meet his gaze, and my heart is racing a mile a minute. A small smile tugs at his mouth.

"I'm going to push past your walls and strip you down. Every chance I get, I'm going to be here." Arousal fills his gaze. "That was the last kiss you get."

Then he climbs off me, leaving me cold and needy.

I groan loudly. "You tease," I say.

His chuckle echoes down the hallway.

With John, it starts with a kiss. It was only a matter of time before I'd want more.

THIRTY-THREE

ALYSSA

Pulling out a plastic sack of breast milk, I place it on the counter.

"This is what I call liquid gold. You do not microwave it. Carefully pour the milk into a bottle, twist the nipple back on, and then heat it in a pot of hot water, not boiling. Warm it for a few minutes and then check it before—"

"Alyssa, I know how to check a bottle on my wrist before I give it to her." John gives me a droll stare. "I did feed her myself this morning. Plus, I helped my parents with my brothers."

This is only the second time that I'm leaving Brooke. She's been glued to my hip since the moment she was born. I know she will be okay and cared for, but my anxiety is through the roof. John suggested he stay home with her while I run errands with his truck. Brooke is out of diapers. I need some baby food and toiletries too. My initial reaction was to reject his offer, but I'm trying to be more trusting with him, and so I agreed. He even gave me money to get my nails done. It was so sweet of him, but I told him it wasn't necessary. I'd rather spend the cash picking us up takeout for dinner since we never eat out. I told him I'd likely buy an overpriced coffee.

"Okay, but do not ever put this in the microwave. It removes all the nutrients."

John picks up the frozen bag and examines it. "So boob juice is liquid gold. Got it." Wiggling his eyebrows, he says, "I bet I could pump out a lot of boob juice from you."

"Oh my God. You are so gross!" I laugh. "Please, for the love of all that is holy, do not spill it. How about I just fill the bottles for you before I leave?"

He shakes his head. "No. I can do it."

I take the bag from him and point to the top of it. "See this right here? All this darker, thick, creamy-looking stuff? It's essential. Sometimes, if it gets stuck, I'll heat it under running water to melt it off the sides, then pour it into a bottle. I'll nurse her one last time before I leave. She should be good for a few hours. My boobs are like rocks, and I need to get the milk out."

John's eyes drop to my chest then back to meet mine. "Just now?" he asks confusingly.

"Yes. Sometimes when she cries, it's like an automatic sensor that goes off and my boobs produce milk. Here, let me have her, and I'll feed her real quick."

Taking Brooke, I sit on the couch. I cuddle her to my chest. Her mouth opens, trying to latch on through my bra.

"Hang on, baby," I say softly. I'm about to lift my shirt when I remember John is standing there. I've never nursed in front of him before. Turning to look at him with a now fussy baby in my arms, I say, "Um, this is kind of awkward."

"What is?"

"You watching as I'm about to breastfeed."

"That's awkward to you after what we did last night?"

My cheeks flame, and my body comes to life thinking about what we shared. Judging by the impish smirk on John's face, he's thinking the same.

John tips his head to the side and just stares. "Would you rather I not look? I could turn around if you want."

I bite the inside of my lip. "No, it's okay, I guess."

"Cool. Because I kind of want to watch."

"Can you hand me the rag next to you, please?" John hands it to me, and I place it under my breast so the milk won't spill onto my clothes. "Thanks."

Unclipping my nursing bra, I pull down the material and Brooke immediately latches on. The first few tugs are always tender for me as she gulps hard. I lean back on the couch as I cradle Brooke to my chest. John sits close by, watching in fascination as she nurses.

"Does it hurt?" he asks.

I shake my head. "It feels a little weird, but my boob returns to normal once she starts drinking. It won't feel like a rock anymore." I reach for his hand and bring it to my hard breast. "Feel that?" I ask. John presses with his fingertips on one of the knots and then yanks his arm back. I laugh. "Now feel this," I say, and reach for his hand again, this time placing it on the soft breast that Brooke is drinking from. "See the difference?" He nods, unblinking.

After a few moments, Brooke slows down as her eyes roll shut. "Oh, no, you don't, baby," I whisper, reaching for the snap on the right side of my bra.

"What did she do?" John asks.

He's so close that I feel his breath on my neck.

"She almost always falls asleep when I nurse her. I need to switch her to the other side before she's out."

Sitting forward, I carefully flip Brooke to the other side. I cover myself up, then sit back and lean into John's side. He drapes his arm across the back of the couch and props his feet up on the coffee table. There's something about this that feels oddly natural. I can't put my finger on it. I rest my head on his chest. John sits with me through the feeding, watching quietly. When Brooke is finished, I stand, but he stops me.

"Can I hold her while she sleeps?" John asks.

"Are you sure?"

He nods. "I want to keep her beside me while I watch sports."

Be still my heart. He makes it so hard to resist him when he does things like this.

I hand Brooke off to John. She senses the change in her sleep because she immediately reaches for his tags and curls up against him. Our eyes meet in recognition. We smile at each other.

"She adores you," I tell him.

"What about her mom?" he asks.

Leaning down, I kiss his cheek. I try to pull back, but he stops me.

John stares up at me. "Uh-uh. Give me those lips," he says.

"I thought you said the last kiss I got was the last one."

"I lied."

JOHN

I HEAR THE KEYS JINGLE IN THE LOCK, AND I JUMP UP.

Alyssa has been gone for only a few hours, but I'm excited to see her. As she's walking in, I reach for the bags of groceries in her hands.

"Hey," I say, happy to see her.

Her eyes light up. "Hey. How's Brooke?"

I chuckle. "She's great. She's drooling all over the floor."

Alyssa asks me a few more questions regarding Brooke. She tells me a box of diapers is in the trunk, so I run out to get them. I don't know what she brought home for us for dinner, but the smell permeates the apartment and makes my stomach grumble. I help her put the items away.

"It's so hot out there. I feel like I need to shower after getting in and out of the truck," Alyssa says. "Do you mind if I take a quick rinse before we eat? I'm sweating."

Walking over to her, I pull her in for a hug. Alyssa leans into me and gives me a little squeeze. She tips her head back and smiles, then she drops her chin on my chest.

"Thanks for today."

My brows knit together. "Why are you thanking me?"

She shrugs. "I don't know. It was just a nice day, and I'm thankful for it. I don't mind bringing Brooke everywhere I go, but it was nice to have a break."

Leaning into her, I drop a quick kiss to her lips.

Brooke's baby babble echoes across the room. Alyssa steps away, but I grab her wrist. I can't get enough of her when she's nearby. I always want to touch her. Before she can escape, I move behind her and wrap my arm around her waist. I tug her to my front and drop my face to her neck. Alyssa moves her neck to the side, granting me access as I press my lips to her skin.

"Johnny," she whispers. "I'm all sweaty. I'm gross and sticky. What are you doing?"

"Just holding you for a minute."

"Why?"

"Why am I holding you?" I ask against her neck. She nods, and I shrug. "Just wanted to, I guess."

Planting one last kiss on the side of her neck, I let Alyssa go. I love the feel of her body against mine.

"Go. Get cleaned up. I'll be waiting."

Ten minutes later, Alyssa walks into the living room, a trail of something fruity following her in the wake. I get up, place Brooke in her playpen, and follow Alyssa into the kitchen.

My nose twitches. "You smell like melon."

She opens the plastic take-out bag and pulls out the containers. "I do?"

My eyes travel to her makeup-free face. I place a hand on her hip, twirl her around, and box her in. I lean down and inhale. My nose skims the curve of her neck. I don't know why I said she gets no more kisses. All I'm doing is torturing myself that way. I give her a quick peck, then pull back.

"Yup. Definitely melon."

She giggles. "It must be my body wash."

"Whatever it is, you smell delicious."

Her eyes twinkle with desire. My gaze drops, and I see her nipples grow hard. My palms skate around her hips. Bending my knees, I reach behind her thighs and lift her up to place her on the counter. I grab her face and kiss her deeply, stroking every inch of her mouth with my tongue. Her arms circle my neck, and her breasts push into my chest. She digs her heels into the back of my legs and scoots closer. Her fingers dig into my back, and I groan from how she kneads me. I want Alyssa to want me the way I want her. I delve aggressively and grab every part of her body I can touch. If she let me fuck her on the kitchen counter, I would right now.

"Do you think we should slow down?" she says, breaking the kiss with a gasp.

I groan loudly but in a playful way. Stepping back, I run my hand down my face and then help her from the table.

"I know you told me to push, but you aren't the only one being pushed. That's the second time you've pushed me away. This isn't easy on me either. You make me feel things in here," I say, pointing to the center of my chest. "I'm not asking for sex. I just want to feel you."

Incredulously, she asks, "How am I pushing you?"

"You're playing with my emotions. One minute, you're all over me—all hot and sexed up, nails digging into my back, your sweet body on mine—and the next, you're pushing me away. You're giving me whiplash. It's partially my fault, but it's hard for me to keep my hands off you."

I pause then mutter about how nothing good can come from a kiss.

"What did you say?" she asks.

"I said nothing good could come from a kiss. Those were your exact words. And you were right. Nothing good has come from it."

The anguish that cuts through her blue eyes makes me feel like shit. I'm not purposely trying to hurt Alyssa, but she needs to know the truth. Just because I'm a guy doesn't mean I don't have feelings.

"One night with you will never be enough, especially after last night. That's all I mean." I lower my voice so she knows I'm not yelling at her. I wish I could explain how I love being with her. "It took all of me not to tackle you to the floor. I see how you are with Brooke, and after I spent all day with her, I have more respect for you than ever. I honestly couldn't wait for you to come home. So, while I said I would keep my hands to myself, it's not as easy as I thought. You're beautiful and a good-hearted, caring mother. Babe, that's sexy as fuck. So last night was a mistake only because I want you more now, and I can't have you. It was a night I'll never forget and probably the best night of my life in a long time."

A deep red colors her cheeks. "Oh," she says.

"Oh?" I chuckle. "This is what's going to happen. We'll eat, watch a movie, and go to sleep together. And when Brooke wakes up in the middle of the night, I'll be the one to get up, not you."

"But you were with her all day."

"Babe, I got this. Now, let's eat and then crawl in bed together."

I want to be near her every chance I can.

THIRTY-FOUR

ALYSSA

I can't remember the last time I slept so soundly. I could get used to this.

I open my sleepy eyes and glance at the clock. 7:00 a.m. I groan inwardly. Brooke isn't even crying. My body is on autopilot.

A strong arm wraps around my waist and tugs. "You're not going anywhere," Johnny grumbles in my ear. He curves around my body, molding himself to me and burying his head in my hair. The heat of his body warms my back. I like being snuggled up next to John. He's like a giant teddy bear. John grabs the blanket and pulls it up. "Shh… Go back to sleep. It's so early for a Sunday."

A soft chuckle rolls off my lips. "This is kind of late for me. Once Brooke wakes for a bottle, I never go back to sleep. I'm wide awake after."

"I already took care of that," he mumbles, and kisses my shoulder. "Brooke took a whole bottle of boob juice and then fell back asleep. She's in her crib."

Speechless, I don't know what to say other than, "Wow. Thank you."

"You're welcome. Now go back to sleep."

"I won't be able to go back to sleep now," I tell him.

"Yes, you can. Just close your eyes."

"You're so bossy sometimes." I giggle.

"Sugar, you haven't seen me bossy. Being bossy would mean I'd take you all sleepy and tired right now. I'd lay you flat on your back and just work my way, nice and slow. Hell, you don't even have to move, I can work it just like this," he says in a husky voice, demonstrating the movements against me.

My body relaxes as I picture him doing it, sliding in and out as he takes his time.

"Your body is so soft and warm right now. I love it," he groans as he slips his hand under my shirt. John's knee nudges between my thighs and sandwiches our legs together. He's wrapped so firmly around me, holding me, and I love it. Dear God, I love every minute of this.

John shifts and wraps his ankles around me, locking me in. We're bound so closely together now. My nipples harden as the tips of his fingers graze the underside of my breasts. My body goes into overdrive, heat spreading through me. He caresses me slowly, gently thrusting his hips against mine as his fingers tease me. My body melts into his. His fingers graze over my breast and I shudder in his hold. He circles my nipple in a feathery, soft touch, and my breathing grows more profound. John continues his torture, moving to my other breast and showing it the same attention. I arch my chest into his touch, and a gasp of pleasure leaves my lips.

"Again," I say softly. "Do it again, please."

"Do what? This?" he asks and pinches my nipple harder, this time not letting up.

My legs scissor between his, but he locks them down and doesn't allow me to move. I struggle in his hold, and it takes me higher to be restrained. Little sounds of desire escape my throat. My head presses into the pillow as I let out a long moan. Breathing hard, my chest rising fast, John moves his hand to cup my pussy.

"Fuck, you're soaked."

I feel a coolness against my chest and peer down. I notice a wet spot on my shirt and realize I'm leaking milk. I'm slightly embarrassed.

"Shit. I'm leaking."

John rolls his hips against mine and groans under his breath.

"Want me to stop?" he asks. I shake my head. "Good, because I wasn't planning on it."

Our hips move against each other's, his dick sliding up and down my plump ass. We're at the perfect angle for him to slide in from behind if we weren't wearing clothes. John slips his fingers into the tiny opening of my shorts, and I bite down on my bottom lip when his fingers delve between my pussy lips. Pleasure soars through me.

"Fuck," he groans when he feels my naked flesh. "You're not wearing panties. Are you trying to kill me?"

As I giggle, his fingers slide between my wet lips. My giggle turns to a moan when John begins stroking me with determination. I try to roll into him to give him better access, but he still holds me. He slides up and down to my opening with two fingers but never slips inside.

"Johnny," I say, my voice breathless. "Take me, please."

"No."

I still in his hold, and when I do, he rubs my clit in circles. John's hips are thrusting against me.

"What? Why not?" I can barely get the words out.

"Because I said no."

"But, John, I need—"

"You need this?"

He begins stroking me so fast that my hips pump into his hand. He bites down on my shoulder and circles my clit simultaneously. An orgasm quickly tingles up my spine. I gyrate against him, needing more. He continues rolling my clit between his fingers.

"Or do you need my cock in you?"

"Ahh," I moan.

His voice is rough as he says, "Say you need me. Say it, or I stop."

"I need you," I beg.

Quickly, he rolls onto his back and lifts his hips. He strips himself of his boxers and then rises up on his knees in front of me. He pulls my shorts off, then he spreads my thighs open to kneel between them. John spits into his hand and uses his saliva as lubrication to stroke his cock. Palming it, he drags the tip up and down my pussy, teasing me so good. He runs circles around my clit and opening with his cock.

"Tell me to stop."

I shake my head. "Fuck me."

John stills. He looks into my eyes, seeking clarification.

"What did you say?"

"I want you to fuck me, Johnny."

"Do you realize what you're saying?" he asks.

I nod. John doesn't waste a second and plunges inside. My body contracts, and I grit my teeth. John pulls back and surges inside again. I gasp in divine pleasure.

"We could always wake up like this if you let us be."

He's rough, and I like it. He pushes his cock in, then he slowly pulls it out. He pushes in again and fills me up.

"I told you I'm going to do whatever it takes for you to see I'm not going anywhere."

He takes my mouth in an all-possessive, heart-stopping kiss. He kisses me, stroking my tongue as he fucks me with his cock.

He groans again. "I want to come inside of you."

The thought makes my pussy contract. He grips my hips and pumps into me.

"Yes," I sigh.

"I was made for your body," he whispers against my neck. "We fit perfectly together." John's hand slides down my waist and over my mound. He teases my clit, and I nearly see stars. I clench my eyes shut, trying to hold back the orgasm clinging to me.

"Feel how I slide in perfectly."

I moan, my impending orgasm coming close to peaking. I squeeze my legs wrapped around his hips at the incredible feeling soaring through me. I'm burning. I'm on fire and ready to explode.

"More, give me more, Johnny."

John's hips pick up speed, thrusting in and out at a pace that kills me. I need more. I want more. I want him to be rough with me. I think it's what I need.

His hands slide up my stomach, kneading my body as he does, until he reaches my face. He cups my cheek, turns my head toward his, and captures my lips. We both moan at the contact, heat spearing through us and tying us around each other. My shirt has wet spots on it. I worry he'll find it gross. I'm shocked and too damn aroused when he leans down, rips my shirt off me, and then tugs a nipple into his mouth. My pussy sings, and I start trembling under him. He moans, his hips pistoning into me. His teeth score my tender skin, and it has me panting.

"I taste your milk," he says, and I blush.

Then he kisses me senseless. His cock carries us over the edge, and Johnny unloads inside me. His cock jerks and twitches. My orgasm tears through me and I sigh in bliss. His body stiffens as his hips take me exactly how I want him to. I let a long breath roll off my lips. John pulls out and falls beside me. His cock flops onto his thigh. He's breathing as heavily as I am.

Kissing my temple, he says, "Think you can go back to sleep now?"

My chuckle is my answer. I'm too busy floating back to reality.

I roll over and curl up to John's side. I throw a leg over his and relax into him as he embraces me. We're sticky, and my breasts are leaking, but I don't care. As much as I've tried to fight my chemistry with John, it's hard. I don't know why I'm fighting it when we blend well. I thought I was weak, but he showed me how strong I am. He's been there for me countless times, proving himself repeatedly. He also gives mind-blowing orgasms.

My eyes roll shut as I feel my body falling. I want to fight John off and tell him no, but I can't. It's pointless when, deep down, I love him.

Yawning, I stretch my arms above my head. My muscles are tight, and my back aches. I can't believe I fell back asleep.

My body warms as I think about what we did. Johnny. His fingers. His dirty mouth. And the pleasure he brought me. A content sigh rolls off my lips, and I smile dreamily. Sleeping in and waking to the smell of bacon and coffee. This is something I could get used to.

I roll out of bed and stroll into the bathroom, where I quickly brush my teeth and throw water on my face. Looking in the mirror, I see the puffiness under my eyes is still there but not as noticeable, thanks to John and the extra sleep I've been able to get. I grab a hair tie and throw my hair into a messy bun before proceeding to the kitchen. I spot Brooke in her high chair shoveling a teething biscuit into her mouth, her little feet kicking in excitement when she sees me.

"How's my little girl?"

At the sound of my voice, my daughter squeals.

Unclipping Brooke, I lift her up and bring her to my chest. Her little arms wrap around my neck. She leans forward and tries to give me kisses Brooke style—open-mouthed and slobber everywhere. I chuckle at her attempt and kiss her cheek. Brooke rests her head on my shoulder. I give her one more squeeze then place her back in her seat before making eye contact with John.

Blood rushes down my cheeks. I suddenly feel shy under his gaze. He's standing in the kitchen, shirtless with his impeccable body, frying bacon.

"Hey," I say softly, biting my bottom lip.

"Mornin'," he says, looking over his shoulder. His green eyes sparkle in the light, and one corner of his mouth tugs up. John turns around and leans against the counter, his stomach flexing and his hands resting on the edge behind him.

"Sleep well?" he asks.

"Very well. Thank you." I smile. "When did you wake up?"

"About an hour ago."

"I was completely out. I didn't hear you or Brooke at all," I say, moving toward him. "Kind of scary how deep I slept."

Stopping just inches from him, I rise on my tiptoes and hover in front of his mouth. He leans down so I can kiss his lips. I pull back, but he's not done yet. John snakes his arm out and wraps it around my waist. He pulls me to him, grips my chin with his other hand, and kisses my mouth hard. He pulls back with a smack.

"Now, that's how you say mornin'."

An easy smile graces my face. "What did you make?"

"Bacon and eggs. I have coffee for you too. I wasn't sure if Brooke could eat this stuff, so I just gave her some baby food like yesterday."

My heart softens at John's thoughtfulness. "Only baby food for her now."

"Grab a seat, and I'll get you a plate."

"Here, let me help," I say, reaching for the cabinet door.

"No, I got it. Get your ass in the chair."

"John, I can help you."

"Babe, I know you can, but let me do this for you."

"Okay, bossy man."

The grin that lights up John's face warms me all over.

He slides a cup of coffee over to me and then sits. "Do you have any plans for the day?"

I give him a bland stare. "No. I'll do some things around the apartment, but if you mean to go out, no. I don't have many friends right now."

"So my brother and his girlfriend are in South Fork. My mom wants us all together for an early dinner. She invited us. She wants to see you and Brooke. It's not too bad of a drive."

I hesitate. I last saw Diane and Clark before the paternity test results. I'm worried how they'll feel about everything.

"Johnny…" I begin, and he silences me with a kiss.

It's a slow, methodical kiss that sends my blood roaring. My tongue entwines with his, melding my heart to him even more. A squeal breaks our moment. We pull away at the same time and look at Brooke. She's squeezing her now smashed cookie in both fists with a big smile, her two bottom teeth showing.

"What do you say, babe? You coming with me or what?"

I blink rapidly a few times. John and his damn kisses.

"Okay."

John laughs. Tilting my head to the side, I ask, "What's so funny?"

"I've noticed any time I ask you a question and kiss you, you answer it with an 'okay.'"

"I do?"

He nods his head and smiles.

"Well, if you would stop kissing me, then maybe I

could think straight." I joke as I wipe the food from my daughter's hands.

"Can't help it. I love your lips. Let's eat and then get ready and head on over there in about an hour or so since we have a little drive. Mama said she wanted to talk to you."

Anxiety curls inside my stomach. What could Diane want to talk to me about?

"Why?" I ask, looking over my shoulder to John.

"I'm not sure, but she's been blowing up my phone, saying she wants to see Brooke again."

A stupid amount of joy floods me. I'm so happy one of her grandmas wants to see her.

"There's that look again. What's wrong?" he asks.

I shrug. Quietly, I say, "Does she know that Brooke isn't… you know?"

I deflate. Shame washes over me. I can't even say the words.

"Babe. Brooke is mine. I don't know what you're talking about."

Emotion climbs behind my eyes. I blink back the tears.

"She knows how I feel about you, how I've always felt about you. She wants to see me happy, and you make me happy. You and cupcake."

"I'm nervous," I admit.

"Don't be. I'll be right by your side the whole time."

I nod quietly. "Thank you."

"For what?

"For yesterday. This morning. Everything."

"I told you I wasn't leaving. Maybe you'll start believing me soon."

Those were John's favorite last words.

THIRTY-FIVE

ALYSSA

I'm a giant ball of nerves as we pull up to John's parents' house with a sleepy Brooke later in the afternoon.

I gently lift her from her car seat while John grabs her diaper bag, and we walk to the door.

"Just breathe," he tells me.

I expel a breath. As if it's so easy. "How did you know?"

"I can feel the tension radiating off of you."

John knocks twice and then opens the door to a home I always wanted—a family with loving parents who accept their children and their faults. The scent of peaches awakens my senses, and I feel a sense of ease.

"My son is home. I've missed you. You look so much bigger," Diane says as she embraces John. She gives him a peck on his cheek.

Diane brings her hands together and turns to me with a kind smile that settles my nerves.

"Alyssa. How are you, my dear? Where's my little pumpkin?"

Before I can answer, Brooke opens her sleepy eyes and reaches for Diane.

"May I?" she asks.

"Of course."

I hand off Brooke to Diane. She walks into another room singing to my daughter. I'm a little stunned. I don't know what to think. I thought there would be some hidden animosity, but there isn't.

As if he read my mind, John says, "I told you."

I elbow him playfully.

A raspy voice echoes around the corner. "Is that my little brother, I hear?"

Coming around the corner is who I presume to be Luke. John's face lights up at the sight of his brother.

"What's up?"

The brothers clasp hands and embrace each other.

"Long time no see."

"Yeah, that's because you're touring the world and shit," John says, beaming from ear to ear.

Luke grins. I can tell right off that he's a charismatic guy. "What can I say? I'm a wanted man."

"Hey now, settle down," a woman says, joining us in the living room.

"Hey, Livy," John says.

She steps up next to Luke and smiles. "Good to see you."

John introduces us, then Olivia turns toward me and says, "Brooke is so adorable."

My face lights up. "Thank you."

"Come on. Let's get a drink," Luke suggests.

John follows his brother outside to the cooler, while I stay inside with Olivia and Diane.

"I could sure use some sweet tea. Would you like a glass?" Olivia asks me.

"Yes, please."

I walk into the kitchen, where Diane gives Brooke a small piece of mashed banana. "She was cryin' for it," Diane explains, shrugging her shoulders like she has no control over a baby. "I told her she needed to wait until dinner, but she wasn't having it."

"It's okay. She's getting ready to move up to the next stage of baby food."

"It's only a matter of time before she's eating dirt," Diane says.

Olivia hands me a glass. I take a sip and wonder if I'm drinking straight sugar water.

"Olivia likes her tea extra sweet," Diane says.

I smile. "Tastes good to me."

"How is South Carolina treating you?" Diane asks.

I shrug. "It's nice, I guess. I don't go out much, but that's because I didn't realize how tired I'd be from staying busy with Brooke. It was an adjustment, that's for sure, but I like it."

"Once you get a bit more situated, you'll be able to get out more."

I nod. I'm not in a rush. I prefer to be home with my baby, where it's safe. But I don't tell her that.

"All John talks about is Brooke. I couldn't wait to see her."

My brows rise. "He does?"

Diane nods. "All the time. He's obsessed and proud. He called to tell me she's crawling."

Be still my damn heart.

Diane looks at my daughter, who is trying to give her sloppy, wet kisses.

"Johnny's been so good to me and Brooke. I don't know what I would do without him."

"The Jackson brothers have big hearts. There's no stopping them once they find something or someone they love. They're in it for the long haul. So what he's doing just comes naturally to him," Olivia says. "Luke is the same way. Things happen for a reason, so don't question it. He's there because he wants to be," she adds.

Hope flourishes inside my heart. Saying John is dedicated is an understatement. That man has proven himself time and time again when I never asked him to. Sure, I've been scared of losing someone who means so much to me, but I'm not testing him.

"Couldn't have put it better myself," Diane says. "Though, I could smack Luke upside the head for taking so long to finally go after you."

Olivia laughs. "I always have that feeling, but about so many other things."

"I'm sure," Diane drawls.

"What did Luke take so long with?" I ask, curious.

"Luke and Olivia grew up together. By high school, they were dating and then continued into college. After college, he just let her walk away!" Diane exclaims, her hand flying in the air.

My brows lift. I look at Olivia. "He did?"

"Kind of, but not really. I hurt Luke by not telling him my plans to continue my education. I didn't tell anyone I was applying to medical school out of fear of being rejected. I kept it a secret until it was all finalized, which was so stupid thinking back on it now. I should have told him, but I didn't, and it backfired. Once he found out, he refused to compromise, so I left." Olivia shakes her head, the smile fading from her eyes. "I don't blame him. I would've been hurt too and probably done the same." She shrugs. "It's all over now, and we're together like we should've been from the beginning. That's all that matters. Sometimes you have to take the good with the bad and deal with it as best you can."

"You really think that it was meant to happen?" I ask. "That you guys were supposed to separate?"

"I do. What's meant to happen will find its way. It always does. And it did."

I think about what Olivia said for a moment and then of John.

"Luke wouldn't have turned to music, and he wouldn't have the career he has now. Music saved us," Olivia says.

I smile, blushing. "I heard some of the songs he wrote about you. They're really sweet."

The sound of sliding doors breaks the conversation, and I look over my shoulder to see John walking toward me with an empty water bottle in his hand. His face lights up, dimples and all showing. John makes my heart beat fast every time I look at him. He walks right up to me, wraps an arm around my shoulders, and kisses my temple as he tugs me to him. Olivia and Diane watch, and it makes my cheeks burn. He goes to hold me from behind, and Brooke begins fussing.

John smiles at Brooke. "Aw, is my little cupcake jealous I have her mommy?" he asks, walking over to her.

Brooke reaches for John, nearly jumping out of Diane's arms. She leans in for a Brooke kind of kiss, then rests her head on the curve of his neck. Her tiny hand runs along John's neck, searching for his tags. He pulls them out of his shirt and hands them to Brooke. She begins rubbing them between her fingers as if they soothe her. John rubs her back gently and moves back to me. Olivia and Diane stand silently watching, their heads tilted to the side.

"When's dinner ready, Ma? I'm starved."

"Now!" She jumps up. "Let's eat," she says enthusiastically.

We begin walking to the dining room, but Olivia places a hand on my arm, stopping me. Looking me straight in the eyes, Olivia says, "I know we don't know each other very well, and I hope that changes one day, but I need to say something."

"Okay…" I say hesitantly.

"Don't question why John does what he does, Alyssa. It's clear how he feels about you and Brooke. Luke told me about you guys. Just that small interaction in the kitchen shows how head over heels in love with you and your daughter he is. It's adorable. Sometimes we don't see what's right before us until it's too late. Don't make the same mistake I did and shut him out. The Jackson brothers are good men," she says, squeezing my arm and walking away, leaving me speechless.

After dinner, Brooke bounces joyfully on Olivia's knees while I help clear the table. John walks outside with Clark and Luke to talk. Being in John's home with his family makes me long for a family of my own one day just like this. My father is long gone, and my mother has disowned me. I've been abandoned by my only family, yet this one took me in and didn't even bat an eye.

"Have you considered going back to college?" Diane asks me.

"I have, but I can't afford daycare, so I can't right now. Maybe one day."

"What about your mother? Is she around to help?"

"She refuses to speak to me. So, no."

Diane spins around, soapy water dripping from her hands. "What do you mean, sweetie? I thought she was past that."

I shake my head. "She hasn't seen Brooke yet."

Diane's eyes nearly pop out of her head. She doesn't say much other than she's sorry. Her shoulders sag in sadness.

Once we're finished, I check on Brooke. She's sleeping peacefully in Olivia's arms. A full belly and some play time will have her napping for at least an hour. I return to the kitchen, and it's just Diane and me.

"Do you need help with anything else?" I ask.

"Oh, you've been such a dear. Everything is pretty much cleaned up. All I need to do is stick the pie in the oven to heat it up." She pauses. "Actually, I want to ask you something."

Anxiety rolls through my stomach. This must be what John was talking about this morning.

"I want you to hear me out and think about what I say before you disagree," she says, and my eyes widen. "How would you feel about allowing me to keep Brooke one weekend a month? Clark and I gave it a lot of thought last night, and I would really like to do it for you. I can only offer one weekend a month right now until I see how I can handle a baby all day with MS, but maybe I could take on more for you down the line. We miss having babies around and would love to have Brooke. You could bring her to me on Friday and pick her up on Sunday."

I blink, and blink, and blink. I'm silent. I don't know what to say. All I know is that my emotions are running in opposite directions because I'm so overwhelmed by Diane's kindness. I don't want to cry, but tears balance on my eyelids. She walks over to give me a hug.

"I'm sorry," I whisper. "I wasn't expecting that. It's really nice of you. I'd love that, and I know Brooke would too."

John too. It makes my heart feel good knowing how happy it would make him. I swallow back the lump that was sitting in my throat. My own mother had never shown unconditional love to me the way Diane has, and it's a lot to take in.

"I raised four rowdy boys. What's one more? A little MS isn't going to slow me down." She winks at me.

I smile so big my cheeks hurt. Once again, the Jackson's big-heartedness hits me hard.

THIRTY-SIX

JOHN

I mimic Luke's pose and cross my legs in front of me and rest back in the wicker chair. I just finished telling him about what happened with Chad and the custody papers.

"Wow." He whistles. "Gotta say, I wasn't expecting that from you."

"She's been through a lot. I just want her to be happy."

Luke nods his head in agreement. "That's a cute kid in there. You seem pretty attached."

I look at my brother with an ear-to-ear grin. "I am. She's got me wrapped around her sticky finger."

"And Alyssa is okay with this?"

I chuckle. "Depends on what time of the day you ask her."

Luke looks at me, and I answer the question written on his face without him having to ask it. "She thinks I'm just going to up and leave if it gets to be too much. She doesn't want that for Brooke. I've told her a thousand times I'm not going anywhere. I think she's finally starting to see it."

"You're young, man. You sure you want this kind of responsibility?" Luke asks, his brows raised high.

"There isn't a doubt in my mind, Luke. She's everything to me."

"And you're a million percent sure? Because there's a kid involved. You can't mess around like that. That baby will get hurt more than you two will."

Isn't that the same thing Alyssa has been telling me? Why doesn't anyone believe me when I say I'm not going anywhere? I love her. And I love Brooke.

"Put yourself in my shoes. What if that were Livy? What would you do?"

Luke takes a swig of his beer. "No question about it. Livy is everything to me and always has been. You know this. I lost her once. I won't lose her again. I refuse. I'd do anything to keep her."

"Now you know what I'm talking about. I may not have lost Alyssa the way you did Livy, but I did lose a little bit of her spirit. She was hurt. I'm trying to restore her."

"I guess I'd be doing what you're doing, then." Luke pauses. He looks at me. "Is she okay?" he asks, and I know he's referring to Alyssa's sexual assault. I had shared my suspicions with him but never confirmed them. I made a promise to Alyssa the truth would stay between us.

I bob my head. "She will be in time."

Luke's quiet for a moment. "Glad to see you've changed. Thought I was going to lose you there."

Sadness creeps through my body. I thought I was losing myself too.

"Nah, I'm too stubborn to leave this world early. Plus,

seeing what I have"—I shake my head—"I never want to leave. I wish I could stay with my cupcake all the time."

Luke rears back. "Cupcake? Dude." He huffs out a laugh. "I don't want to know what you call Alyssa behind closed doors."

I bark out a laugh. It feels good talking with my older brother. "That's what I call Brooke, you ass."

"Man. Who are you, and what have you done with my brother?"

I chuckle. "Find the right girl, and she can change everything."

"Cheers to that."

Standing up, I walk into the kitchen to get another water bottle and overhear the women talking. I chose not to drink so I could safely drive us back to South Carolina.

"You'll take what?" I ask, walking into the kitchen. I stop where Alyssa is sitting and drape an arm over her shoulders.

"Alyssa here has just agreed to let me watch Brooke one weekend a month."

I look down at Alyssa, shocked. "Is that so?" I ask, and she nods, smiling. "You're okay with my mom watching Brooke the whole weekend?"

"I am."

"Do you have any idea how much she loves babies?"

Alyssa smiles wider and bobs her head. I lean forward and kiss her forehead then wrap my arms around her back. I tug her to me. I love Alyssa a little more and more each day. It's killing me not to tell her, but I don't want to scare her off when I just got her back in my life.

"Speaking of Brooke, where is my little girl?" I ask.

"She's asleep in Olivia's arms. I offered to take her, but she insisted on holding her."

We walk into the living room. Brooke is sound asleep, sprawled out on Olivia, with her thumb hanging out of her mouth.

"Hey now! Don't get any ideas," Luke says to Olivia as he sits beside her. "I want you all to myself before we start popping out little hellions."

"But Luke," Olivia whines. "How cute is she? Look at her chunky thighs. The little rolls." Olivia picks up her foot and shows Luke, who shakes his head.

"I'm sure Alyssa wouldn't mind letting you babysit when you suddenly have baby fever. Until then, you're all mine."

Luke throws an arm around Olivia's shoulder. He carefully pulls her to him and kisses her cheek. The love between Olivia and Luke is felt all around the room.

"So, are you two finally tying the knot, then?" I ask.

Olivia looks up but doesn't answer. She purses her lips together and elbows Luke playfully.

"Luke knows I would be his wife in a heartbeat. He just won't ask me."

Luke barks out a laugh. "How can I ask you when you remind me all the time? It has to be a surprise, baby."

"Aw, come on, Luke. Put a ring on it." I wiggle my eyebrows.

"She reminds you?" Clark asks.

"No, I don't!" Olivia denies.

"She leaves magazines flipped open to pictures of rings that she likes. As if I don't know what she's doing."

Clark tries to keep a straight face. "She does?"

"And flowers that she likes." Luke grins like a fool. "She has it all planned out. All she's missing is the groom."

With an exaggerated sigh, Olivia says, "I take back everything nice I have ever said about you. I don't want to marry you now."

"Well, that's good because I never asked."

"Luke Jackson!" Mom hisses.

"I'm just playin', Ma. Calm down." Looking at our father, Luke says, "Dad, tell her to relax, will ya?"

"Relax, sugar." Dad turns to my mom.

Olivia pinches Luke's arm and glares at him. "You take that back, Luke."

"Nope." She pinches him harder, and Luke winces with a grin.

"Well, as much as I'd love to watch you two lovebirds, we need to hit the road soon. We have a few hours of driving ahead of us, and I want to spend as much time with my girls as possible before I have to go back to training tomorrow."

THIRTY-SEVEN

ALYSSA

Looking into the mirror, I hook an earring into my ear.

Four months have passed since that day at John's parents' house, and everything is going well between me and John. Almost too well. I'm worried that something will cause strife between us, but nothing has. Once I stopped doubting life, John was everything he said he would be— my strength, my rock, a father to my daughter, and most of all, my other half.

I love him so much. I haven't told him yet, but I want to. I think he loves me too. He just hasn't said it yet.

I contacted my mother, but she declined any kind of relationship. She told me she wasn't ready and then hung up the phone. She's upset because she wanted more for me, but I have more than I could have asked for. Brooke is the light in my life. I never knew how much joy a child could bring until she was born, which makes it hard to understand my mother's rejection. The pain is still fresh, but John works to erase it every chance. I hope one day she'll come around.

Just thinking about John makes my heart soar so high. He's a true gift I didn't know I needed in my life. He's my best friend, my confidant. I'm so caught up in John that I can't imagine my life without him.

When the anniversary of Jace's death came, John had a rough few days. Leading up to it and then after. I made sure to be his rock while he relived that tragic night. We drove down to South Fork so John could visit Maryanne and Ford, and Brooke and I stayed with Diane. That night when he returned to his mom's house, I had never seen him so drained. We stayed in his old room. John collapsed on me and quietly cried. He was suffering. He's still grieving, and I imagine will for a long time.

I stare at myself in the mirror. Curls cascade down my back, and I'm wearing a smoky eye and nude lipstick. I slip into a black satin dress and matching high heels, and I'm ready to go. The eye makeup and black dress make my blue eyes pop. I can't remember the last time I felt this beautiful.

Today is Olivia and Luke's wedding, and I'm attending it with John. Luke proposed soon after we saw them. From what I was told, Olivia wanted more time to plan her wedding, but Luke wanted to marry her as soon as possible, so he hired wedding planners to get the ball rolling. When I asked Olivia how the proposal happened, she smiled dreamily and said, "It's a story for another day."

The bathroom door opens, and John saunters in, wearing a form-fitting tux and looking more attractive than ever. My jaw actually drops at the sight of him. Desire hits me hard. I remember the first day I met him. He was covered in dirt and riding a four-wheeler with Jace by his side. I smile. A lot has happened since then.

"What are you smiling about?" he asks, kissing my forehead.

"Just thinking about the first day we met."

John grins. "You were so reluctant to get dirty that I made it my mission to get you as filthy as possible."

"I knew you did!" I laugh. I slap his chest playfully. "Your persistence paid off."

John grabs my waist and pulls me close so we're inches apart. I grin. His hands skim down my back and over my butt. He presses his hips into me and groans.

"You're not allowed to wear this dress."

"What? Why?"

"Because you look so damn good I could eat you." John wiggles his eyebrows and grins. "Turn around so I can see how you look."

I spin around slowly, and John whistles in approval. "I'm going to need you to change, babe. You look too damn good. I don't want to fight anyone who looks at you. You look stunning."

I flatten my hands on his lapel and say, "Johnny, whose bed am I in at the end of the night?"

He grins. "Mine."

"And who's the most amazing father my daughter could have?"

"Me."

"Who's my best friend…with benefits?" I chuckle.

He lifts a brow and yanks me to him. "It better be just me, babe," he mutters against my lips.

"Who has the ability to render me speechless with just a kiss, making me forget everything around me?"

311

This time John's dimples appear with his grin. "I do?"

"Sure do. Each time."

"Is that so?" he says before kissing me. Thanks to my high heels, I easily wrap my arms around John's neck. "As much as I would love to continue, we need to get going. I can't wait to be alone with you tonight. The things I'm going to do to you." He trails off.

I shiver. I can only imagine.

"I want a love like that," I whisper as I watch Luke and Olivia dance to their wedding song. He holds her close and focuses solely on her. Two hearts beating as one. It's a beautiful moment between them that I almost feel like I'm intruding.

"Dance with me," John says, putting his hand out.

"Go," Diane says when I look over my shoulder at a sleeping Brooke in her stroller. "I'll watch Brooke sleep."

"Are you sure?"

"Positive. Go dance, sweetie."

Before I can respond, John pulls me onto the dance floor and spins me around to his chest. He wraps an arm around my lower back and embraces me intimately, chest to chest, cheek to cheek, and lets out a satisfied breath. We begin swaying slowly to the music in the background. I fit perfectly against him.

He dips his chin close to my ear. "I love you, Alyssa," he says as we sway. I draw in a breath and squeeze his shoulder. "I love you so much. You're my heart, and so is Brooke. There isn't a minute that goes by when I don't think of you both. After watching my brother and Livy

312

tonight, I want it all. You're what I want. You and Brooke Elyse. Say you're mine forever." My heart is hammering against my ribs. "Seeing my brother and Livy tonight made me realize I want that with you one day. I want us. But if you don't see more for us, I need to know so I stop pushing for something that isn't there for you. I'll never stop loving you or being there for Brooke, but I need to know if you see me in your future."

I swallow thickly. Pulling back, I look into his green eyes. "I want what you want. I want the same thing for us. I love you, Johnny."

His jaw falls open. His eyes widen, and I know he's shocked to hear me say those three little words.

"You do?" he asks.

I nod. "Yes."

"You swear?" he asks once more.

"I love you so much it scares me," I tell him.

"I want all of your heart, not just a fraction. No more friends-with-benefits shit. You're mine, and I'm yours. That's it."

I'm smiling from ear to ear and nod my head feverishly. "You're mine. I want us. I want a man who will love me at my worst. I want a man who will love my daughter as his own, and you do, Johnny. You do that and so much more. You're a father to Brooke, which means more to me than anything else."

His eyes grow dark, his lips an inch away from mine. "I am her father, Alyssa."

"You are. You really are."

I choke up. John is Brooke's father in every sense of the word.

"So this is it. No going back." A grin spreads across

John's face. "No going back. Because I don't know if I could deal with not having you."

Tears fill my eyes. I smile so big my cheeks hurt. "No going back."

I stand on my tiptoes and press my mouth to his, breathing in his goodness. Wrapping my arms around his neck, I slant my head and kiss him hard. John uses the opening to slide his tongue along the seam of my parted lips. His tongue meets mine, but this time it's different. The kiss is different because we are fully devoted to each other now, heart and soul. No going back. Warmth spreads throughout my body, and we moan into each other, our kissing picking up speed as we devour each other like it's our last night on earth. I'm his, all his.

"I'm yours, Johnny. Forever. You're my family now. You and Brooke."

"I love you," he says, making my heart flutter.

"And I love you. I should've told you the first time you said it to me," I tell him. "I regretted not saying it." He angles his head, and I answer his unasked question. "It was the night of the accident. We'd just returned from the hospital and were lying in my bed."

He kisses my forehead. "Repeat it now, and you're forgiven."

My eyes light up and I giggle. "I love you, Johnny."

"Once more for good measure."

I look deep into his eyes and say, "I love you so much."

He grins so big I feel his happiness. John is a sweet-talking, rough around the edges country boy. Who'd ever guess that the city girl in me would fall so hard?

John and I are inseparable for the rest of the night. At times, we hold Brooke and dance with her, but when it slows down, it's just the two of us. Diane doesn't mind staying with our daughter while we fall more in love. John never takes his eyes off me, proving how much he loves and wants me. Not that John needs to. I know he does.

He makes me whole.

Yesterday may be gone, but tomorrow is a new day. I have a guy who loves me and my daughter unconditionally. Most men consider babies baggage, but John jumped right on the boat as if it were meant to be.

And maybe it was.

EPILOGUE

JOHN

The drive down to South Fork is quiet and somber. Brooke had long fallen asleep in the back seat of the truck. Alyssa sits beside me with her feet propped up on the dashboard and her seat laid back. My thumb circles her open palm while her other hand rests on her growing belly. Her hair billows in the wind as she stares at the passing trees.

She's pregnant with my baby this time. A boy.

It's been three years since Jace left this world, and not a single day goes by that I don't miss my friend. His death is still raw. Time hasn't made it easier; I've just learned to live with it. I have a feeling I'm going to be mourning his loss for the rest of my life.

I often visit Jace's Facebook page just to look at old photos and videos to relive the good times we had together. I scroll through posts and read each one, sometimes even dropping a line on the page myself. I know I should stop, but I can't. I miss him so fucking much.

Once things settled down, Alyssa returned to college at night and received a Bachelor of Science degree. She wants to be a nurse. Alyssa told me she wanted a job that would always be in demand and one where she could help others. I knew her need for stability was a result of her upbringing. After speaking with Olivia about what to expect in the medical field, Alyssa is now set to take her registered nursing license in a few months, right before our baby is born.

I let up on the gas a little, my heart slowing as I approach the place that cost Jace his life. The tree now has a rope of silk flowers wrapped around it that has faded due to the sun. Right next to it is his remembrance cross with fresh flowers that Maryanne replaces every couple of weeks. A presence surrounds me. I swear I can feel him. It's the same feeling that appeared when I did nine months of deployment this past year when an explosion happened just a couple of feet away from me. My life flashed before my eyes again. That day, I knew I'd been spared because of Jace.

Why did he have to go? Why did that tree have to be there? If only he hadn't reached for his cell. If only I hadn't asked Alyssa to call Jace. The same what-ifs play through my mind every time I'm in town. If only I could turn back time. I wipe my eyes and look in the rearview mirror at the white cross-shaped sign behind me. My chest tightens, and my heart aches for my friend.

A few minutes later, I pull into the cemetery and park the truck. I step out and go around to the passenger side to help Alyssa out. I love watching her belly grow with my son. I spoil her and shower her with love every minute of the day. Reaching into the back, I lift a sleeping Brooke to my chest and then close the door.

"Daddy?" she says groggily.

I rub her back. "Shh. Let Mommy hold you for a minute."

"No," she wines and throws her arms around my neck. I shrug. Brooke is a daddy's girl through and through.

"Ready?" Alyssa asks, and I nod.

"Well then, come on, baby, let's go see Jace," she says and slips her hand into mine. She always knows when I need her most without saying a word.

Damn, how I love this girl.

Hand in hand, we stroll down the aisle, passing dozens of headstones. The overgrown grass tickles my ankles, and my heartbeat hammers against my ribs as we reach Jace McConnell. The last time I visited this spot, I poured Jace a drink and sobbed. I haven't been back since, and I despise myself for that, but I couldn't bring myself back just yet.

"Take a breath." Alyssa squeezes my hand, giving me courage.

Stopping in front of Jace's headstone, a rush of emotions flows through me. I wasn't expecting to cry, but I can't stop it from happening. The tears pour out and Alyssa embraces me. I still can't believe he's not here.

"Want me to give you some alone time with him?" Alyssa asks quietly.

Looking down, I see the depth of love, sincerity, and strength in her eyes. Alyssa had been with me when Jace was in the accident. She had felt my pain and stayed by my side that night. She belongs with me right now. I need her.

"No, I want you here with me."

I exhale and hand Brooke over to Alyssa. She fusses, so I remove my tags and hand them to her. Brooke grips them in her hand, then she rests her head on Alyssa's shoulder.

Crouching down, I say, "Hey, buddy. How you doin'? It's been a while, and I apologize for that. It's been a rough few years without you. I wish I could give you a bullshit story about why I haven't been back, but I haven't been able to let go. Your death still hurts all the time." I sigh, the guilt hitting me harder than ever. "Ford lives in Tennessee now. Can you believe he snagged an older woman? Remember how he loved his younger girls with wide hips? Well, this one is the complete opposite. He said she's a cougar." I laugh and hear Alyssa snicker. "I almost don't believe it myself."

Sobering, I grow serious. "So, I know I brought you a drink the last time I was here." I look up at Alyssa with glossy eyes and mouth, "I'll explain later." I turn my head back to the marble lettering and stare at it. "I don't have a drink this time, but I have something even better." I take a deep breath. "My son is growing inside Alyssa, and we're going to name him Jace after you." A knot clogs my throat, and I struggle to get the words out. "Man, I wish I wasn't sitting here talking to a piece of stone. I wish you could be here right now. What I wouldn't give to go back to that night and do it all over again." I shake my head and close my eyes. Tears roll down my cheeks. "A little piece of me died with you that night. I haven't been able to let go. I haven't been ready to say goodbye, to accept it. Doing so makes me feel like I'm saying goodbye to you forever, and I hate that feeling."

Standing up, I reach blindly for Alyssa's hand. Taking

one last long breath, I exhale at the clear blue sky. The world works in mysterious ways. No one knows what is ahead of them. If I've learned anything, it's that life has taught me to live in the moment and have no regrets because it could all be gone tomorrow.

I miss Jace and always will. The longing for my friend never goes away. I know that Jace is looking down and watching over us, and that eases the sorrow in my heart. I'll never forget him or the memories we share. Those will always be with me, and I'll hold on to them until my time is up here.

"You're always with me. Until then, this is our last goodbye."

The End.

ACKNOWLEDGMENTS

Hold On to Me is the second novel I published and is one of my favorites. The original version was written in third person omniscient and published in 2015. Soon, I learned that point of view held people back from reading the book. I've always loved this story more than others. I wanted to give these characters a fighting chance, so I decided to rewrite the book to first-person present tense and republish the story as new.

Only I was intimidated by the process. I was overwhelmed. I was too close to the story and couldn't see how to sort the chapters, keep the plot, or decide which point of view to delete. Extensive revisions were required. I attempted a few times but had no luck until one of my editors offered to assist me. We came up with a plan and never turned back.

Mattingly Churakos, you helped make a dream a reality. The second republication would not have been possible without you. Thank you for the hours you spent painstakingly going through every sentence and converting each word. This rewrite was challenging, and you didn't back down. From the bottom of my heart, thank you for helping me rewrite Hold On to Me.

Nadine, we've come full circle. Hold On to Me is the novel that started it all for us. We're still a team a dozen books later and ten years of publishing. You're the peanut butter to my jelly. You understand my stories and see my visions. Thank you for editing another book and treating my manuscript like it's your baby. p.s. I will never use the find and replace again. Although, the Chad-a-fits was a priceless moment and the funniest mistake I've ever made.

Alyssa and Brittany, thank you for beta reading. The early drafts were embarrassingly messy, and significant revisions had been made, but that didn't hold you back from helping me republish this book. Both of you loved the original story to pieces. Your feedback on the second edition meant a lot to me. Thank you so much for beta reading Hold On to Me.

To the readers who read the first edition and loved the story as it is, you're one of the reasons why I never stopped writing. One day, I was standing in my kitchen reading a review shortly after Hold On to Me was released when the feeling hit me right in the gut that writing books is what I was supposed to do. I was motivated by your passion for more of my words. That day, I decided to write fiction romance for the rest of my life.

Teamwork makes the dream work.

ABOUT LUCIA

Lucia Franco has written over a dozen romance novels. Her emotional stories often include an age gap and forbidden love.

Her novel Hush Hush was a finalist in the RWA 2019 Stiletto Contest. Her novels have been translated into several languages.

Lucia resides in South Florida with her husband, two boys, and five pets. She was a competitive athlete for over ten years – a gymnast and cheerleader – which heavily inspired the Off Balance series. When she isn't writing, you can find her at the beach getting slammed by waves or wandering through her butterfly garden.

Printed in Great Britain
by Amazon

60032213R00188